# LUCKY NUMBER 6

## Julia Shraybman

Black Rose Writing | Texas

ISBN: 978-1-68513-649-9
LIBRARY OF CONGRESS CONTROL NUMBER: 2025934577
PUBLISHED BY BLACK ROSE WRITING
www.blackrosewriting.com

Printed in the United States of America
Suggested Retail Price (SRP) $21.95

*Lucky Number 6* is printed in Minion Pro

*As a planet-friendly publisher, Black Rose Writing does its best to eliminate unnecessary waste to reduce paper usage and energy costs, while never compromising the reading experience. As a result, the final word count vs. page count may not meet common expectations.

# PRAISE FOR
## *LUCKY NUMBER 6*

"It was difficult to put this well-written book down, and it kept me turning the pages as fast as possible. The ending was a big surprise. I did not see it coming or expect it at all."

–*Readers' Favorite*

# LUCKY
# NUMBER
# 6

# CHARLIE

Giovanni's Coffee Shop wasn't my usual spot. It was too far from the little apartment Mammina and I called home in Rogers Park, on the far north side of Chicago—a place we'd lived ever since Dad left. The apartment was small, just two rooms with a leaky faucet that no one ever fixed and windows that stuck if you tried to open them. The floors creaked with every step, and the walls were so thin I knew the couple next door's favorite TV shows better than their names. Mammina worked long hours at the factory to make sure we could stay there, and we did our best to take care of it. It wasn't much, but it was ours. The neighborhood was loud and busy, full of families like ours—immigrants and their kids—coming together to create a patchwork of shared stories in languages I didn't always understand. I liked it that way. It felt safe. It felt like home.

Both sides of my family were from Italy, and I loved my Italian roots. I hadn't been to Italy yet, but Mammina's stories—I affectionately called my mom "Mammina"—made it feel as if I had. She'd tell me about the olive groves and vineyards, bustling markets, and the quiet cobblestone streets of her hometown. As a little girl, I'd sit wide-eyed, soaking up her stories about village festivals, with everyone dressed in colorful clothes, dancing to music that made you want to twirl. She'd talk about picking fresh figs, their juice sticky and sweet, and swimming in the Mediterranean, the cool waves splashing against her skin, breathing in the salty air that made her feel alive.

We always talked about going to Italy together someday, where we could walk the same streets and see all the places she told me about. Oh, and my name—it's a shorter, American version of "Carlotta," the name my grandma had picked. But to everyone else, I was just Charlie.

Anyway, going downtown wasn't something I did much, so when I did, it felt kind of special, like a treat. I loved walking around and staring up at the buildings. The buildings were huge, towering over everything, but I didn't feel small. I liked looking up at them, noticing how different they all were. The streets were always packed—tourists with their cameras, businesspeople rushing by without noticing anyone, and street performers trying to catch someone's attention. And then there was the Chicago River, cutting through it all, its green water almost too bright to believe, like it didn't belong but somehow made the city what it was. I could stand on the bridges for hours, watching them lift for the boats, wondering how something that old and heavy could still move. Sunlight bounced off the glass and steel, making the whole city look like it was glowing.

Lately, I'd been coming downtown for a different reason. I'd been accepted to Northwestern University and was checking out the city campus. That's when I stumbled across Giovanni's Coffee Shop for the first time. The name caught my attention—it reminded me of my Italian roots, and I couldn't resist going in. I stepped inside, hoping it might feel like the cafés Mammina always talked about—warm, inviting, with the kind of charm that made you want to twirl.

"*Ciao, bella,*" a voice called.

An older man with a broad smile stood behind the counter. "Welcome, I don't remember seeing you here before. I'm Giovanni, but you call me Gio. Always nice to meet another Italian girl, you know?"

I smiled. "Hi, yeah, it's my first time here."

"Well, *benvenuta*, welcome! Make yourself at home. Try my coffee. It's really good here. Coffee is good. Life is good."

His enthusiasm was impossible to resist, and by the time he handed me my cup, I already felt like I belonged. As he worked, I glanced around the café. It felt cozy, like a warm hug you didn't realize you needed. The scent of fresh coffee wrapped around me, familiar and safe. Little Italian flags hung from the walls, and soft music drifted through the air. The whole place had an easy, welcoming feel, like it was meant to make you want to stay a little longer.

Then I took a sip. Smooth. Warm. So good, it caught me off guard. The kind of coffee that stayed with you, even after the cup was empty, like all the best things in life. After that, every trip downtown led me back here. Not just for the coffee, but for the way it felt to be there.

Giovanni's quickly became my haven, a place where I could let my thoughts wander. Every visit started the same—Gio greeting me with a big smile and a *"Ciao, bella!"* He wouldn't let me sit until I told him about my day—classes, Mammina, and even my boyfriend, Jason. It was the kind of fatherly warmth I'd never known but always missed. And the best part? My spot by the window, where I'd sit for hours, watching the city move around me, thinking about everything ahead—graduation, college, a new life waiting to begin.

But today, that perfect bubble burst. It shattered so suddenly I barely had time to catch my breath. Just when you think you have everything figured out, life throws you a curveball. It's strange how the moments you think will last forever can vanish in an instant, like a flame snuffed out before it even burns. A perfect future can vanish in a heartbeat.

From that moment on, I knew my life would never be the same again.

# MATT

Damn. Ten in the morning, and the place was packed. The coffee shop buzzed with people talking, the hiss of the coffee machine, and the clatter of cups and plates. The smell of fresh coffee and pastries was a welcome distraction from the corporate grind—brief, but I'd take it. Anything to hold off the usual weekday dread.

The office felt like a slow death. Petty gossip, pointless meetings, politics over nothing. Every day dragged into the next, each one exactly the same, stretching out like a dull, gray line. Just the thought of going back made my stomach churn.

But this place was different. The moment I stepped inside, something shifted. The weight lifted, even if just a little. Here, I could actually breathe. The energy was nothing like the monotony of my daily routine. The hum of conversation, Giovanni's easy banter as he worked the counter, the constant flow of people—it all reminded me there was more to life than gray cubicle walls. It hit me every time. Sharp. Unforgiving. A reminder of the gap between the life I had and the life I wanted. One thought hammered in my mind: *I was meant for more than this.*

"What's up, Gio?" I waved.

Giovanni ruled behind the counter, his kingdom of espresso machines and steaming milk untouched by the outside world. He was mid-fifties, maybe, but moved like someone half his age. With his slicked-back hair and an old-school charm straight out of a black-and-white film, he had a laid-back swagger that made people linger a little longer.

But it wasn't just the effortless cool—there was something about him that made the café feel like home. He never forgot a name, never let a cup go empty without a friendly nudge to stay for another. He flipped between English and Italian as he chatted with customers, his jokes landing as smoothly as the espresso he poured. His wave and easy grin could turn a bad day around before you even took your first sip. And, like always, he had my back—tipping his head toward Tom's table, where my coffee waited.

"You're the man, Gio. The absolute best. This is why I keep coming back."

"This is why everyone keeps coming back!" Giovanni replied with a grin. "*Grazie, amico.* Enjoy your coffee."

As I headed toward Tom's table, I couldn't help but notice the girl in line. She was gorgeous—brown hair spilling down her back and a lemon-yellow dress that fit her just right. She was laughing with the girl behind her, eyes bright, completely in the moment. For a split second, our eyes met, and damn, my heart did this weird little flip. I glanced away just as fast, not wanting to look like some weirdo staring too long.

I dropped into the seat across from Tom with a deep sigh. "Thank God it's Friday. Just one more day of dealing with work crap, and then I can forget about it for a while." I took a sip of my coffee, and the caffeine kicked in, sharp and instant, like flipping a switch. This stuff wasn't just good—it was the best coffee in town, no contest.

Tom chuckled, but it didn't quite reach his eyes. He looked beat, and the stress on his face was hard to miss. He lost his IT job six months ago and still couldn't land anything. I'd even tried to get him a spot at my company, but the hiring freeze slammed that door shut. Everywhere you looked, companies were slashing jobs left and right.

Guilt nagged at me. Here I was, complaining about work while Tom was just trying to land a damn job. I knew I should've felt lucky to still have a paycheck, but it was hard to be grateful when the office grind was bleeding me dry.

"What is it you even do again?" he asked.

I rolled my eyes. "Seriously, man? You know this," I said. "Finance at WFZ Technologies. Same corporate grind, same dead-end meetings, same people complaining about the same crap every day. And don't even get me started on my boss. The guy breathes down my neck over the dumbest shit. I need a change of pace, you know?"

Tom stirred his coffee absently, staring into the cup. "I'm just messing with you. But yeah, at least you've still got a job," he said. "I've been out for months, and nothing's coming up. Burning through my savings just to keep my head above water, and the bills don't stop. I can't even get a callback." He paused, then looked up. "But I've been thinking... maybe this is my shot to do something different. Our shot. I think I've got a solution for both of us."

Leaning forward, eyes locked on mine, he said, "What if we finally open that bar we've talked about since college?" His fingers drummed a rapid beat on the table, eyes gleaming. "Bro, imagine this—a killer bar downtown, packed with gorgeous women and epic tunes."

I wanted nothing more than to ditch my soul-sucking job, but we had to be realistic. "I'm with you, man, but let's be real," I said. "That kind of thing takes serious cash. Plus, the economy's shaky, and what bank's gonna loan us money when we've got nothing to back it up?"

Tom leaned back, crossing his arms with a grin. "I've still got 20K stashed, and you said you've got twenty-five. That's almost fifty grand to get this thing rolling!"

"But how the hell are we gonna come up with the rest of the money?" I replied. "We need to make sure we have enough for rent, equipment, inventory, staff . . ."

"Let's hit up the casino," he said. "It's worth a shot."

I shook my head. "I don't know, man. What if we blow all our savings and it tanks? We could lose everything."

Tom didn't even hesitate. "If I don't find another job soon, I'll lose all my savings anyway. And you've still got your job. It's not like you're quitting right away. Think about it—what if we actually hit it big? That's the beauty, bro. Life's about taking risks. If you don't, are you really living? And let's be real. Winning is everything, winning is the ultimate goal. Plus, we're not just gambling for the fun of it, we're gambling for our future. We're gambling for our dream."

My pulse quickened. The idea was reckless, insane—but maybe that's why it felt so damn tempting. The thought of never going back to my job had a dangerous pull.

Tom gave me that look—the one that said he wasn't letting this go. "Come on, man. You really wanna be stuck in a job that's killing you? And your dad, dude, I've known him for ages. He always had these killer ideas, but he never went for them."

I exhaled, staring down at my coffee. The safe answer was no. But then Tom brought up my dad.

For thirty years, my dad toiled in a warehouse, underpaid and miserable. Every day he came home looking like the world was crushing him. He'd talk about quitting, chasing his dreams—but he never did. Fear held him back. He had us to think about—me, my younger brother, my mom. So instead, he'd disappear into the basement with a bottle of whiskey, drowning in the weight of everything he'd never done. Watching him waste away like that was heartbreaking. Every swig, every sigh of resignation, chipped away at him—and at me. The man who once seemed invincible was fading, slowly eaten alive by a job that took more than it ever gave back.

But at my college graduation, I saw something I hadn't seen in years—a gleam of hope in his eyes when he told me how proud he was. It's a moment I'll never forget. It wasn't just about being the first in my family to go to college. It was about him seeing a glimpse of something more in my future—something he felt he'd missed out on. I wanted to make him proud again, to show him that all his sacrifice and hard work meant something. I wanted to be the one who took the risks he couldn't, who chased the dreams he had to leave behind.

"I'm all in, man! Let's do this!" I declared. "We can do this. I know we can."

"Hell yeah! Always trust your gut!" Tom shouted, slamming his fist on the table. We both burst out laughing, ignoring the stares. "You'll see. We'll bust our asses, hustle, do whatever it takes. And when we finally open those doors, when we hear the music pounding, when the place is packed, man—it's gonna be worth it."

Tom kept talking, fired up, but my focus had already drifted. Across the room, the girl in the yellow dress laughed, tipping her head back, her brown hair catching the light. She was still talking to the younger girl with black hair, who looked barely eighteen. She was stunning— not just in the obvious way, but in a way that made her stand out. Confident. A little mysterious. I couldn't look away.

She grabbed her drink and turned to go. Now or never.

I nodded toward her. "Tom, you see that girl in the yellow dress? I'm thinking about asking for her number. Think I'll come off like a creep?"

"Absolutely. She's way out of your league." Tom smirked. "But go for it. Just don't blame me when you're sulking in the bathroom."

I grinned, masking the nerves twisting in my stomach with a shot of fake confidence. "Watch and learn, my friend."

But just as I stood up, Tom's face went pale.

"What the fuck?" he muttered.

The door slammed open. Two figures in black ski masks burst through the door, locking it behind them. Shots exploded into the air. The café erupted—screams, chairs scraping, tables crashing. *Was this a robbery? A terrorist attack?* I had no clue, and no time to think.

Tom was crouched low, his face bloodless. "Get down, man," he whispered.

I hit the floor, my heart hammering. My hands were shaking, my legs useless beneath me. I held my breath and forced myself still. *Don't move. Don't breathe. Stay invisible.*

Everything else dropped away—the girl in the lemon-colored dress, the job I hated, the dreams I had yet to chase. I glanced at Tom. His eyes were squeezed shut, his lips moving in a frantic whisper. A prayer? A plea? I couldn't tell.

The shots still rang in my ears. Sobbing. Scuffling. My stomach clenched. Nausea creeping up my throat. Life was paper-thin. One second, solid. The next—gone. All I could do was pray we would make it out of this alive.

# ALEXANDRA

The coffee line crawled, but nothing could kill my vibe. I'd just aced my last final, officially conquered college—what were a few extra minutes compared to that? Besides, Giovanni's Coffee was too charming to complain about. The murals on the walls turned the place into a tiny slice of Italy, rich with color, like someone had captured the golden light of Venice and brushed it across every inch of the café. It felt almost sacred, like stepping into history itself. Pretty incredible for a coffee shop.

For the first time in years, the future wasn't some distant goal—it was here, waiting. All those sleepless nights, the caffeine-fueled study sessions, the sheer grind—it had all led to this. College was in the rearview, and I was ready for what came next. A weekend of celebrating, sure, but beyond that? The life I'd been working toward. A dream job, success, everything I'd imagined.

My phone buzzed. Mom.

"Hi, honey! Mazel tov!" she practically shouted. "Your dad and I already made reservations for after the ceremony. I'm so proud of you—Northwestern, top of your class! My brilliant girl!" Half the café probably heard her. Wouldn't be surprised if someone started clapping.

I laughed, rolling my eyes. "Thanks, Mom. You've already congratulated me like ten times."

"I can't help it! I'm just so excited." She softened, just a little. "Besides, I'm your mother. I get to be excited. I love you that much."

"I know, Mom, you're my biggest fan, and I love you for that," I said, smiling. "I'm stoked too! I've got that interview with the amazing ad agency next week. Fictive Creative Company. Remember I told you about it last week? I'm so nervous—it's like the best of the best, like, Beyoncé level."

"You're the Beyoncé of advertising, honey," my mom said, beaming. "You're better than Beyoncé. They'd be crazy not to hire you."

"Thanks, Mom." I glanced at the counter—still three people ahead of me. "I should go. I'm actually at this place called Giovanni's Coffee. This place is packed, and I need to figure out what to order."

"Okay, okay. Get something delicious!"

"I will. Love you."

I tossed my phone back into my purse and studied the chalkboard menu when a voice chimed in behind me. "Hey, that's awesome."

A girl, maybe eighteen, with olive skin and deep dimples, smiled at me. She wore a white Rolling Stones T-shirt and faded jeans. "Sorry," she added quickly, tucking a strand of long black hair behind her ear. "I don't mean to intrude. It's just—the line is long, and I overheard. I just got into Northwestern."

"That's amazing! Congrats. What's your major going to be?" I asked.

She grinned. "Thanks! Journalism. I hope it's okay I just started talking to you. I'm Charlie, by the way."

"Alex."

Charlie tilted her head toward a guy walking past. "Oh, he's cute. That guy was totally checking you out. Maybe you should go talk to him."

I caught his glance just before he quickly looked away.

Charlie smirked. "See? Busted."

I just shook my head. "Nah, I'm good," I said. "I don't need any distractions right now. I've got that big interview next week."

"I really hope you get it," she said, looking impressed. "What made you want to go into advertising?"

Charlie's question caught me off guard.

My mind flickered back—high school hallways, the clang of lockers, the cafeteria where I always sat alone, tracing the edges of my book with my thumb to keep my hands busy. Jennifer Smith and her perfect friends, their casual cruelty sharpened to precision. All I wanted was to be part of the popular crowd, but instead, it was nonstop bullying.

"Look at the dork with the ugly clothes." Laughter, not loud, but loud enough. My face burning, my shoulders curling in as if I could shrink away from it.

Sometimes, I still felt like her—that girl with glasses too big for her face, sitting alone, pretending not to care. Maybe part of me still *was* her. But I'd learned. Perception was power. In advertising, people like me got to decide what was cool, what people wanted. Of course, I wasn't about to spill all that to a stranger.

"Honestly? I love the creativity of it," I said instead. "And the challenge."

She nodded like she got it. "That's really cool."

Just then, the person in front of me moved up in line. "What are you getting?" I asked. "I've never been here before."

"Their regular coffee is amazing."

"Good to know. I think I'll go with a cappuccino." I pulled out my phone. "Hey, let's swap numbers. If you ever need advice about school, I'd be happy to help."

Charlie beamed. "That would be awesome."

We traded numbers, grabbed our drinks, and said our goodbyes. I was about to sit down at a table to read a book when the door slammed open. Two men. Ski masks. Guns.

A crack—gunfire.

The hum of the café shattered. Screams tore through the air.

People dove to the floor. I did too, my body moving before my brain could catch up. My hands hit the tile. My breath tumbled out, fast and uneven. The world around me sharpened, brutal and cold.

This was real. Not a fire drill. Not a movie scene. Real. Happening now. The men locked the doors. The lock clicked. We were sealed inside.

Under the table, I sucked in a shallow breath. Panicked whispers crackled through the air. Footsteps scuffed against tile. My mind ricocheted between thoughts—my mom, my dad, the future I'd just been so sure of.

I wasn't ready for this to be the end.

Somewhere, someone sobbed. A chair tipped over, crashing hard. I pressed my palms against the cool tile, trying to steady myself.

Outside, the world kept moving. Traffic hummed. People walked past, oblivious.

But inside, reality had changed. No script. No exit. Just terror, closing in.

# OLIVIA

As I stepped into Giovanni's Coffee Shop, the scent of fresh espresso wrapped around me. The coffee grinder churned, steam hissing as the barista worked behind the counter. Voices murmured over the clinking of cups, the familiar rhythm of my second home.

"*Ciao*, my dear!" Giovanni's voice rang out before I even reached the counter. His face lit up, eyes crinkling with warmth. "And how is my favorite doctor today?"

Giovanni—Gio, as I called him—wasn't just a café owner. He was a friend, a constant in the chaos of hospital life. He stepped from behind the counter and pulled me into a quick hug, the scent of coffee beans clinging to his apron.

My husband, Owen, often joked that I spent more time here than at home. The hospital was my first home, Giovanni's my second, and our actual house a distant third. I used to laugh it off, but he wasn't wrong. Here, I had space to just be.

"Beautiful necklace," Giovanni said, nodding toward the white gold necklace from Tiffany's resting against my collarbone. "*Molto bella!*"

I touched it lightly, smiling. "Today's actually my thirty-sixth birthday. Owen surprised me this morning."

"Ah! *Buon compleanno,* my bella!" His hands lifted in an animated gesture. "Owen, he is a true gentleman. Back home, when a man loved a woman, he didn't just say it—he showed it.

Gifts, gestures, little things that meant everything. My papa once brought my mama a necklace, gold and diamonds, shining like stars. Every time she wore it, he would puff out his chest and say, 'That's my bella.'"

His smile flickered, nostalgia pressing at the edges. I knew he missed Italy, but his wife, Sofia, had convinced him to move to America for a better future.

"But today," he said, shaking off the memory, "everything in my shop is free for you. A birthday gift."

"Gio, that's too kind—"

Before I could finish, my phone buzzed. Owen. I shot Gio an apologetic smile and picked up.

"Hi, honey."

"Hey, birthday girl." Owen's voice was warm, familiar. "Just wanted to remind you there are more surprises waiting at home. Think you can finish early?"

Owen never missed my birthday. No matter how relentless our careers—me as a surgeon, him as a broker—he always made time for us. Ten years, and that hadn't changed. Our marriage wasn't perfect, but it was solid. Real. Built on something steady. Through it all, he was my anchor. My best friend. My home. We had weathered it all—the endless hours, the heartbreak of negative pregnancy tests, the petty arguments over dishes and TV shows. The big moments. The small ones. The ones that nearly broke us. And through every high and low, he was there. Showing up. Choosing us.

"I'll do my best," I said, smiling.

Then—

A gunshot cracked through the air.

Screams. Chairs scraped against the floor as people dove for cover. My phone slipped from my fingers, crashing onto the tiles.

Two masked men stormed in, rifles raised. A second shot exploded into the ceiling. Plaster rained down, the acrid scent of gunpowder thick in the air.

Through the chaos, Owen's voice crackled from my fallen phone. "Olivia? What's going on? Are you still there?"

A shoe came down hard, crushing it.

"Hands up!" one of the gunmen barked, his voice sharp, commanding.

Across the room, Giovanni's hand twitched toward something behind the counter. The taller gunman snapped his rifle toward him. "Don't even think about it."

Gio lifted his hands, jaw tight, eyes blazing. "What do you want? You come into my shop—my American dream—and destroy it? Let these people go."

Tables lay overturned. Bullet holes gaped in the ceiling. The stench of smoke and metal clung to the air. Everything Giovanni built—gone. Fear coiled tight in my chest. *Would I see Owen again?*

The gunman's finger curled around the trigger. "Say one more word, and I'll put a bullet between your eyes."

Gio didn't flinch. "You think I'm scared? I've seen worse than you."

A sick glint flashed in the man's eyes. "Oh yeah? What if I start shooting them one by one? Wanna test me?" Gio held his ground, silent. The gunman let out a slow chuckle, the sound muffled behind his mask. "That's what I thought."

He turned to the rest of the coffee shop, his voice booming with menace. "Pay attention, all of you! From now on, you do exactly as we say if you don't want to be next."

*Next.* The word settled like a stone in my stomach.

Two small girls huddled together, clinging to their mother's dress. Their tears had dried, but the fear in their eyes was still raw. My heart clenched as if they were my own daughters.

A chill swept through me. Owen and I had just started IVF. What if I was pregnant? What if I never got to know? The nursery, the whispered baby names, the future we dreamed of—it could vanish before it even began.

The girl next to me softly whispered a prayer, "Please, God. Please save us." She was a teenager, no more than seventeen or eighteen, with an olive complexion, thick black hair, and a pretty oval face. She was wringing the bottom of her Rolling Stones T-shirt, the fabric twisting in her trembling grip. Her eyes were wide with terror, darting around the room as if looking for an escape that didn't exist. "You have the power to save us all. You just have to save us," she pleaded under her breath.

In that moment of fear and uncertainty, I wished that I believed in God. Maybe if I did, I could pray for a miracle, for a way out of this nightmare. But I had never been religious. Never found solace in the idea of a higher power. As a doctor, I had seen the worst of humanity and the best. Life and death weren't divine interventions. They were brutal, unpredictable realities.

Instead, I clung to the one thing I knew for sure—my love for Owen. It had carried me through the toughest times, held me together when everything else felt like it was falling apart. Even now, in the face of terror, it anchored me. Owen's face flashed in my mind—his smile, his laugh, the way he held me when the world felt too heavy.

That love would stay with me. Even in the dark. Even in death.

"Will it hurt?" the girl whispered, and I realized she was talking to me. "Do you think it will hurt when they shoot us?"

"No, you won't feel a thing," I lied. "Trust me, I'm a doctor." Holding on to her hand tightly, I whispered, "Maybe we'll be rescued soon. The police will come."

Maybe. Just once, maybe. It was the same thought that ran through my mind in the operating room. Maybe, just maybe, we can save this patient. The same fragile hope cancer patients hold onto, believing the next round of chemo might work. The same delusion passengers cling to when a plane starts to plummet, praying it won't hit the ground. The same desperate belief a soldier has when he's bleeding out, willing his comrades to find him in time.

Hope. It's what keeps us breathing. Until it doesn't. Until all that's left is the quiet acceptance of what comes next.

"I hope so," the girl murmured, her voice breaking.

"What's your name?" I whispered.

"Charlie."

"I'm Olivia. Listen to me, Charlie," I said. "No matter what happens, I will try to save you. As a doctor, I promise you that."

"Help me, please."

A pained groan snapped my attention to the floor. An elderly man clutched his leg, his face contorted in agony. How had I not noticed him before?

The second gunman, the quieter one, suddenly pointed his rifle at the man's head. "Get up! Get up right now! Or I'll put a bullet through your skull!"

The old man's hands trembled as he reached for his glasses. "I can't," he stammered. "I think I twisted my ankle when I fell. Please don't shoot me."

I moved without thinking, kneeling beside him, placing a steadying hand on his shoulder.

"Try to stay calm. I'm a doctor. Let me look."

The gunman's eyes narrowed, his grip on the rifle tightening. "Figure out what's wrong with him," he ordered.

I examined his ankle. Swollen, bruised. "It looks like a sprain," I said. "I'm going to help you up. Can you put your arm around my shoulder?"

Before I could lift him, the first gunman stalked forward and snarled, "Fuck, Billy, you're such a softie. Who cares what's wrong with him?" He turned his rifle on me, eyes dark with rage. "I thought we told everyone not to move."

"I understand," I said carefully, forcing my voice to stay even. "But this man needs help. Let me help him."

The gunman pressed the barrel of his rifle against my temple.

"I said shut up!" he yelled.

I closed my eyes, my pulse pounding. Time slowed. Every heartbeat, every breath, felt like it could be my last. *If I died here, would Owen be okay?* Would he move on? Find happiness without me? A sharp ache cut through my chest, but beneath it, a certainty settled, I wanted him to live, to keep going, even if I wasn't there. Even if this was the end for me.

Then, just as suddenly, the gunman dropped his rifle back to his side with a scoff. He shoved me behind Charlie. "Stay put, or I'll make sure you never move again."

He kicked a chair so hard it clattered against the ground, the crash making people flinch.

"Well, sit down," he barked at the old man.

The elderly man barely moved, still gripping his ankle in pain. The gunman lost his patience, grabbing him by the arm and yanking him up before shoving him into a chair. "Jesus, why are you so damn helpless?"

The old man let out a low moan but said nothing.

"You are a disgrace," Giovanni said suddenly. His voice was steady, but his eyes burned. "*Eh, ma chi sei tu?* He is an old, helpless man. And you—" His lip curled in disgust. "You are nothing but a coward."

The gunman strode over and struck him across the head with the butt of his rifle. The crack of impact echoed through the room. Giovanni crumpled to the floor, blood streaking down his face.

A woman gasped. Two young girls clung to their mother, sobbing into her dress. Their shoulders shook violently, their cries muffled but raw.

A young man near the counter surged forward. "You son of a bitch!" he spat.

Billy moved fast. He grabbed the man by the shoulder and drove a brutal punch into his stomach, sending him crashing to the floor.

"Matt, no!" his friend cried out, reaching for him, but the first gunman swung his rifle toward him, freezing him in place.

"Anyone else want to play hero?" His voice was sharp, coiled with menace. He let the question hang, scanning the room, daring someone to challenge him. "No? Good. Now shut the fuck up!"

I clenched my eyes shut, hot tears slipping down my cheeks. Giovanni groaned from the floor, the sound rattling through the heavy silence.

Then, the gunman's voice cut through it all. "Alright, listen up!" he shouted. "We're gonna play a little game. Do exactly as we say, or there will be consequences." He turned to Billy, and snapped his fingers once, as if setting the tempo for their twisted game. "Now, let's have some fun. Everyone, start counting off from one to six. We'll start with the old man."

And just like that, the twisted game began. Each number spoken felt like a noose tightening around our necks. The gunmen's laughter slithered through the room, a sick melody, a cruel reminder of how powerless we were. In the distance, sirens wailed. Taunting. Too far. Too late.

We had to get out of here. I had to survive. For Owen. For the dreams we hadn't even started living.

But deep down, I knew there was no hope for us to be saved.

# CHARLIE

"K-Keep... keep counting!" The gunman's voice snapped through the air, spit flying with each barked order.

Two men with guns had turned us into pawns in some twisted game. Nothing made sense. My pulse pounded like a trapped animal—fast, desperate.

We stood in line, voices shaky as we counted from one to six. Olivia, the doctor I'd just met, was behind me, and I clung to her hand like a child—not eighteen anymore, just something small, breakable, desperate for someone to tell me it would be okay.

I should've been last in line, but Olivia had stepped away to help an elderly man. When the gunman shoved her back, she stumbled behind me. By then, I'd already counted ahead. I knew I'd get Number 5. My favorite number. The one I always picked for luck. I wanted to believe that meant something. That it was a sign.

"Please, God. We're trapped. I'm scared. I don't know what to do." My lips barely moved. My heart ached for Mammina. She had no one else. If I died here, she'd be alone. "If I can't be there, please... please watch over her. I love her so much."

Praying gave me something to hold onto. Just for a moment. Just long enough to pretend they might change their minds. That at the last second, something human in them would win. That even the darkest hearts had a flicker of light somewhere. And that, somehow, goodness would still find a way.

But fear dug in deep. Time stretched, warping the space between the life I had and the one I might never reach. My future—college, Jason, the life I'd mapped out—felt thin, fragile. Glass about to shatter.

I had just finished high school, but the graduation day I'd imagined was slipping away. While everyone else would be tossing their caps into the air, I'd be missing. No photos with Mom. No arms around Jason. And no chance, finally, to see if Dad would show up after thirteen years of silence. Would he even care? Would he even miss me?

I wanted to text Jason. Just three words: *I love you.* But my fingers wouldn't move. If they saw me reach for it—if they thought I was trying something—they'd kill me before I even hit send.

"Six," a young guy said. The one who'd tried to protect Giovanni.

The gunman's head snapped toward him. "By the exit. Now. Stand with that girl."

The girl was Alex. She was sobbing, her hands pressed against her face.

The guy didn't move. "Why?" His voice stayed steady. "What are you planning?" His friend grabbed his arm, a silent warning. Stop.

The gunman didn't answer. He just shoved him, hard. "Move." Then, louder: "Next!"

"One," the guy's friend replied. "Two," the woman beside him choked out.

The counting crawled forward, step by step, until it landed on me.

Olivia gripped my hand tighter. Her whisper shook. "Charlie, no matter what happens, I'll try to save you, okay?"

I wanted to believe her. But how?

"Shut the fuck up!" The gunman's eyes locked on me. "Your turn. State your number."

My throat closed. "F-five."

"Next!"

"Six," Olivia said, her voice thin.

The gunman's lip curled. "You. With those two." He pointed toward the exit. "You get to leave. Look, they're already being pushed outside."

I gasped, my fingers slipping from Olivia's. *Six had been my number.*

"Why?" Olivia demanded, grabbing my hand again. "She's coming with me." Her fingers tightened. Her eyes pleaded. *Trust me.*

The shooter ripped her hand away, his voice like ice. "Because, Doctor, six is the number of the Devil." He seized her wrist. "We're Satanists, and we're selecting three sixes from the crowd to survive. Consider yourself lucky that you're one of them."

A drop of sweat slid down Olivia's forehead. "No. No, no, no!" She fought his grip. "You sick fuck! You got it wrong! I'm not six—she is. I was in front of her! I only moved to help that old man! I'm five! She's six!"

The gunman chuckled. "Luck's a bitch." His eyes slid to me. "She got the short end of the stick. You got lucky. She didn't." He didn't look away. His stare was cold. Absolute. "Don't worry. We've got something special planned for her."

Something inside me cracked. Hot. Sharp. Olivia's tears meant nothing—I didn't want her pity. She got to live. I didn't.

The shooter's stare burned through me. *This was it. My fate was sealed.* And the fear of what came next made it impossible to breathe.

# MATT

"What do you think they'll do to us?" Her voice trembled. "Why pull us from the line?"

Even in this nightmare, she was stunning. The smudged mascara didn't change that. In another life, I might've asked her out. Gotten to know her.

But this was the life we had, and in this one, we were just pieces in someone else's fucked-up game.

"I don't know," I said. It was the truth.

My blood ran cold as I caught Tom's stare from the line. His expression was unreadable—sharp, intense, full of something I couldn't place. Was he waiting for me to move? Planning something? No way to tell.

The sound of muffled crying and frantic whispers pressed in around us. It was suffocating, like the air had already run out.

The counting dragged on, deliberate. Each number stretched, feeding their sick pleasure. Every second cut like a blade. *Why us? Why pull us? What made us different?*

I wanted to fight. My mind scrambled for options—grab a chair, throw it, make a scene, yell for everyone to scatter. For a second, it almost felt possible. But it wasn't. We were trapped. They had the guns, the control. We had nothing.

I turned back to her. "What's your name?"

"Alex." Her voice trembled. "You're Matt, right? I heard your friend yell your name when you took that hit."

I nodded, just as one of the gunmen stepped forward, raising his rifle. Instinct took over—I grabbed Alex's hand. She squeezed back, tight, like it was the only thing keeping her here.

A lump formed in my throat. Dad's tired eyes. Mom's warm smile. I saw them so clearly, like they were right in front of me.

"I love you, Pops," I whispered under my breath. And Mom. She deserved to hear it, too. "I'm sorry for being such a shitty teenager." I thought about all the slammed doors, the yelling. The way the kitchen smelled like warm cookies, how she always hummed while she baked. The way I'd taken them for granted. The idea of them not knowing, of never getting the chance to say it, scared the hell out of me.

Beside me, Alex let out a shaky breath. "Please. Just one call. Just to hear my mom's voice."

The gunman ignored her. Instead, he yanked open the coffee shop's door. "Get the fuck out, both of you."

We froze.

"Wait, what?" I asked.

"You're free to go."

We exchanged a look, equally lost. "Why?" I asked.

"Move," he snapped. "Quit asking so many damn questions."

"No." My voice came out firm. "Let her go, but I can't leave my friend."

Tom's gaze locked onto mine. His brow furrowed, arms crossing like he was asking, 'What the hell's going on?'

"What about the others?" I demanded. "Are you letting them go, too?"

The gunman didn't answer. He just shoved me out, hard.

As I stumbled backward, my eyes found Tom's again. He shook his head, quick and sharp, something urgent in his face. A warning. A command. *Don't fight this.*

*No. No fucking way.* I lurched forward, but the gunman was faster—he slammed the door, the force of it rattling through my bones.

The bang echoed like a gunshot. Tom was still in there.

And for all I knew, I'd just walked out of his grave.

# CHARLIE

I stared at the shooter, silently begging for even a flicker of mercy. Fear tangled with desperation, drowning out Olivia's shaky breaths. She kept glancing at me, eyes tight with worry.

Then his phone rang.

"Yeah?" His voice snapped, sharp and impatient. A pause. His grip tightened around the gun. "We're not talking." He hung up, jaw clenched.

The other shooter shifted. Billy. I'd heard the first one say his name earlier when Olivia was helping the old man, but I hadn't had time to process it. Now, it stuck. "Who was that?" he asked.

"The police."

Billy tensed. "Again?"

The first shooter scoffed, gripping the phone. "Yeah, again. They won't stop." His gaze flickered to Olivia, lingering a second too long.

Then, the phone rang again. This time, I caught a glimpse of the screen. Mom. Something flickered in his eyes—hesitation, doubt—but it vanished just as fast. He slammed the phone off.

A voice cracked through the megaphone outside. "Jimmy. Billy. It's Mom." Her voice wavered. "Please—don't do this. This isn't who you are."

Billy sucked in a breath. But it was the other shooter—Jimmy—who went rigid. Billy turned to him. "Jimmy," he said, voice unsteady, "maybe we should talk to her."

For the first time, I had his name. Jimmy.

"No!" the first one snapped. "We don't need to talk to anyone. We have to finish this. Block all your thoughts."

"Jimmy, Billy, please, listen to me," their mother begged. "You remember the camping trip? That summer? The fire crackling, the fort you built together? We laughed. We were happy. Please—come back to me."

Billy shut his eyes. A breath shuddered out of him. For a moment, hope flickered. Maybe he didn't want this. Maybe he could stop it.

"But Jimmy," Billy whispered, "it's Ma. It might be our last chance."

"I know you don't want to do this. You don't have to do this," their mother continued. "For the love we shared, please end this nightmare."

For a moment, I thought they might actually listen. But that hope didn't last.

Jimmy shook his head. "I said no." His hands curled into fists. "What good would that do? It'll just mess everything up." His attention snapped to Olivia. "You. Do what I told you."

Tears burned my eyes as hope crumbled. Olivia was free. But it should have been me. My number. My turn. The unfairness of it coiled inside me, tightening like a vise. How could Olivia take my place? It wasn't supposed to happen like this. Fate had cheated.

"You have to let her go!" Olivia screamed as the man dragged her toward the door. She fought—kicking, breathless, sobbing. "No—no, this isn't happening! She prayed to God, not me. I didn't pray—I'm a nonbeliever! I took her place! I took her place!" Her desperate cries fell upon deaf ears as he pushed her out the door and onto the street.

Through the closing door, I caught one last glimpse of Olivia as the officers led her away. Then, the door shut. A heavy quiet settled over the room.

Jimmy exhaled sharply, then turned to Billy. "Get ready."

Billy hesitated. A moment too long.

Jimmy's voice dropped, low and final. "Now."

I swallowed hard. "Dear God, I know miracles happen. I've seen the impossible become possible. Help me believe that there's a way out of this darkness—"

A crack of gunfire tore through the prayer. Someone gasped. A body hit the floor. Then another. I stood frozen as the brave man's friend took a bullet to the heart and crumpled. One by one, they collapsed. Then, Giovanni's eyes met mine—just for a second, filled with something like regret—before he, too, went down.

Then—the pain. A bullet punched through my back. Air fled my lungs. My body folded. I hit the floor. The world tilted, spinning out of reach.

Agonizing pain blurred everything. Giovanni's voice drifted through my mind. "Try my coffee. It's really good here. Coffee is good. Life is good."

*Life isn't all that good, Giovanni. There's so much evil in it.* The thought flickered, slipping away—then everything went dark.

# MATT

I squinted against the blinding glare of ambulance lights and flashing patrol cars cutting through the dark. Sirens wailed. Officers rushed forward, their voices sharp, urgent. "Over here! Hold your fire, they're the hostages!"

A piercing cry cut through the crowd. "Alex! My daughter! Let me through! Alex!"

"Mom!" Alex sobbed, collapsing into her mother's arms.

We were out. Safe. But it didn't feel real. My limbs were sluggish, the air too thick to breathe—like my body hadn't caught up to the fact that I was still standing. Tom was still inside. I tore away, sprinting for the coffee shop. I didn't get far. Strong hands pulled me back.

"What the hell are you thinking, kid?" the officer yelled into my ear. "You trying to get yourself killed?"

"I have to go back!" I fought against his grip. "My friend! He's still inside!"

Another hostage stumbled out. I barely noticed. My eyes locked past her, waiting. Tom would come. Any second now.

But he didn't come. No one else did. Then—a crack. Sharp. One shot. Then another. Screams tore through the night. Time slowed, then snapped back too fast.

I hit the ground hard, my hands clutching my head.

Tom. He wasn't just a buddy—he was family. We built treehouses, raced bikes down hills we had no business being on. Survived every scrape, every dumb decision, always knowing the other was there. He always had my back. Always.

And now—just like that—he was gone. I gasped for air, but it barely reached my lungs. Everything was wrong. Too still. Too final.

Tom's laugh echoed in my head—cracking up over some stupid inside joke, daring me to one more round of some dumb bet we never finished. His voice, calling my name like he was right beside me. Like he was still here.

My breath hitched. The flashing lights blurred, streaking across my vision. Sirens twisted into something distant, warped and unreal. I sucked in air—not enough. Never enough. My chest clenched, my fingers digging into the pavement like I could hold onto something. But there was nothing. No more late-night plans. No bar with our names on the door. No Tom. Just silence where he should've been. I gasped again, but it came in ragged bursts.

"This can't be happening!" I choked out, my fists slamming against the ground.

"Sir, you can't be here," a police officer said behind me.

"Like hell I can't," a voice shot back. "I got every damn right. He's my son."

My dad. His arms wrapped around me, pulling me in. I didn't fight him. I couldn't.

"Matt, c'mon, kid. Let's go home."

I sagged into him, my body giving in. But my mind wouldn't stop. Regret tore through me like claws, each *if only* cutting deeper. If I'd stayed. If I'd done something. If I'd just given him my number. Maybe it would've been different. But it was too late for maybes. The echoes of gunfire had faded, leaving nothing but an awful, suffocating stillness.

I clung to my dad, wishing I could turn back time. One more moment with Tom. One more chance to tell him what he meant to me. But that chance was gone.

Tom wasn't just my best friend. He was the one who pushed me when I hesitated, who knew what I was thinking before I said a word. He was the kind of friend you don't get twice. He was my family. And now—just like that—he was gone.

And with him, part of me was too.

# OFFICER DAVIS

Night swallowed Chicago, sirens carving through the dark. Giovanni's Coffee Shop—once rich with espresso and lively chatter—was now drowning in flashing red and blue. Police had locked down the block, patrol cars sealing the perimeter. Officers strung crime scene tape across the street, forcing the crowd farther back. Murmurs. Raised phones. Wide eyes. Nobody looked away.

They watched in horror, powerless to stop it. Some hoping, some praying—not that it would make a damn bit of difference. This was spiraling. A hostage situation teetering on the edge of bloodshed. And we were running out of time.

At the command post across the street, my headset crackled with clipped radio updates.

*"Perimeter secure."*

*"Still no response from inside."*

*"Negotiator making contact again."*

I already knew how this would go. The suspects never answered. No demands. No threats. Just silence.

Then—gunfire.

*"Shots fired inside!"*

I didn't hesitate. "Move in! Go, go, go!"

We hit the entrance fast and hard, moving in a tight stack, bodies low, weapons up.

I took point. "Flashbang out—three, two, one."

A detonation—blinding white light, concussive force rattling the air. We surged in. Clear left. Clear right. No movement. No sound.

Then the smell—burnt coffee, blood, gunpowder. Bullet holes punched through murals of Italian immigrants. Tables overturned. Somewhere, water dripped. I stepped over shattered glass, scanning for movement. My stomach clenched.

No Giovanni behind the counter. No knowing grin. No extra shot of espresso waiting for me. No joke about my retirement. This had been my place. My table in the back. My coffee poured before I even ordered

I swallowed. Hard. I'd seen death before. Too much of it. Enough to earn every white hair on my head. But nothing like this.

Just blood. Just bodies. Close-range. Precise. Execution-style.

Bodies sprawled across the floor, limbs twisted, clothes soaked in blood. A woman in a business suit lay near the entrance, her hand outstretched toward something—a phone, maybe. A teenage boy slumped against the counter, hoodie drenched. A man had died shielding a woman, arms locked around her in a final, futile act of protection. I thought of Maria, my wife of three decades. How she held me close this morning, like she always did—like she knew one day, I might not come home.

And there, crumpled in the wreckage, was Giovanni. His white apron stiff with dried blood. His thick, slicked-back hair, always neat no matter how busy the café got, was matted with gore. How the hell was I going to tell his wife, Sofia? His sons, Lorenzo and Alessandro?

When the first call came in, we did everything by the book. Secured the perimeter. Called in a negotiator. No response. We ran the plates on every car near the café. Reached out to the owners. Only one remained unaccounted for. It was registered to Jimmy and Billy Miller. Brothers. No record. No motive.

At first, just a name. A lead. But then—confirmation. Security footage from a nearby storefront showed the Miller brothers parking outside minutes before the attack. One of them stepped out, hauling a duffel bag. Heavy. Weighted. The kind that could carry weapons.

We brought in their mother. She pleaded trough a megaphone for them to surrender. No answer. Negotiator tried again. More time passed. Nothing. Not a damn word. They wouldn't talk. They wouldn't negotiate.

Then they let three hostages go, and for a second, I thought—*maybe. Maybe we had a shot. Maybe this wouldn't end in blood.*

Inside the café, the back door creaked open. I raised a closed fist—hold.

Two figures stepped out, black ski masks hiding their faces. Rifles at their sides, fingers loose on the grips. Jimmy and Billy Miller.

"Police! Drop your weapons!" My voice hit the walls like a gunshot. No movement. No flinch.

They just stood there—too still, too calm. My finger tightened on the trigger. "Last warning—drop your weapons and put your hands up!"

Nothing. Not even a shift in posture. No fear. No hesitation.

I signaled to my team to hold fire. The air was thick with waiting, each side locked in a silent standoff. One wrong move and we'd be pulling more body bags.

I adjusted my grip. "Is there anyone else here besides the two of you?" I asked.

The taller one stood firm. The leader. He didn't need to speak to prove it—the way his brother kept glancing at him, waiting for permission, said everything. He tilted his head slightly, as if entertained by the tension in the air.

Cold. Amused. "No one left but corpses." He studied me for a long moment, unreadable behind the mask. Then, softly—"And what makes you think we're afraid to die?"My trigger finger tensed.

Then—a sound. A faint, shuddering breath. A girl lay on her stomach near the counter, blood streaking her shirt. Late teens, maybe younger. She wasn't moving. Alive? I couldn't tell. I needed to keep the Miller brothers focused on me. "You let three hostages go earlier. Why them?"

The leader didn't answer. Instead, he turned to his brother. "You ready, Billy?"

Billy nodded. He exhaled slow. "Let's do this."

Their hands moved. I started to pull the trigger. But they didn't raise their rifles toward us. They turned them inward. Barrels pressed under their chins. Two gunshots. Two bodies hit the ground. Silence.

Then my radio crackled. "Tactical Medic, move in," I said, my voice rough. "It's over." A beat passed. "One possible survivor. A girl."

"Sir—look!" One of my officers pointed.

A woman with long black hair strolled toward us, her dress pooling at her feet. She moved through the chaos, stepping over broken glass and bodies—unhurried, untouched. Her jet-black hair framed a face too composed for the carnage around her. Too much makeup. Not a drop of blood on her. Not a tremor in her hands. She was smiling. Not a hostage. An ally of the brothers?

She knelt beside the brothers, tilting her head like she was listening for a heartbeat.

"Hold your positions," I said, leveling my weapon. "Ma'am, put your hands up."

The woman silenced me by placing a finger on her lips. Then, without urgency, she rose and strode toward the rear exit.

"Ma'am, stop right there!" I shouted, but she didn't break her stride. "Stop!" I yelled again. She didn't.

I fired—low, aiming for her leg. The bullet never landed. It dissolved midair, vanishing in a wisp of smoke. I tightened my grip, steadying my aim. *What the hell?* I fired again—same result. The bullet vanished like smoke. She smiled. Then, without a word, she opened the back door and slipped out.

I caught up with her in the alley. The lone streetlamp flickered, moths swarming in its sickly yellow glow. She stood beneath it, waiting. She didn't run. Didn't speak. Just watched me.

Then she laughed. Low. Rich. Like I was the punchline to some private joke.

"You'll never catch me," she said, running a hand through her black hair. Her long, manicured nails caught the light. "Best of luck if our paths cross again."

I steadied my aim. "Who the hell are you?"

She just smiled.

Then she vanished into thin air before my eyes.

I went still, staring at the empty space where she'd been. No footprints. No sound. No goddamn explanation.

Then, just as I took a step back, a breath—too close to my ear.

A voice. Soft, almost playful.

"See you soon."

I spun around, gun raised—nothing there. Just the flickering light. The empty alley. And the feeling of something watching.

My fingers twitched against the grip of my gun. I wasn't imagining that. I knew what I saw.

And I had no goddamn explanation.

# MATT

"Ladies and gentlemen, the winning number is . . . Red 15!" the MGM Grand roulette dealer yelled. My stomach dropped. *Fuck.*

The ball clattered to a stop. Cheers. Groans. Mutters of disbelief. I just sat there, staring at the table. Losing. Again. Telling myself the next spin would turn it around. But it never did.

Across the table, a guy clapped, raking in his chips. His watch caught the flashing lights, and for a second, I hated him. Not because he won. Because he could still feel the high of it.

Two years had passed since the shooting at Giovanni's Coffee Shop. Two years, and I was still stuck. Same dead-end corporate finance job, same shitty boss, and now, almost no savings at all. Dad would be so damn disappointed.

The casino throbbed with sound—slot machines ringing, chips rattling, voices layering into a steady rhythm of risk. Dealers swept up winnings. Cards snapped against felt. Held breaths. Whispered prayers before the ball dropped. Vegas fed on people like me. Chewed them up. Spit them out.

And the women. Another game. Another gamble. They moved through the crowd, dressed to kill. Sharp smiles. Knowing eyes. Just enough skin to make sure you looked. Their laughter wove through the chaos, lifting it, stretching it.

I should've felt something. The charge of it. The energy. I didn't. Nothing but weight. Heavy, pressing, turning every breath into work.

So I drank.

I flagged down a waitress. "Vodka. Neat."

The last one still burned in my throat, but I needed another. Something to dull the edges.

Vegas pulsed around me, alive with movement. With risk. With want. But I was just a ghost, drifting through the neon, chasing something already gone.

But no one needed to feel sorry for me. I was all right. I wasn't dead. I was still breathing. I wasn't lying in some coffin. And yet.

*"Winning is everything, winning is the ultimate goal."*

I rubbed my temples. Trying to drown out Tom's voice. Because I knew that voice. Because I shouldn't be hearing it. But there he was. Sitting next to me, like he'd been there the whole time. Leaned back, arms crossed, that same cocky grin. Tom.

*"Winning is the whole fucking point."*

I gripped my empty glass. The condensation slicked my palm, cool and damp. I tried to focus on that, instead of the fact that my best friend—the guy who should be here for real—wasn't.

Because that was the truth. Tom was gone.

Two years, and I still couldn't let him go. That's why I kept coming back. Not for the money. Not even for the game. For him. Some desperate, pathetic hope that maybe if I won big enough—if I pulled off some impossible fucking miracle—I'd make it all mean something. I'd open that bar. Like we always planned. Like he always wanted.

"Ladies and gentlemen, place your bets for the next round, please!" the dealer's voice snapped me back.

A bearded guy on my left placed his chip on Black 10. Then— *nope*—after a slight hesitation, he started counting out more chips, spreading them across random numbers. His short-sleeved T-shirt exposed a long, jagged scar from elbow to wrist. Car crash? Bullet? "Why are you staring at me?" he asked, not pissed off, just curious.

I cleared my throat. "Sorry, man. I didn't mean to stare. But . . . what happened to your arm?"

He rubbed his beard. "Oh, this? It's from my time in Afghanistan. We were on a mission, got ambushed. Those motherfuckers just started shooting at us. I took a bullet." He took a slug of his beer and smacked his lips.

*Afghanistan. We got ambushed. Those motherfuckers just started shooting at us.* "Sorry to hear that, man," I said, swallowing hard. *But we weren't in Afghanistan. We were at the café. We weren't in some goddamn war zone, in godforsaken Afghanistan. How the hell could they just start shooting people?*

He shrugged. "Scar doesn't bother me. Just reminds me I'm still here. It's my head that's the problem. Can't shake the evil shit I saw."

A dull pain pulsed behind my eyes. *Now, everyone start counting off from one to six! We'll start with the old man in the chair!* The thoughts just kept coming. I had to stop talking to this guy.

There were eight other people playing—seven men and one older woman with thick foundation and red lipstick. She was watching me. Hard. After another few minutes, she wasn't even trying to hide it. She crossed her legs, making her black dress ride up her thighs, and tossed her long black hair over her shoulder.

She leaned in closer and whispered, her tongue dancing over my ear. "Want me to blow on your chips for good luck?"

Three $5,000 chips lay in front of me. *Shit, this is all I've got left.* This wasn't even my money. It was Tom's dad's money. "I want you to have it," he'd told me almost exactly one year ago. "I know it was his dream to open the bar with you."

"I can't take your money."

"Take it. I know it's not enough, but it's something. Just do me one favor, yeah?"

"What's that?" I asked.

"Name the bar after my son."

I closed my eyes and rubbed my temples, trying to push everything out of my head. One last bet. This was it. My last shot.

I exhaled sharply, pushing the memory down. "Sure. I'll take all the luck I can get."

She took the chip between her long, manicured fingers. Blew on it. Kissed it. Slow. Intentional. Like a promise. "Here you go," she said, sliding it back into my palm. "Hope this brings you some luck, friend."

"I hope so too," I said and managed a smile.

She raked her brown eyes over me. "How old are you? Twenty-five?"

"Twenty-eight."

"You're very handsome. Dark hair, blue eyes, muscular shoulders . . . just the way I like them." She swirled a thin black straw in her drink.

Her makeup was too heavy, almost clownish under the casino lights. But beneath it, she might not have been half-bad. Not that it mattered. I wasn't interested.

As if reading my mind, she recrossed her legs and placed her chip on Black 6. The number grew. Bigger. Warping, stretching, filling my whole vision. *Now, everyone start counting off from one to six! We'll start with the old man in the chair!* My chest seized. Sweat stung my eyes. *Oh my god, we are all going to die! Start counting!* I blinked hard. Focus. Just focus. I wiped the sweat away, forcing myself to look at the game, the dealer, the chips in front of me—anything but that goddamn number.

"There you are, man. I've been looking all over this casino." Sean appeared behind me—my college roommate for four years. Chubby face, cheeks that always turned pink when he got excited. Tonight, he was squeezed into a too-tight brown blazer and jeans that had seen better days. I used to roast him for his terrible fashion sense, but now? Didn't even matter.

"What are you doing?" he asked. "Haven't you lost enough money?"

I glanced away from the table. I fucking hated the number six. Anything that reminded me of it, I stayed clear of.

"Too much money. I think I may have a gambling problem."

He snorted. "You think?" His voice dropped. "Two years, man. This is all you do. Drinking and gambling. I only came because it's Derek's bachelor party, but this?" He gestured at the table. "This isn't fun anymore."

"That's enough, man." My jaw tightened. "You know how much I hate it when you start lecturing me."

Sean exhaled. "There has to be an end to this," he said, almost pleading. "I can't keep watching you throw your life away."

"Dude, I never asked you for shit," I snapped. I knew I was being a jerk—Sean was a good friend, and he didn't deserve that. But I didn't need his concern and attention. I didn't need anyone's concern and attention. I just wanted to be left alone. "I'm fine. I need to gamble to win money. I need money to open the bar. The bank won't give me a loan, and I don't want to waste any more time."

I could die tomorrow. You could die tomorrow. Anyone could. Nobody knows how much time they have left. Nobody.

Sean ran a hand through his gel-slicked hair and let out a breath. "Man, I don't know how much more of this I can watch." He shook his head. He rubbed the back of his neck, his eyes flicking away before he spoke. "You know I've got your back, right?"

"I'm fine," I lied.

He studied me for a second, then just nodded. Giving up. "Make your final bet, but after that, we're leaving. Derek and the guys are waiting. They wanna hit the clubs."

I didn't feel like hitting the clubs, but I didn't want to argue anymore either, so I just nodded.

The waitress returned. "Vodka?"

I nodded, ignoring Sean's stare. "Thanks." I slid a ten onto her tray as she set the shot down with practiced ease, a smile playing at the corners of her mouth. When she turned to Sean, he ordered a beer, gave her a wink. Her smile dropped so fast, I almost laughed.

"Last chance to place your bets!" the dealer called.

The energy shifted. The tension thickened as people piled chips onto the table.

"Here we go," I muttered, heart pounding. Tom always had a thing for the number nine, which was his birthday—November 9th.

"I need to hit the bathroom. Be back in a sec. Good luck, man," Sean said, tapping my shoulder before heading off.

I reached for my chips, ready to place them on Red 9, when the woman's hand slid over mine—the same one who wished me good luck. And then, before I could react, she shoved all my chips onto Black 6. *What the hell?*

"Trust me on this," she said, calmly reapplying her red lipstick in a tiny compact.

The room closed in. Pressure clamped down on my chest.

"Don't fucking touch my chips." My fingers curled into a fist. "I hate number six." My teeth clenched. "I'm not betting on six."

She only smiled. Unbothered. Like she already knew something I didn't.

Then—my body locked up. Her lips moved, but she didn't speak. The words came from inside my head. "Trust me on this."

I tried to move. Nothing. Not numb. Not in pain. Just... disconnected. Like my body wasn't mine anymore.

I tried again. *Move. Just fucking move.* Nothing.

She was still watching me, her red lips curving—pleased. Her brown eyes darkened, pulling me in. The longer I looked, the deeper I sank. Like slipping into warm water. My limbs, too heavy to lift.

The casino noise stretched, warped. Laughter. Voices. Glasses clinking. Everything blurred, pressing in like a bad dream.

The dealer's voice cut through the suffocating fog. "Bets are locked."

*No, no, no. Don't spin the wheel. I'm going to lose all my money. I'm going to lose it all!*

I needed to move. I needed to do something. But the dealer's hand was already in motion.

The wheel spun. Too fast. The ball clattered against the frets, ricocheting, bouncing, spinning, jumping. Still, I couldn't move. Frozen. Locked in place. The other players leaned in, chasing their next big win—except for her.

Her eyes stayed on me. Unblinking. Unmoving. Holding me there. A slow, knowing smile.

The waitress returned, setting Sean's beer on the table.

And just like that, it released me. The pressure snapped back. My body lurched forward, gasping, hands shaking.

"Here you go."

"Thank you." I heard my own voice, but it felt distant.

The woman with the black hair laughed, chatting with the guy next to her. I cleared my throat. She didn't even glance at me. Like I wasn't there. Like none of it had happened.

Sean came back to the table. "How'd you do?"

I slammed back my shot and stood up. I wiped my mouth, my fingers still trembling. "Sean," I whispered, my voice unsteady. "We have to leave . . ."

"And the winning number is 6, black!" The dealer's voice rang out.

A roar from the table. Applause. Excitement. A slap on someone's back.

"Wait—what?" My voice shook. That couldn't be right.

"I think he said Black 6," Sean replied. "Why? What number did you bet on?"

"Black 6," I said, barely above whisper.

Sean's jaw dropped. "You . . . you did what? How much did you bet?"

"Fifteen thousand dollars."

Sean stared at me, then let out a stunned laugh. "Oh my god, man, you just won five hundred and twenty-five thousand dollars!" He grabbed my shoulders, shaking me, his voice a sharp crack against the noise. "A bet on a single number pays 35 to 1!"

The words barely registered. Slowly, I turned to her. But she was gone. No chair pushed back, no drink left behind. I scanned the room, searching. How the hell did she know that number was gonna hit? Was she working with someone in the casino? Was this all some elaborate setup? My gaze flicked across the casino floor.

Nothing. Not even a trace. Like she had never been there at all.

# ALEXANDRA

The heat slammed into me the second I stepped outside—thick, stifling, like a sauna I never signed up for. Not just hot—melting. The sun bore down, relentless. I checked my phone. Seven thirty a.m. And, of course, no bus in sight. Fantastic. If I was even a minute late, Lisa would have my head.

Lisa—my nightmare boss—found flaws in literally everything I did. No matter how hard I worked, she found something to nitpick. And if, by some miracle, I met her impossible standards, she moved the goalpost again. She liked watching me scramble. I wasn't an employee—I was a puppet, and she yanked the strings.

Sweat trickled down my back, my clothes already sticking to my skin. My makeup was slipping. My hair—frizzy, hopeless—was losing its battle against the humidity. Not exactly the effortless, polished look expected at Fictive Creative Company, where the unspoken dress code was *hot and flawless*. I fanned myself with my hand. Useless. This day was off to a spectacular start.

A car screeched past—sharp, sudden. My breath hitched, my shoulders locked, and I stumbled back. Not again. Not the first time. Every loud noise felt like a threat. Every flash of panic, too real. My therapist called it PTSD.

My life changed the day of the shooting. The world felt sharper, darker—like danger could be lurking anywhere. I was always bracing for something to go wrong. But I was still here, and I knew I should be thankful for that. Today was a new day. The thought almost felt forced, but I had to remind myself that every day was a gift. Even when it felt more like a burden. But maybe if I told myself enough times, it would start to feel true.

At the bus stop, only three others were waiting. A teenager with a backpack and headphones, lost in his phone. An elderly man, deep into a book, occasionally glancing up to check for the bus. And then, *her*.

A woman stood at the stop, wrapped in black—long hair, heavy makeup, a sweeping dress. Thick foundation. Purple eyeshadow. Eyeliner winged past her lids, exaggerated and dramatic. Lipstick, a deep gothic red. She looked like she'd stepped out of a *Victorian vampire novel*. How was she not melting in this heat?

My purse buzzed. I pulled out my phone, hoping for good news. No such luck. My heart sank.

"Alex, what the hell happened to you? Why aren't you in the office?" Lisa's voice snapped through the line, followed by an obnoxious throat-clearing. Fingernails tapped against her desk—impatient, sharp.

I forced a bright tone. "Hi, Lisa! How are you?"

"Don't." A clipped pause. "Just tell me why you're not in the office."

I rifled through my bag, searching for my bus pass. *Damn it, where is it? And where is the damn bus?*

"I'm waiting for the bus," I said. "The first client meeting's not until nine, so I still have time."

"Yes, the meeting is at nine, but this isn't a *nine-to-five job*, Alex. I need you here now." Lisa's voice dripped impatience. She practically sneered the words, like the concept of normal working hours was beneath her.

My eyes landed on a stick nearby, and I indulged a little fantasy of bringing it to the office and whacking Lisa over the head with it. Instead, I bit my tongue and did my best to keep my voice calm. "I'll be there in twenty or thirty minutes. The bus should be here soon." That was, of course, if the damn bus ever showed up.

God, I needed coffee. Coffee was a necessary evil these days. Every sip dragged me back to that day at the café. But without caffeine, I could barely function—especially after nights like last night. Another nightmare. The shooters. Charlie. The sheer panic. It felt like some sick preview of my future, like I was speeding toward something inevitable. *No. Don't go there.* I shook my head, forcing the thoughts away. It was just the PTSD, like my shrink always said.

*Where is my bus pass?* I kept shuffling through my purse.

"Why can't you take a cab?" Lisa asked, like it was the most obvious solution in the world.

"Because I can't afford cabs," I said, then immediately wondered why I always felt the need to justify myself to her. "I can only afford public transportation," I added, digging deeper into my bag. And a tiny two-bedroom city apartment with a roommate. So tiny, you couldn't even fit a cat in there. Not even a tiny cat. Not even a fucking tiny cat!

"Whatever, just get here!" Lisa barked. "I need to see the presentation again before the meeting! And, then you and I are meeting with Cindy from HR."

My stomach lurched. Cindy from HR? My mind immediately spiraled into worst-case scenarios. "Wait, why are we meeting with—"

Lisa hung up before I could finish. *Great.* I exhaled sharply and shoved my phone back into my purse. We'd never had to meet with HR before. The only interaction I'd ever had with them was during some company-wide town hall where they droned on about some policy updates. I'd zoned out halfway through. Could that be why?

*No. No way.* I worked too damn hard for them to fire me. I stayed late. Sacrificed my weekends. Meanwhile, Lisa was on her tenth vacation with another boyfriend. No, they wouldn't get rid of me. I was too valuable. They wouldn't dare.

"Tough boss?" The woman with long black hair had clearly been eavesdropping. "The woman on the phone," she said. "Your boss?" There was a strange glint in her eyes, like she already knew the answer.

And then, somehow, my brain checked out and my mouth took over. Before I could stop myself, I was unloading my entire life story on this complete stranger.

"Is she my boss? Oh yeah, she's my boss. Her name is Lisa, and I can't stand her . . . like really seriously can't stand her. My god, the woman is the boss from hell! But I love my job and the company, I swear. I love it so much."

I didn't know why I was saying this. The words just kept coming. The woman listened, a small, unreadable smile playing on her lips.

"Advertising isn't just a job for me. It's why I get out of bed every morning. It gives me purpose. I pour my heart into every project, every client. What can I say? My job is my raison d'être! You see, two years ago, I survived this shooting. It was . . ."

I sucked in a sharp breath. My throat tightened. The teenager pulled off his headphones. The old man closed his book. I could feel their eyes on me now, but the words kept spilling. Like a dam had cracked open.

"It . . . it was the scariest moment of my life. The coffee shop was packed, and when chaos broke out, I felt trapped. I thought I was going to die." My voice cracked. "Sadly, a lot of people did die." I barely noticed when the first tear slipped down my cheek. "Even now, the thought of being trapped in a crowded bus makes my skin crawl. But I have to get to work." I was shaking now, swiping at my wet cheeks with the back of my hand. Her smile widened. "I never thought I'd make it out alive, but somehow I did. I was lucky to be the sixth person in line when the shooters played their twisted game."

The old man got up, tucking his book under his arm, and walked away. Just turned and crossed the street—like he needed to put as much distance between us as possible.

Still, I kept talking. I didn't know why.

"After it was all over…" I swallowed hard. "I didn't know how I'd ever move on from what happened. But this job became my escape. Not many people understand." I forced out a weak laugh. "My mom thinks I work too much, always telling me I should get out more, meet new people."

The woman was still watching me. Too closely now. Her smile hadn't faded, but something about it felt…different. Like she'd been waiting for me to say all of this.

"Shhh." She lifted a finger to her lips. The expression softened. Almost tender. Almost kind. Beneath the layers of makeup, she had beautiful features.

"I know what it's like to have a tough boss," she said. "It can be a real struggle. In fact, I'm dealing with something similar myself."

Her voice was so gentle, so unexpectedly warm, that I suddenly felt exposed, foolish. I glanced at the teenager—still watching. Surprisingly, he'd stuck around. A much-needed cool breeze ruffled my hair and skirt.

"This wind feels nice, doesn't it?" she said.

I swallowed. Finally, I managed, "I'm sorry… for dumping all of that on you."

She waved it off, like it was no big deal. "Don't let your boss get to you. Things will get better from here."

The bus pulled up, and I nearly sagged in relief. I couldn't get away fast enough. But as I was about to step onto the bus, I suddenly remembered that I couldn't find my bus pass. "Oh no, I don't think I have my—"

"Honey, your bus pass is right there." She pointed to my shoe. I'd been standing on it the whole time. "You must have dropped it."

"Thank you," I murmured, bending to grab it.

Her phone buzzed. She barely glanced at it. "It was nice talking to you."

I hesitated. "Yeah… you too."

"Best of luck to you," she said to my back as I boarded.

I made my way to the back, scanning for an empty seat. When I finally sat down and looked out the window, the woman was nowhere to be seen.

***

"Hey, Alex, tell me about your date on Saturday! Spill the tea, girl!" Bruce exclaimed.

I quickened my pace toward Lisa's office, Bruce hurrying to keep up. "Uh, it was painful," I blurted. "I'm sorry, but I really have to run to this meeting. Can we catch up later?"

"Oh, Lisa can spare another two minutes." He grabbed my elbow. "You cannot just drop a bomb like that and walk away. Was he a total disaster? Did he fail to meet your impeccable standards?"

I sighed. While I adored Bruce, he had this relentless need to cling to his curiosity until he'd wrung out every last piece of gossip. And honestly? This news wasn't even that interesting!

"Fine, but just two minutes, okay?" I said, shooting him a firm look. "You know how terrible my boss is, right?"

"Oh, darling, I think you mean our boss. And I pinky-promise to only take two minutes of your precious time," he replied.

Bruce straightened his flashy purple tie and leaned against the wall, striking a casual pose next to the gallery of client photos and artwork. I'd walked past them a million times, but somehow, I always noticed something new. The bold colors. The vibrant, chaotic energy. This office didn't just house ideas—it was one. Everywhere you turned, there was something to catch your eye: quirky wall art, sleek typography prints, edgy installations that probably cost more than my rent. Walking through the office felt less like work—more like wandering through a living art gallery.

"I swear, I'm never going on a blind date again," I groaned. "My mom swore he looked like a movie star. I probably should've asked *which* movie star. Let's be real—bald, fat, and rocking crooked teeth is *not* my idea of a Robert Pattinson look-alike."

He threw his head back and laughed out loud. "Darling, a blind date is better than no date at all. I mean, come on, it's been two whole years. It's about time you got back out there!"

"You sound just like my mother." I rolled my eyes. "But honestly, I haven't been ready these last two years. But now... I think I'm ready to try."

"You're destined to meet someone absolutely fabulous, you just need to get out there more. I mean have you seen yourself? You are drop-dead gorgeous!" Bruce said, flashing a smile. "And I was really hoping your date would have a hot friend for me, but alas, we can always hope for the next one!"

I teasingly tapped his chin. "When have you ever had trouble meeting guys? You're total eye-candy!"

He nodded solemnly, fully aware of his charm. "Speaking of guys, I finally had the pleasure of meeting my new neighbor. The cute one I've been gushing about? Fate united us in an enchanting elevator ride. Me, being the social butterfly that I am, couldn't resist a chat. And what do you know? His name's Matt. He's got this thrilling dream of opening a charming bar. Naturally, I had to mention my gig at the ad agency." He sighed dramatically. "One problem. He's, uh… into women. But I can introduce you to him."

I wasn't listening anymore. Kyle, the VP of Advertising, and Cindy from HR had just stepped into Lisa's office and shut the door behind them. My stomach dropped. This wasn't good.

"Oh my gosh, Cindy and Kyle just walked into Lisa's office and closed the door."

Bruce barely looked up. "And?"

I turned to him, glaring. "Cindy. As in Cindy from HR."

He rolled his eyes. "I know who she is, darling. But seriously, who cares?"

"I care! Lisa told me we were meeting with HR, but she didn't say anything about *Kyle*." My pulse kicked up. "Now I'm freaking out even more. Should I go knock? Or wait it out?"

Bruce rubbed his chin. "Perhaps waiting would be safer," he suggested. "Maybe it's good news. Lisa's horrible, and you went to Northwestern. You'll always land on your feet."

"I love this job! Why would I need to 'land on my feet' somewhere else?" My voice came out sharper than I intended. "Why don't you go find a new opportunity?"

Bruce gasped dramatically, clutching his chest. "Darling, don't be crazy. This place is like walking through a fashion magazine. Where else would I work?"

"Well, you're not the one at risk of getting fired. Lisa loves you. Me? I'm in trouble. And it's all because of you." I jabbed a finger at him.

Bruce staggered back, horrified. "I can understand that you're upset, but I fail to see how any of this is my fault."

Before I could argue that he'd distracted me with his date interrogation, the door to Lisa's office flew open.

"You can't fire me—I quit!"

Lisa's voice boomed down the hallway.

Bruce and I exchanged wide-eyed looks. "Did Lisa just... quit?" I asked.

Kyle and Cindy emerged from the office. As they approached, I panicked, flipping through my folder like I was deep in work. Bruce, of course, remained completely unbothered. He straightened his tie, flashed his most charming smile, and greeted them like we were at brunch. "Well hello there, how's your morning?"

Kyle's sighed. "Not as great as I was hoping, but okay," he said and then turned to Cindy. "I'll catch up with you in the next meeting."

Cindy nodded. "Just don't be late. We're discussing vacation policy changes." Her Chanel heels clicked as she strode away. Of course they were Chanel.

Then Kyle turned to me. "Congratulations, Weisman. You're the new Director. Unfortunately, we can't discuss what happened with Lisa, but you'll be taking over her role."

"What?" Bruce and I blurted it at the same time.

"But I've been here longer," Bruce protested.

Kyle gave him a tight smile, the corporate equivalent of a shrug. "Sorry, Bruce. Alex just has... a stronger connection with clients."

"She does?" Bruce asked.

Kyle didn't blink. "Yes, she does." He turned back to me. "Make sure the meeting with Dr. Olivia Jones goes well today. She's seeking our help to promote a charitable fundraising event at the hospital aimed at finding a cure for diabetes."

I nodded quickly. "Absolutely! I'm on it. Let's do this." I replied, maybe with a little too much enthusiasm.

Kyle seemed pleased. "I have faith in you, Weisman." He started to leave, then paused, rubbing his forehead. "Oh, by the way, Lisa should be out of here in the next half hour. Then the office is all yours."

Bruce's voice pulled me back to reality.

"So, um, are you like my boss now?" he asked.

I swallowed. "I guess so."

Bruce sighed dramatically. "Fine. I shall resume my work."

What the hell just happened? It felt like I'd stepped into some weird alternate reality. Lisa quitting. My sudden promotion. And then, that bizarre encounter with the lady from the bus stop flashed in my mind, wishing me good luck.

Then I shook my head—what an absurd thought.

I flipped through my folder, double-checking that everything was in order. And then, something slipped out from between the pages. My bus pass.

"Huh, that's strange," I pondered, picking it up. I reached into my purse. Another bus pass. The one I had stepped on earlier.

I turned the new pass over, and it slipped from my fingers and fell to the ground. Bold scrawls of "666" and a creepy smiley face stared up at me.

# OLIVIA

The Daily Grind's gaudy neon sign glared at me, as if daring me to come in. After the shooting, the new owner had wiped away every trace of the past—new door, fresh coat of paint, a flashy new name. But no amount of remodeling could erase what happened here.

My heart ached. I missed Giovanni's warm smile, the way he'd greet customers like old friends. Two years later, his absence still cut deep. The shop had lost its heart. The familiar faces—the morning regulars—were gone.

I'd tried reaching out to Sofia and their sons more times than I could count, but they shut me out completely. The last time I spoke with Giovanni's oldest son, Lorenzo, he said they just needed space. "It's not personal," he said, "we just can't deal with it right now." I understood, but the rejection still stung.

I glanced at the door, debating. The new owner—whoever he was—lacked Giovanni's warmth. Truthfully, I couldn't even remember his name.

I could have kept walking. Should have. But instead, I took a slow breath and stepped inside. Giovanni would have wanted the coffee shop to continue running, even if it no longer bore his name. His legacy lived on, and that thought gave me a small glimmer of comfort.

Inside, it felt like nothing had happened—conversations murmured, cups clinked, espresso thick in the air. But everything had changed. The wooden tables had been swapped for sleek, modern ones. The stiff-backed chairs replaced with deep, cushioned couches. Greenery now crawled along the walls, framing generic coffee-themed prints where Giovanni's Italian murals had once been. Every trace of him—of what this place had been—was gone.

There were no reminders of the shooting. No broken glass. No splintered wood. Just a fresh coat of paint, the clatter of cups, baristas calling out orders, voices overlapping—life moved on.

To the people here, I was just another customer. But this place held ghosts. And for those of us who remembered, the scars ran deep.

"I'll take a medium latte with skim milk and no sugar," I said as I fumbled for my wallet. Time was ticking—surgeries, patients, a dozen things waiting back at the hospital.

The cashier barely looked up as he punched in my order. "Medium latte, skim milk, no sugar!" he echoed to the barista. "Name?"

"Olivia," I replied.

He scrawled it on the cup, handed me my card back, and I stepped aside, already glancing at my phone.

I should have been checking my schedule, making sure I was ready for the next case. Instead, my mind pulled me elsewhere. To Charlie. Still in a coma. Still fighting a battle she didn't know she was in.

I had insisted on taking her as my patient—not only because I thought I could save her legs, but because I owed her that much. When I found out she had survived, relief nearly knocked me off my feet. Others hadn't made it out. But survival had come at a cost.

The bullet that lodged in her spine had caused irreversible damage to her nerve center, rendering her paralyzed from the waist down. I had promised her mother I would do everything in my power to save her legs. Two surgeries later, all I had to offer was the truth no one wanted to hear. If she wakes up—and that's still an if—she might never walk again. I couldn't help but feel like I had failed her *again*.

Charlie's mother refused to accept it. Every day, she sat by her daughter's bedside, whispering the same plea. *Wake up. Walk again.* As if saying it enough times could make it true. Hope was cruel like that. Charlie's mother clung to it for her daughter, and I clung to it for Owen.

A year had passed since he left, but I still wore the Tiffany's necklace. My fingers often found the pendant's delicate curves, tracing them without thinking. I could still feel the brush of his fingers against my skin as he fastened the clasp, his voice low as he told me how beautiful it looked. I should have taken it off long ago. But I didn't. Maybe I couldn't. Maybe it was the last thing holding me to something that no longer existed. Pathetic, really—but I couldn't help it.

I let out a slow breath. It was going to be a long wait. My phone screen lit up again, pulling me back to the present. Daniel.

*"How's your morning going?"*

We had worked together for years, but somewhere along the way, he became more than just a colleague. When Owen left, Daniel became my lifeline. Without him, I don't know how I would have held it together.

Even after grueling nights at the hospital, when exhaustion dulled his eyes as much as mine, Daniel still came over. He'd sit beside me, a silent presence in the darkness, keeping me from drowning in my own company. He'd bring food, knowing I wouldn't eat otherwise, and put on *Friends* because he knew it was my favorite. Even when laughter felt impossible, he tried. And that meant everything.

Two college-aged girls next to me started talking loudly. One blonde. The other dark-haired, with a face so familiar my breath caught. *Charlie.*

Or at least, for a second, that's who I thought she was. Lately, it felt like I was seeing her everywhere. Maybe she didn't even resemble Charlie at all. Maybe my mind was just desperate to find pieces of her in strangers, no matter how far off the mark.

"Hey, did you know there was a shooting here two years ago?" the brunette asked.

"What? Are you serious?" the blonde replied.

"Yeah, it was crazy. Fourteen people were killed. Sixteen, if you count the shooters."

*If Charlie doesn't make it, the death toll will rise,* I thought. I wondered if she could hear us, if she knew how long it had been. Was she trapped in her mind this whole time, suffering in silence? I just wanted her to wake up. She had to wake up.

The blonde scoffed. "Nah, you're lying."

"She's not lying." The words left my mouth before I knew why. "I was there."

Both girls gasped, the blonde eyeing me warily. "What's it like being back here again?"

"It's like a wound that never heals," I said, surprised at how easily the words came. Maybe it was the loneliness since Owen left—maybe even talking to strangers offered some relief.

"Why do you keep coming here then?"

*Yes, why?* I had asked myself that same question every time I entered the coffee shop. For a while, I had stopped.

"It's close to my work," I replied, though I knew that wasn't the whole truth. "But honestly, it's more than that. I feel like I have to come here. It's like visiting a grave—it helps me stay connected to the ones who didn't make it. Even though I didn't know most of them, it brings... some kind of solace."

The barista called their orders. The girls exchanged awkward glances, grabbed their drinks, and hurried out.

The pain of not being able to save those you want to help . . . that was what hurt the most. I had sworn to save lives, but that day, I had failed. And if I lose Charlie too... it's too much. My hands trembled as I wiped away tears, but they kept coming, unstoppable.

"Olivia, your medium latte is ready!"

The barista's voice cut through my thoughts, startling me.

Sniffling, I reached for the cup, hoping for warmth, for comfort. I took a sip. Weak. Like everything else lately.

I took another sip, glancing at my phone to check my schedule and realized I had completely overlooked a meeting. In forty minutes, I was supposed to meet with Lisa, the hospital's advertising director, to discuss the fundraising event for diabetes research. A cause I cared about. One I'd eagerly volunteered for. Especially now, when there was no one waiting for me at home.

Absentmindedly, my eyes drifted to my left hand, where my wedding band used to be. Owen's last words crashed in.

"You don't need me anymore," he said, his voice flat, as if he had already made up his mind.

"That's not true! Of course I need you. I love you. Please don't leave."

"Bullshit!" he snapped. "You spend every waking minute at the hospital."

"I have to help Charlie!" I protested. "I survived the shooting; I took her place. I was supposed to suffer, not her."

"When will you accept that this isn't your fault?" Owen argued. "This girl has consumed your life. There's no room for me anymore. We gave up on having kids, and I'm losing you more and more every day. I can't watch you destroy yourself—it's too painful. I'm done."

And just like that, he was gone. In an instant, my marriage unraveled. Our divorce wasn't finalized yet, but I knew it was just a matter of time. Holding on to hope seemed foolish. He wasn't coming back.

I shoved thoughts of Owen aside and headed for the exit, moving too fast, too lost in my own head—until I accidentally stepped on a woman's foot.

"I'm so sorry," I apologized.

She straightened up, adjusted her bag, and flipped her long black hair over her shoulder. The heavy makeup—dark purple eyeshadow, deep red lipstick—belonged on a stage, not a morning coffee run. Striking. A little intense. Completely out of place in the daylight.

"It's all good," she said, brushing it off. "You seem to be in a hurry."

"Yes, a bit," I said, offering a weak smile and reaching for the door. "Sorry again."

"No worries. Good luck today, Doctor."

I froze. How did she know that? I wasn't wearing scrubs, no badge, nothing that would give it away. Just a beige business suit—ordinary, forgettable.

"Excuse me, do we know each other?" I asked, turning back to her.

She smiled and handed me a business card. "You dropped this."

I glanced down. My name. Spelled perfectly. But the rest was wrong. All of it. The title. The hospital address. None of it matched.

"This isn't my business card," I said, holding it up. "I'm a surgeon, not a family physician. And this doesn't even resemble my card. Where did you get this?"

Her smile faded. "Oh, I'm sorry. I must have confused you with someone else."

A chill curled through me. "Yes, you most definitely have," I said, suddenly needing to get out of there. "Sorry, I'm in a hurry."

Her gaze sharpened, lingering a beat too long. Watching me. Measuring something. "Good luck with your day."

"I appreciate it," I muttered, even though luck wasn't something I believed in anymore. The only luck I wanted? For Owen to walk back into my life. For Charlie to wake up.

Exiting the coffee shop, I waited patiently for the traffic light to turn green.

Two pigeons brawled over a scrap of bread while people at nearby café tables lingered over late breakfasts. A woman in a sunhat threw her head back, laughing too loudly, her voice rising above the hum of traffic. A kid yanked at his mother's dress, pointing at a dog trotting past. Meanwhile, all I could think about was the sweet relief of air-conditioning.

The light turned green, and I stepped into the flow of pedestrians heading toward Michigan Avenue. Then, a shift. A prickling awareness at the back of my neck. I glanced sideways. She was there. The black-haired woman stood outside the café, watching me. Smiling.

"Lady, watch out, that cab is about to hit you!"

The scream barely registered before I saw it—the taxi, barreling toward me.

*Move.* My body wouldn't listen. My feet cemented to the pavement, my breath strangled in my throat. Then—silence. Like a switch had flipped, the street vanished. I wasn't here anymore. I was back in the shooting. Charlie and I, mid-conversation. The old man on the floor, his face twisted in agony. The shooter's voice like ice.

*"Because, Doctor, six is the number of the Devil. We're Satanists, and we're selecting three sixes from the crowd to survive. Consider yourself lucky that you're one of them."*

The weight of his words crushed my lungs. The air thinned, my throat closing. Through the whispering wind, I heard it.

*Six. Six. Six. Lucky number six.*

A hand grabbed my shoulder, yanking me back to reality. I hit the pavement hard, tumbling onto the curb. A gust of wind rushed past— the cab missing me by inches. Still disoriented, I blinked up at the man who had just pulled me back from death—tall, late twenties, dark hair damp with sweat, eyes sharp with concern.

He extended his hand to help me up.

"Are you all right? Let's get off the road and onto the sidewalk," he said.

As we stood, I noticed a small crowd had gathered. Someone asked if anyone had caught the cab's license plate, but I wasn't listening. I was searching for her. She was gone. I swallowed hard. Had I imagined the way she watched me? The way she smiled? I'd never believed in things like hypnosis or mind games, but for a moment, I'd felt—pulled. Trapped in something I couldn't explain. Maybe it was stress. Maybe shock. That was the logical answer. But logic didn't explain the way my skin still prickled.

"It was a reckless cab driver," the young man said, shielding his eyes from the sun. "I tried to get the license plate, but it sped off. Anyway, are you okay? You're trembling. Do you want to go to the hospital?"

I shook my head. "No, thanks, I'm a doctor. I'll be all right."

"Sorry about your suit," he added, pointing to the coffee stain spreading across my jacket. My empty cup lay on the sidewalk.

"Dammit." I exhaled, brushing at the fabric. "How am I supposed to clean this before my meeting?"

"Sorry," he said, rubbing the back of his neck. "It was the only way to get you out of the way."

"It's not your fault," I replied, still a little shaken.

"I'm Matt, by the way," he said.

There was something familiar about him. I searched his face, trying to figure out where I'd seen him before, but nothing came to mind.

"Olivia." I reached into my purse and pulled out a business card. "Here, take this. Like I said, I'm a doctor. If you ever need anything, reach out. I owe you one."

He slipped it into his wallet. "Thanks. Hope your day turns around."

"Thanks," I replied, gingerly touching my scraped knee. "First, some weird lady with black hair and too much makeup wishing me good luck, and now this…" I sputtered, realizing too late I'd said it aloud.

His gaze sharpened. "What weird lady?"

"Just a stranger I ran into this morning," I said, glancing at my watch. 10:05. I was late. Could this day get any worse? "I'm sorry, but I have to run. I'm late for a meeting. Thanks again."

"Wait, hold on." He took a step closer. "Have we met before? You look familiar."

Strange. He thought the same thing. But I had no time to dig into it now.

I shook my head, already backing away. "Maybe. But I really have to go. Keep my card—we'll figure it out later."

As I hurried away, an unsettling feeling gnawed at my gut. Meeting Matt felt like more than coincidence. But I had no time to dwell on it.

Just then, a text from Daniel lit up my phone: *Charlie woke up. You need to get to the hospital right away.*

I stopped cold. My hand flew to my mouth. Could this be real?

*Be right there.* I quickly texted back.

Then, I fired off a quick message to reschedule my meeting and took off toward the hospital. As if my life depended on it.

# CHARLIE

"Charlie, it's Mammina. Can you hear me?"

Her voice, warm as ever, was a ray of hope.

"I'm here with you, and I love you so much. I know you're strong, and I believe in you. You can fight this. Please don't give up, Charlie. You have so much to live for, and I need you. Jason also needs you. Please come back to us."

I'd been aware of their voices from the beginning. Even in a coma, I heard everything. My body felt heavy. Unresponsive. But my mind? Light. Almost detached.

*Mammina, it's me, Charlie. I can hear you, but I'm trapped inside my own body, and it's so frustrating.*

I wanted to tell her that I was fighting to come back. But the words wouldn't come. I wanted to walk again. Live a normal life. But I didn't know if that was even possible. The doctors were trying to save me, but I already knew the truth. The bullet that struck my spine had caused irreversible damage. I'm paralyzed from the waist down. My chances of ever walking again? Only four percent.

And that was *if* I ever woke up.

"Charlie, baby, can you hear me?"

Jason's voice cut through the fog—gentle, steady, but cracked with pain.

"I'm here, by your side. I visit you every day, and it's hard to believe that two years have passed. I miss you so much. But I won't give up on you. I'll be here for you every step of the way."

His words pulled me backward—into us. We had known each other since we were nine. Jason lived down the street, and we spent hours playing tag, hide-and-seek, and chasing each other around the neighborhood. Saturdays meant cartoons, video games, snacks, and secrets.

But as we entered our teenage years, things changed. One summer night, sitting on the swings in his backyard, we talked for hours under the stars. I remember the way the air smelled of the neighbor's barbecue, how the heat clung to our skin, how even the mosquitoes didn't bother us. At some point, we grew quiet. Jason looked at me like he was seeing me for the first time. Then—he leaned in. His kiss was hesitant, shy. But it felt right. From that moment, we just knew.

Jason didn't get into Northwestern, but he was planning to attend Indiana University. He promised to marry me after we finished college. Even with the distance, I knew in my heart nothing could change what we had. We dreamed of a future where nothing could tear us apart, where our love would only grow stronger with time.

But that was before the bullet tore through my body and shattered our dreams. We would never get back what we had before. No more morning runs. No more skiing down the slopes. We wouldn't walk down the aisle. Or explore the streets of Italy. The life we'd dreamed of was gone.

*Why us? Why now?*

"Look at her, Ms. Moretti! She's lying there like a vegetable, wasting away. Who are we kidding here? She's never gonna wake up. It's been two years already."

His words hit me hard. Was that what I was? A vegetable? I couldn't move. I couldn't speak. Maybe he was right.

"Charlie is not a vegetable, Jason," Mammina said firmly. "She's still here with us."

Jason exhaled sharply. "I'm sorry, Ms. Moretti," he said. "I just love her so much. I wish I could've taken that bullet for her. It's just not fair, and I'm just so angry. Why did she have to be the one who got hurt?"

"I know it's hard to accept, Jason," Mammina said softly. "But sometimes life can be unpredictable and cruel. We can't change what happened, but we can still hope and pray for Charlie to wake up."

*But Mammina, it wasn't fair. Why couldn't I have been one of the lucky ones? That last number six was supposed to have been me.*

"Any word from Charlie's father?" Jason asked.

"No, Jason. It's been two years, and he hasn't even checked in once," Mammina replied, her voice tinged with bitterness.

"Do you think he knows?" Jason asked.

"He should. Charlie's name was mentioned in the news. But he hasn't reached out to us, and I don't know if he even cares."

It hurt to think that he might not care at all.

"It's time to go, Jason. We'll come back tomorrow."

Their voices faded. The door clicked shut.

And I was alone again.

Two years of loneliness. I should be used to this by now. But how do you get used to loneliness? How do you adapt to the aching emptiness that fills the room when everyone leaves?

I clung to memories like lifelines. Jason's eyes when he talked about our future. Mammina's lullabies when I was scared. But memories weren't enough. They never were.

Then I realized it. I wasn't alone.

Someone was watching me.

And then, someone was talking.

At first, it was just a whisper, barely audible. But then— the voice grew louder.

"Charlie, can you hear me?" the voice said. "It's me, I came to visit you. You look so fragile, like life has drained you of everything. But don't you worry, soon we'll fix that. You see, I know you can hear me. You can't see me, but let me describe what I look like. I'm a woman with long black hair. I wore extra makeup today, especially for you. And soon, dear Charlie, very soon, you'll be free.

Just wait and see."

# ALEXANDRA

"Thanks for making time for me, Dr. Richardson," I said, clutching my coffee cup as I sank deeper into the ridiculously comfortable burgundy couch. If therapy couldn't fix me, maybe this couch could. I managed a weak smile, trying to find solace in the little things, even if my brain still felt like a tornado had blown through it.

As soon as Dr. Olivia Jones rescheduled our meeting, I called my therapist and snagged an appointment. My promotion might've looked like a win, but underneath, I was a mess. Between last night's nightmare, my mini-meltdown at the bus stop, and the creepy writing on that bus pass, one thing was clear—seeing Dr. Richardson wasn't a whim. It was a full-on emergency.

Dr. Richardson sat across from me, flipping through his notebook while the room glowed with soft, warm lighting. A framed photo of his wife and son rested on his desk, right next to the peace lily he loved to use as a metaphor for personal growth—*resilience, healing, the whole "journey" spiel*. Behind him, the wall practically screamed *overachiever*, with his Stanford PhD, awards from the American Counseling Association, and a lineup of other fancy accolades on display—all basically saying, *Look how much better I am at life than you.*

Tissue boxes sat within easy reach—I usually went through them fast. The clock on the wall ticked softly, each second a reminder that time was moving forward. Maybe I was, too.

Dr. Richardson finally looked up, offering that familiar, gentle smile—equal parts encouraging and *let's unpack your trauma*.

"I'm always glad to see you, Alex," he said, adjusting his glasses and crossing one leg over the other. Mid-forties, salt-and-pepper hair, green eyes that caught everything. Warm but professional—the perfect balance of reassuring and perceptive. "I can tell something's bothering you. The way you keep chewing your lip gives it away. Let's start with your nightmare. Can we dive into that?"

I curled my fingers around my coffee cup, bracing myself. "Yeah."

"Tell me, what did you dream about?"

"That girl again," I sighed. "The one I met in the coffee shop right before the gunmen stormed in."

His expression remained steady. "Charlie?"

I nodded. Weirdly enough, she'd been popping up in my dreams for two years. Strange, considering our interaction had been so brief. Just a stranger. A girl I'd talked to for a few minutes. But when I found out she'd survived the shooting and was in a coma, it hit me harder than I expected. She was so excited about college. Now she might never wake up. Still, I never visited her. Never reached out to her family. What would I even say?

Still, in my dreams, she was always there.

"It was different this time," I said. "I couldn't see her, but I could hear her. And somehow, I just knew it was her."

Dr. Richardson didn't interrupt, just nodded and scribbled a note in his notebook.

"I dreamt the shooters didn't let me go," I continued. "Instead, they locked me inside a small, dark box where I couldn't breathe. I screamed for help, but no one could hear me."

His brow furrowed slightly. "A small, dark box this time?"

I frowned. "Yeah... why?"

"It's just interesting," he mused, tapping his pen against the notebook. "Before, it was always a coffin. This time, it changed."

I shook my head. "I don't know. I really don't. It just felt... different, you know?" I hesitated, gripping my coffee cup tighter. "Like my claustrophobia got a lot worse." I exhaled sharply. "You know how bad I get with enclosed spaces. The coffin was bad, yeah—but at least it was just pressing down on me from the top." I swallowed. "That box? It was everywhere—pressing in from all sides. Tighter. No air. No way out." I ran a hand through my hair. "It was suffocating. Worse than before. Way worse."

"Did Charlie say anything to you in your dream?" Dr. Richardson asked.

"Yeah." I shifted in my seat. "She said she was in trouble. That she needed my help."

His pen stilled. "Just like in your other dreams?"

"Yeah, and just like before, I asked what kind of trouble, but she wouldn't say. She just kept repeating, 'Help me, Alex. Help me.' But I couldn't help her because I was trapped and couldn't escape." I chewed my lip, thinking. "It's strange, isn't it? Why do I keep dreaming about this girl? I didn't even know her—not really." Dr. Richardson didn't interrupt, so I kept going. "And why doesn't Matt ever show up?"

Dr. Richardson's head tilted. "Matt?"

I nodded. "The guy who held my hand during the shooting. The last time I saw him, he was on the ground, sobbing. His father was there— I think. My mom told me to go home, and I didn't argue." I swallowed. "I thought about messaging him afterward on social media, but… I don't know. I didn't want to seem like a stalker." Exhaling, I shook my head. "Still, for all the times I've thought about him, he's never once shown up in my dreams."

Dr. Richardson leaned back, studying me carefully. "Like I've said before, Alex, dreams are your mind's way of processing trauma. This girl—Charlie—probably represents something deeper. Maybe the part of you that felt powerless that day. Or the fear and vulnerability you're still carrying. And then there's survivor's guilt—you made it out, but she's in a coma. It's not unusual for those emotions to show up in your dreams." He watched me for a moment. "Have you thought about visiting her? Seeing her in person might help you heal, too."

I shook my head, fast. "I can't, Doctor. I can't see her like that."

"I get it," he said gently. "But facing that fear might be the key to unlocking these nightmares."

I sighed. "I just don't know if I can handle it."

Dr. Richardson nodded. "It's a process. One step at a time. But let's go back to your dream—was there anything else? Any details that stood out?"

I took a sip of my coffee, stalling. "Yeah," I said slowly. "She warned me—told me something dark was hanging over me, something I couldn't escape. And while she talked, I couldn't breathe. Like something clamped down on my chest, squeezing the air out. Like I was on the brink of something... bad." I exhaled, trying to shake the feeling. "Then I woke up screaming. And after that? My day got *weird*."

"Weird how?"

I told him about the woman at the bus stop. How I couldn't stop talking—spilling my entire life story to a total stranger. "It's like my brain wasn't mine," I said. "I told her everything—the shooting, my job, how much I hate my boss."

Dr. Richardson just nodded, jotting down notes.

"And here's the weirdest part," I went on, my words picking up speed. "She looked... off. Like something out of a horror movie. Too much makeup, long black hair, total witchy vibes. And I just kept talking—until she touched my hand. That's when I snapped out of it. Then the bus came, and she wished me good luck."

He adjusted his glasses, pausing before responding. "Alex, I think this is all part of the PTSD. The trauma from the shooting has impacted your ability to process emotions, so your mind is drawing connections that aren't really there."

I narrowed my eyes. "Maybe. But how do you explain this?" I reached into my bag and pulled out two bus passes. "I thought I lost my bus pass, and this woman pointed out it was under my foot. Then when I got to work, another bus pass fell out of my folder. And look at what's written on the one from the bus stop." I flipped it over, revealing a bold '666' and a creepy smiley face.

He studied it for a moment. "It's unsettling, I'll give you that," he said. "But it's probably just a prank. Chicago's full of strange characters. Maybe some kid decided to get creative with a bus pass."

*Honestly?* I rubbed my forehead. He wasn't wrong. The city was full of weirdos. And bus stops? Prime real estate for creepy pranks. Probably just someone messing with people. *Probably.*

I forced a shrug. "You're right. Just a dumb joke."

Dr. Richardson smiled. "Try to relax, Alex. Keep your focus on the positive. I know it's hard, given everything you've been through, but daily mental exercises can help. Okay, so let's talk about something good. Anything come to mind?"

I grinned. "Guess what? My terrible boss got fired, and I got her job. Totally out of the blue! And after this session, I'm meeting Bruce for lunch to celebrate."

His smile widened. "Fantastic news! Keep your sights on the positive, and make time for fun—it's the best way to shake off stress. And remember, when anxiety or panic hits, breathe. Stay focused on the good."

"Positive vibes," I repeated, half-joking but making a mental note to stick with it.

He stood, walking me to the door. "And don't forget to get some exercise. Oh, and go easy on the alcohol."

I smirked. "I'll try. But hey, a little wine never hurt anyone, right?"

We both laughed.

"I'm glad you're smiling," he said, opening the door. "Healing takes time. But much like my peace lily here, you'll keep growing."

I nodded. "Thanks, Doctor."

"I look forward to our next session. And remember, you can always call if you need anything in between."

As I stepped outside, I promised myself I'd focus on the positives. But no matter how hard I tried, that nagging feeling—the one whispering that something wasn't quite right—just wouldn't let go.

"No," I told myself firmly as I walked out into the sunshine. "Cut it out. It's a whole lot of nothing. Channel your inner Dr. Richardson, focus on the positive, and go enjoy lunch with Bruce before heading back to work. Life is good—you're a big boss now."

Then I spotted Bruce, deep in conversation. I squinted, stepping off the curb. And when I saw who he was talking to, my stomach flipped. *No. Freaking. Way.*

# MATT

Olivia darted across the street and disappeared into the crowd. I stayed put, hands on my hips, thinking.

*"First, some weird lady with black hair and too much makeup wishing me good luck, and now this…"*

The words rattled loose in my head. A woman with black hair. Not *the* woman. *A* woman. Coincidence. Had to be. Too many people in this city. Too many women with black hair and too much makeup.

Then why did my stomach feel tight?

The woman at the roulette table. The way she moved my chips. The impossible win. The way my body had stopped listening to me, like I'd been hypnotized. The way she looked at me—like she already knew the outcome. And now, a random stranger—completely separate— mentioning a woman with black hair?

A horn blared. A cab skidded to the curb, tires screeching. My muscles tensed. A flash of memory—the cab that almost hit Olivia.

I shook my head. *No. Enough.* Tom's dream. That's what mattered.

Lucas, the real estate guy Sean had put me in touch with, wanted me to check out the building again. I had a bar to open.

I exhaled, squared my shoulders, and climbed into the cab. "West Loop," I said, giving the address.

Inside, I leaned back, exhaling hard. The seat smelled like old leather and stale cigarettes.

The driver glanced at me in the mirror. "Rough morning?"

I hesitated, not answering right away. "Something like that," I finally muttered.

The driver nodded, like he got it, and turned his focus back to the road.

I stared out the window. The city blurred past, but my mind was still stuck in the street, replaying Olivia's words. Turning them over, trying to make sense of them.

*Enough.* I rubbed my temples.

The cab jolted over a pothole. My body snapped forward, hands catching the edge of the seat. I let out a slow breath.

For a second, I could hear him. *Smile, bro. This is it. We're making our dream come true.*

I turned. The seat was empty. Of course it was. It always was. My stomach tightened. I stared out the window. Didn't let myself look again. Because if I did—he'd still be there. Smirking like always. Like nothing ever changed. I faced forward again, pressing my fingers against my temple. *Stupid. He's gone.*

Ten minutes later, the cab pulled up to the curb. I stepped out, fixing my shirt where it clung to my back. I glanced up at the building. Steel and glass. Sturdy. Dark windows, clean lines. No frills, no bullshit.

West Loop. The perfect spot. Plenty of foot traffic to stay packed. Plenty of business to keep the money flowing. A bar would fit here— not just fit. It would thrive. This was it. I dialed Lucas.

"Lucas, listen, man, I don't want to waste any more time looking at other options," I said, heat pressing down, sweat prickling at my neck. "This is it."

Lucas exhaled. "Matt, maybe we should check out a few more places first. I don't want you rushing into this."

"I've passed this building every day for years," I said. "Always thought it could be something."

Tom did too. Every time we walked by, he'd nudge me, grinning.

*"This is it, Matt. This is the one."*

Back then, I just laughed, shook my head, told him he was crazy. A bar? We barely had enough cash for rent, let alone some dream like this. But now? Now, it wasn't just an idea. It wasn't just some wild plan we joked about on late-night walks home.

A bar. *Our* bar. A place that actually meant something.

Lucas hesitated. "Alright," he said. "Just making sure you're sure."

"I'm sure, man. This is it. I'm positive," I said.

Then Lucas dropped a bomb. "Landlord wants three months payment upfront," he said. "I tried negotiating, but with your limited renter's credit, he wouldn't budge. He's had bad experiences with renters in the past."

The street noise dulled.

"How much?"

"Rent for a spot this size in the city is around fifty grand a month." He paused. "So you're looking at one hundred fifty K upfront."

My stomach lurched. That was too much money, and I hadn't even factored in the other costs yet.

*"Jesus, Matt. You're really doing this?"*

I could almost hear him. Almost see him. But he wasn't there. *He never was.* Tom. Hands in his pockets, grinning the way he always did. Like nothing could touch us. Like we had all the time in the world. We didn't. This should have been our moment. But he was gone. And now it was just me.

I took a step back. Turned. My heart was racing. This was insane. *Too much. Too risky.*

Another step away.

And yet.

I turned back and stared at the building—the future it held, the life it could breathe into what we built. Tom's dream. *Mine too.*

*Who was I kidding?* This wasn't just his dream. It was ours. Always had been. I'd told myself I was doing this for him. That it was about honoring him, keeping his dream alive because he couldn't. Because someone took that from him. But maybe saying it was for him was just an excuse. Because I wanted this too.

My throat tightened. If I failed, I wasn't just failing myself. I was failing him. *It was too much. Too risky.*

My stomach clenched. I wanted this. *No—needed it.*

I swallowed hard. The fear was still there, pressing in, but so was something else. Something stronger. *Screw hesitation.* "I'm in."

"You sure about this?" Lucas asked.

"Yeah," I said, my voice steady, even though my pulse was anything but. "I'm sure."

Lucas promised to talk to the landlord and get the contract over to me tomorrow.

I hung up and ran a hand through my hair, pacing a few steps before stopping. My nerves were tangled, but beneath them was something stronger. I felt what Tom was talking about.

I could almost see it—the doors swinging wide, people flooding in, the bass shaking the walls, drinks clinking, voices rising. A grin tugged at my face. This was gonna be worth it.

I tilted my head back, staring at the cloudless sky. "You see that, man?" I whispered. "You better be watching."

The air stayed still. No response. Just the city moving around me. Just me, standing there.

I wiped the sweat from my forehead and shoved my hands into my pockets, swallowing the lump in my throat. "I won't let you down, Tom." The road ahead wouldn't be easy. That didn't matter. "I'm ready."

And this time, I believed it.

I checked my watch. 12:15 p.m. Sean was meeting me for lunch in fifteen minutes, but there was someone I needed to call first. Actually, two.

I dialed my boss. "Hello," he answered.

"Hey," I said. "Just calling to let you know—I quit."

A beat. Then I hung up. Just like that.

I dialed again. After a few rings, my dad picked up. "Hey, son. What're you up to?"

I stepped to the edge of the sidewalk, dodging a jogger as I brought the phone closer to my ear. The sun was relentless, beating down on my shoulders. I hadn't told Dad about the money yet. I was waiting for the right moment. Now that I was taking the leap with the bar, this was it—the right moment to tell him everything.

"I quit my job," I said.

There was a pause. Not a long one, but just long enough to feel it. Then came the sigh, low and drawn out. "You quit your job? What the hell are you gonna do now?" His voice was tight, the kind of tight that pressed in, like a fist gripping too hard. I stared down at a crack in the pavement, scuffing it with the toe of my shoe.

"Matt, you can't just quit your job. You've got bills, responsibilities—a future to think about," he said. "You can't just toss your job aside without a plan. I sure as heck hope you've got a plan. So, what's your plan now?"

"I'm opening a bar," I said, gripping the phone tighter. "I know it sounds crazy, but hear me out. I won five hundred and twenty-five grand at the casino over the weekend, and it's finally given me the chance to make our dream real. I want to honor Tom's memory. But it's not just his dream—it's ours, Dad. Mine and his."

There was another pause, longer this time. "Listen, Son, running a bar ain't no cakewalk. It takes some serious elbow grease and dedication. You gotta know what you're doing, and you don't have any experience. You think just because you hit it big once that Lady Luck is gonna keep on smiling at you? Hate to break it to you, but luck runs out faster than you can say 'bottoms up.'"

This wasn't the conversation I was hoping for.

"I'll hire people who can help me," I replied.

"You can't trust just anyone these days," my dad said gruffly. "What if they're stealing from you behind your back? Have you thought about that? "

"I hear you, Dad," I said, straightening my shoulders and lifting my chin like he could see me through the phone. "But I've got a solid plan, and I'll make sure to hire the right people. I thought you'd be proud of me."

"Son, I didn't send you to college to become a bartender," he said, his voice rising. "You have a degree, for Christ's sake. You could have a steady job with benefits and a retirement plan. You know how hard it is to make ends meet. I've been working in a damn warehouse for thirty years and I still struggle to pay bills. I thought I taught you the value of money." He let out another heavy sigh. "What if the bar fails? You'll be right back where you started, with nothing to show for it. You could invest that money and retire early, travel the world, something your mother and I could only dream of. Don't be foolish, Son."

"Sometimes you've got to take risks, Dad," I said, jaw clenched. "And if it doesn't work out, at least I'll know I tried. I can't live my life afraid of failure."

He went quiet. I pictured him rubbing his temple, the way he always did when he was deep in thought.

"Well, I hope you know what you're getting into. I just don't want to see you regret this," he finally said.

I hung up and leaned against the brick wall. The heat pressed into my back, but I barely noticed. The call sat like a stone in my chest. I stared at the sidewalk, turning his words over in my head. *Was I making a mistake?*

"Matt?" a cheerful voice called, snapping me out of my thoughts. I looked up and forced a smile. Bruce—my neighbor. Friendly guy, maybe a little too friendly. We'd met recently in the building, but last time, I had to cut our conversation short in the elevator—I was in a rush. Running into him again wasn't a surprise. He'd mentioned working at an ad agency in the city, though I couldn't remember which one.

"Well, hello there!" he exclaimed, spreading his arms wide. "What brings you to this corner of the world?"

"See that building right there?" I said, nodding toward it. "That's where my new bar's gonna be."

"That's so exciting! It'll be an absolute travesty if Alex and I aren't on the guest list for the grand opening." He clapped his hands together. "I'm envisioning a night filled with finest bubbly, divine cocktails, and outrageous fun."

"Thanks, man," I said, appreciating his enthusiasm. It felt good knowing someone else believed in my dream. "By the way, who's Alex?"

"Alex is not only a cherished friend but also my new boss whom I'm meeting for lunch around here," Bruce glanced across the street and suddenly lit up. "And speak of the devil—there she is!" He waved big, like he was flagging down a taxi. As she approached, he grinned. "Alex, meet Matt—my neighbor and future bar owner."

I couldn't believe it. It was *her*. The girl from Giovanni's. What were the chances? Everything from that day came back. Her laugh cutting through the noise of the coffee shop. Her eyes catching mine in the line. The way she squeezed my hand when we thought we were going to die. Afterward, I'd tried to find her. Searched online like an idiot. Scrolled through faces that didn't match, wondering if our connection had been real or just something I imagined in the chaos.

And now? She was right here. Even more stunning than I remembered. Her brown hair fell over a crisp white blouse, tucked into a beige skirt. She slipped off her sunglasses and pushed them into her hair. When her eyes met mine, I saw it—she recognized me too.

We stood there, silent. I didn't know what to say. Should I ask how she's been? Should I say anything at all? My mind scrambled for words, but I knew one thing: I couldn't let this chance slip away.

"Hey, it's been a while. How have you been?"

"I've been okay," she said softly. "How about you?"

"Hanging in there. Taking it one day at a time," I said. I tried to sound casual, but the tightness in my chest gave me away. "You know how it is. Just trying to get through."

She nodded. And in her eyes, I saw it—the sadness. A weight. A pain that never leaves. I knew that kind of pain. The kind you carry and can't put down. The kind that sticks with you long after surviving what no one should. How does anyone stay okay after that?

Bruce's eyes lit up. "You two know each other? Do tell me, from where?"

I hesitated. Diving into the painful details with someone I barely knew wasn't exactly appealing, and Alex seemed to feel the same. Clearing my throat, I said, "We had a brief encounter a few years back."

I thought I saw a flicker of disappointment on Alex's face, but maybe I was imagining it.

Bruce grinned like a mischievous cat. "Well, well, well. We simply must fix that," he said, snatching my phone before Alex could object. He quickly punched in her number and handed it back to me. "Okay, darlings, we simply must dash! We're on our lunch break and time is of the essence," he announced, practically dragging Alex away.

As they disappeared, I heard Alex's voice trailing behind. "Bruce! That was so awkward!"

I wanted to chase after her. It felt like fate, but I stayed where I was. I had her number now. No need to rush.

I checked my watch—12:30, and Sean was still a no-show.

And then I saw her.

The black-haired woman from the roulette table. Across the street. Watching me. Even from here, I could tell her face was still caked with makeup.

I didn't think. I moved. I darted into traffic, dodging cars, ignoring the horns, the curses. She started walking away. No. I wasn't letting her go. Who was she? Why was she here in Chicago?

I grabbed her by the elbow. She turned, and my stomach sank. It wasn't her. Not even close. Just an old woman with barely any makeup, wrinkles creasing her face. "What the hell do you think you're doing?" she snapped. Embarrassed, I muttered an apology and stepped back.

Sean's hand clamped onto my shoulder. "Dude. What the hell was that? You almost got hit by a car."

His voice snapped me back. The cars. The woman. The old woman. *Not her. Not her.* I swallowed hard. Heat crawled up my neck, my heartbeat a hammer in my throat.

"I thought she was someone else," I said.

Sean's eyes narrowed. "Who?"

"The woman at the roulette table in Vegas," I said. "Black hair. She blew on my chips for luck and called the winning number. She was right next to me. I thought I saw her again."

Sean frowned, looking at me like I'd lost it. "Matt, there was no woman at that table. It was all guys. Are you feeling okay?"

No. I remembered her. I knew I did. Black hair. A low, close voice. The way she leaned in, effortless, and slid all my chips onto Black 6. I could still hear her voce. *Trust me.* Sean was wrong. He had to be.

"What do you mean? She blew on my chip for luck," I said, the memory sharp and unshakable. I could still feel her breath on my hand, warm and close, like it just happened.

Sean didn't flinch. "Man, I remember that night perfectly. There was no woman. That table was full of guys. You sure you're feeling okay?" He clapped a hand on my shoulder.

Doubt clouded my mind. "I don't know, man. I don't feel okay," I said, the words tight in my throat.

I pressed my fingers into my temples. The pressure wasn't helping.

Sean's voice softened. "You're just stressed," he said. "You're doing something big with the bar. Tom would be proud. Maybe that's why you got lucky."

I nodded, but his words didn't settle me. I wanted to believe him. I wanted it to make sense. But something didn't add up. I tried to steady myself, to pull it all together, but the more I reached for control, the more it slipped through my fingers. The street felt off. Tilted.

The last time I felt fear like this was in the coffee shop, staring down the barrel of a gun, death close enough to touch. But this was different. This fear had no shape, no face. It was a shadow inside me, twisting my thoughts, pulling them apart.

What the hell was happening to me? Was I losing my grip? Was I hallucinating?

# OLIVIA

The elevator took too damn long. I shifted from one foot to the other, my shoes squeaking against the floor. It did nothing to ease the restlessness needling under my skin. When the doors finally slid open, I stepped inside and jabbed the button for the third floor. Daniel's text wouldn't leave my head:

Charlie woke up. You need to get to the hospital right away.

*Please, let it be true.*

The elevator doors slid open with a ding. I stepped out fast, my feet moving on instinct. As I passed the front desk, I spotted Kate fidgeting with a stack of papers she couldn't seem to organize. Her pen tapped against the desk, restless. Her gaze flicked to the clock—over and over.

"Is everything okay, Kate?" I asked.

She let out a small, almost inaudible breath—like she'd been holding it too long. She set the stack of papers down with exaggerated care, as if finally allowing herself a moment of stillness. Then, with a nervous half-laugh, she wiped a hand across her forehead, the motion lingering just a bit longer than necessary. "Dr. Jones, there's a patient waiting for you. I wasn't sure when you'd be in today," she said. She leaned in closer, lowering her tone. "Honestly, I was getting a bit nervous. I didn't know what to tell him, and he was becoming somewhat confrontational. Mentioned filing a complaint."

Her words caught me off guard. I wasn't supposed to have any appointments—I'd cleared my schedule for the ad agency meeting.

"Who is it?" I asked, glancing toward the patient area. "Are you sure there's an appointment? I don't recall one."

Kate nodded toward an older man with snow-white hair and a disheveled beard in need of a trim. He sat nervously, fidgeting with a pen, muttering to himself as if locked in a heated internal debate.

"His name is Joe Davis," she said, gesturing toward the computer screen. "According to the schedule, he has an appointment."

"Joe Davis?" I repeated, the name unfamiliar. He wasn't one of my regular patients.

A knot of frustration tightened in my chest. It wasn't about Joe Davis—it was about Charlie. I needed to be with her, but I couldn't ignore a patient.

With a reluctant nod, I took the folder from Kate.

"Mr. Davis," I began as we entered my office, "please have a seat. I apologize for keeping you waiting. How can I assist you today?"

He took a deep breath, his eyes flickering between me and the chair, as if unsure whether to sit. Finally, he did, crossing and uncrossing his legs, rubbing his knees as he slowly exhaled. "I came to you for a consultation," he said quietly, swallowing before continuing. "I've been having... issues with my brain. I think I might need surgery."

I carefully flipped open his folder, scanning the pages as I listened. His medical history was thorough—notes from his primary care physician, test results, MRI scans. But when I looked at the scans, I frowned. There were no abnormalities. Nothing in his file explained why he'd been referred to me.

"What kind of issues?" I asked.

He gripped the edge of the chair, his fingers trembling—just slightly, but enough to catch my eye. Like if he let go, he'd fall to pieces. "I've been seeing things, Doctor," he confessed, his gaze unwavering. "I've been seeing her. All the time. But no one else can see her."

"Seeing who?" I asked, my curiosity sharpening.

"The woman who vanished before my eyes two years ago," he replied. "She just disappeared into thin air."

*I couldn't fix this.* I could repair tissue, stop a heart from failing, but I couldn't stabilize whatever was unraveling in his mind. He needed real help—help beyond my training. This wasn't something I could cut away or stitch back together. He needed a psychiatrist, not me.

"Mr. Davis," I said, choosing my words carefully, "I appreciate your honesty, but—"

Before I could finish, his voice escalated into a shout.

"I know you! I recognize you now!" His voice sharpened, his finger jabbing toward me. "You're the doctor who made it out! Do you remember me?" His breath came faster. "Officer Davis. I was in charge of that hostage crisis."

I froze.

*Hostage crisis?* The words knocked something loose in my memory—flashes of an officer questioning me after the shooting, younger than this man, his face blurred at the edges.

I searched his features for familiarity, but they didn't match. Nothing clicked. Had he really been in charge, or was he just making this up? But why? What was the point of lying?

*It didn't add up.*

What did make sense, however, was the state of his mind. The fragments of the trauma started to align, and I nodded, a quiet understanding settling over me.

I felt a surge of empathy for him.

"No, I'm sorry, I don't remember," I said, the words thick with regret. "That day... it was too difficult to remember anyone clearly. Honestly. But I can feel your pain."

I wanted to help, to say something that would ease whatever was breaking inside him. But I wasn't the kind of doctor he needed. He needed therapy, not surgery.

"Yes, 'too difficult' is one way to put it. It was hell. That's what it was," he said, his voice raw with agony. "It was hell, and it still is. I used to be Officer Davis, but not anymore. I lost my job, my wife left me.

Now I'm just a bum, a nobody. And it's all because of her—the vanishing woman. She gave me everything I ever wanted after that horrible day at the coffee shop."

He paused, his eyes drifting into some far-off place, as if reliving something only he could see. "I received a reward, a medal of honor, for how I handled the hostage situation, even though I had failed. I failed them, you see." His breath hitched between words, his voice barely holding steady. "Then came the promotion, a corner office, the admiration of my peers. But she took it all away. A female officer— impersonating an affair that never even happened—ruined my reputation and stripped me of my job. It was like she offered me the world, only to snatch it back." His eyes snapped back to mine. "And do you know how I know it was her?"

"No," I said, my voice quieter now.

He slammed his fist onto the desk. A case of pens and pencils tipped over, spilling onto the floor in a sharp clatter. He was shouting again, his voice cracking with pain, each word heavy and charged, as if it couldn't escape fast enough. "Because I saw her right after I got fired! She was laughing and then said, 'You got what you deserved.' Now she's everywhere— following me, stalking me! She's trying to destroy me, and no one else can see her! I asked people—do you see that woman? They all said no. So I figured if I could fix my brain, maybe she'd disappear. Maybe she'd stop messing with my mind." He leaned forward, his face twisted in torment. "Do you understand, Doctor? Do you see why I'm here?"

It became painfully clear that this man's trauma had spiraled into delusion. His mind was unraveling. Surgery wouldn't fix this. It never could. I needed to end this appointment. Now.

"Mr. Davis," I said firmly, "I truly sympathize with your suffering, but brain surgery isn't the solution for these issues. You need to consult a psychiatrist who specializes in trauma and psychological disorders. They're better equipped to help you."

"I've seen hundreds of doctors!" he shouted, leaping from his chair and pounding his fist on the desk again. "Nobody can help, dammit!"

I forced my voice to stay level, controlled. "I'm sorry, Mr. Davis, but I must conclude this appointment now." I rose, stepping back slightly to maintain space. "I'll send a recommendation to your primary care doctor. In the meantime, it's critical that you seek the appropriate mental health care."

As I walked past Kate, I lowered my voice and instructed, "Be prepared to call security if needed."

When I finally reached Charlie's room, Daniel was waiting just outside, his brow creased in that familiar way that always felt like a warning. My heart sank. That look never came with good news—just another blow in a day already full of them.

"Olivia, I'm sorry," he said the moment he saw me. "Charlie had a coma arousal event earlier, but she's gone back to being unresponsive. I texted you because I thought—hoped—it might be something. I should have waited."

I knew coma arousal events all too well. Those brief moments when a patient in a coma opens their eyes or moves, but it rarely means anything. Just a brief flicker of brain activity or the side effect of medication.

A cold knot tightened in my chest. "Damn you, Daniel," I said even though I knew it wasn't his fault.

"I'm sorry, Olivia," he sadly replied. "But you know her condition is bad."

I looked through the glass door. My heart ached at the sight of Charlie, tangled in wires and machines, a tight blue cap clinging to her head. The only sound was the steady beep of the monitor, a relentless reminder of what she wasn't.

Jason sat by her bedside, his shoulders trembling with each sob.

Jason. Young, good-looking. He'd been by her side every day for the past two years. I couldn't help but admire his loyalty. He hadn't left her. Not like Owen left me. He stayed. Through everything. And if that wasn't love, I wasn't sure what was.

"Olivia, have you thought about the possibility of letting go?" Daniel asked, his voice even. I blinked, the words stuck between my throat and the noise of the hospital, as though they couldn't quite reach my ears.

I stared at him, my mind struggling to catch up with his words. "What do you mean?"

His gaze didn't flinch. "I mean, have you thought about the possibility that it might be time to start discussing discontinuing life support for Charlie? We haven't brought this up with her mother yet, but maybe it's time," he repeated, his voice calm, too calm. "I've been thinking about it a lot lately."

My fingers dug into my palms, the pressure sharp, grounding me, as if I could stop the world from shifting. "No," I said, the words barely leaving my mouth. "I haven't thought about it. I can't even begin to imagine . . ."

He rested his hands on his thighs, his fingers tapping once, then stilling. "I know you care about this girl, but how long do we continue treatment when there are no signs of improvement?"

I clenched my jaw, the muscles in my neck tight with the effort to keep my voice steady. "But we also have to consider the emotional toll it would take on everyone involved," I shot back. "And what if we give up too soon? What if she can still recover?"

Daniel's breath hitched, his fingers tapping briefly on his thighs before he clenched his fist. "But what if she doesn't?" His voice cracked, his composure slipping. "Every day brings false hope, and it's tearing her family apart. That boy in there. And you, too, Olivia."

"I've long passed that point," I said, the words sharp and bitter, a quiet exhale of everything I hadn't said before.

Daniel couldn't understand. No one could, not unless they'd lived through what I had—what Charlie had, or the others who were there that day, two years ago, in that damn coffee shop. People claim they get it, but it's just a lie they tell themselves to make it easier.

Daniel waited, silent, as if expecting me to say more. When I didn't, he spoke. "I still think we should discuss this option with Charlie's mother."

The words landed like a slap. My muscles stiffened. "I disagree, and I won't do it. Charlie is all that woman has," I said, my voice catching, the anger sharp in every syllable. "I can't bear the thought of giving up on her. If you want to have that conversation, fine. But know this, Daniel—I'll fight it until the bitter end." I took another deep breath, trying to steady myself. "Now, if you'll excuse me, I'm going to check on her."

He didn't argue, but the softness in his voice made it clear the conversation wasn't over. "Okay."

As we entered, Jason shot to his feet, the chair skidding back with a jarring screech before toppling over. His eyes, red-rimmed and frantic, darted between us, as if trying to decide which of us deserved his anger.

"I'm just here to check on Charlie," I said, holding up my hands as if to calm him. Daniel bent down and picked up the chair.

"Lady, you've been checking on her for the past two years," Jason snapped. "Nothing has changed. Nothing. Look at her, she's still in a fucking coma. I've been coming to see her twice a day, and it's the same every time. Why can't you do something about this? Jesus, you're a fucking doctor! Can't you wake her up?"

Daniel stepped forward, trying to diffuse the tension. "Hey, hey," he said, placing a hand on Jason's shoulder. "We're doctors, not gods. We're doing everything we can."

Jason jerked back like the touch burned. "Fuck off, man!" he shouted, his voice raw and cracking. Tears streaked his face as he glared at us, his chest heaving. "I love her. I love her so much. We were supposed to be together." He wiped his sleeve across his face, rough and quick, like he was trying to scrub the grief away. "Do you know what it's like to lose someone you love?"

I knew that pain too well. "Yes, I do."

But Jason wasn't listening. "You know she got into Northwestern," he choked out. "She didn't think she would get in, but she did. She had her whole life ahead of her. We were supposed to be together, and now I don't even know if she'll ever wake up again. Why can't you make her wake up?"

I wanted to say something—anything—but the words tangled and died before they reached my lips. I finally managed, "Look, I want her to wake up, too." The words felt thin, useless. Jason gave me one last hollow look before turning and walking out of the room, his shoulders hunched under the weight of his grief.

There was no reaching him—not now, maybe not ever. His pain was too raw, too overwhelming to be consoled.

I turned to Daniel. His eyes met mine, full of a painful truth. "Do you feel it now? The endless torment, this soul-crushing helplessness . . . There's nothing we can do. We're prolonging her suffering. Everyone's suffering."

I nodded, swallowing hard against the ache that rose in my throat. "Okay," I said finally. "Let's talk to her mother."

# CHARLIE

*Talk to my mother about what?* I wondered, as the footsteps faded, leaving the room in a thick, suffocating silence.

Then, that same voice returned, whispering too close, too intrusive. "Isn't Jason a sweet boy? He loves you."

When you're in a coma, the world doesn't vanish—it changes. Your body is still, your voice silenced, but your senses remain wide open. In the quiet, you hear things you'd never noticed before—the way people speak, the rhythm of their voices, the tiny pauses between words. You begin to understand what they're not saying, the hidden meanings behind their words. You can't respond, but you become a sharp observer, piecing everything together like a puzzle. It's like being a detective, reading the tone, sensing the truth beneath the surface.

That's how I knew something was wrong with this woman. Her voice lacked the warmth of someone kind. When she called Jason a *good* boy, it felt off, like she was mocking me. It was as if she knew something I didn't—that maybe his love wouldn't last. Her presence felt strange, and she only spoke when the room was empty, as if she had something to hide.

"Charlie, don't be afraid. I'm your friend," she purred. And in that moment, it hit me—she could read my thoughts. "There's an explanation for everything. And you, dear Charlie, have a significant role to play." Her voice grew darker with each word. "You're such a *nice* and *kind* person," she said, mockery dripping from every syllable. "But soon, everything will change," she hissed, and I felt a cold breeze stir, creeping through me. "The world, dear Charlie, can be an incredibly cruel place. Some people get what they don't deserve, while others suffer for no reason." Then she added, "Let's start by thinking about your daddy, and how he left you and your mother."

The past unfolded before my eyes, vivid and raw, like I was reliving it all over again. I was back in our familiar living room, clutching my beloved brown teddy bear. The room smelled like Daddy's aftershave and the coffee he made in the morning. He stood by the door, tall and strong in his gray Chicago Bulls hoodie, his duffel bag and old suitcase—scuffed, worn, covered in travel stickers—sitting on the stained beige carpet.

"Daddy, are you leaving us?" I asked.

"No, baby girl. Why would you think that?" Daddy replied.

I pointed to his suitcase. "If you're not leaving, why do you need a suitcase?"

Daddy's lips curled into a smile. He scooped me up into his arms, and I buried my face in his hoodie, breathing in the scent of him. "Daddy's just taking a little trip, sweetheart."

I wrapped my small arms around his middle, holding on like I could somehow keep him there. "I love you, Daddy."

With a tender kiss on my forehead, he whispered, "I love you too, my sweet girl. I'll always come back to you. You're my everything."

When he left, I rushed to the window, pressing my palms flat against the glass, desperate to catch one last glimpse. Daddy saw me, blew me a kiss, and I returned it, my heart hopeful, wishing it would follow him wherever he was going.

"What are you doing?" my mother asked behind me.

I didn't turn around. "Waving to Daddy," I replied. My eyes stayed on his car as it drove away, getting smaller until it was gone.

Mammina chuckled, but it was a sad sound. "He won't be back, baby girl. And the sooner you accept it, the better off you'll be." Then she walked out of the room.

"He will be back! You'll see!" I yelled after her.

But days bled into months, and months into years, and he never came back. No calls, no postcards—nothing. Not even a message on my birthday. And now, lying here—trapped between life and death—Mammina's words echoed in my mind. A painful reminder, sharp and relentless, that he never bothered to check in.

"Now, you see him for who he really is, a massive disappointment as a father," the voice said.

In that moment, all the excuses I'd clung to for so long, the reasons I told myself he hadn't come back, crumbled away piece by piece. The truth of his absence tore through me—ruthless and undeniable—shredding every excuse I had ever made for him. I couldn't deny it anymore. He wasn't just absent. He was a piece of shit, plain and simple.

The realization hit me hard, like a punch to the gut that stole my breath. All those years of waiting, of weaving stories in my head, trying to understand why he wasn't there—they were nothing but lies. He didn't care. He never had. And now, in this moment, I finally saw him for what he really was. Not a misunderstood man, not someone who needed more time and would come back to be a caring dad. Just a selfish, irresponsible asshole who abandoned his family.

"Good, good, dear Charlie," the voice whispered, syrupy sweet—like a lullaby sung just a little too slowly, a little too carefully. "We're making splendid progress here. But don't fret too much. Your brain is exhibiting concerning signals once again. The doctors may believe you're starting to awaken again."

A pause. A chuckle.

"Yes, one day you'll open your eyes. I assure you." A breath, soft as silk. "We're on the right track. But not yet. Not yet."

The voice curled around my ear, then slipped inside—pushing into the space where my own thoughts should be.

"When that moment comes… you won't be you anymore."

Dread slithered through me. *What did she mean? What would I be when I finally woke up?*

# MATT

Lunch with Sean felt like pushing a boulder uphill. He talked, and I nodded at the right moments, let out a laugh when expected, but his words slid past me, weightless. My head wasn't there. It kept circling back to what he'd said. *There was no woman at the table.*

No woman.

I couldn't let it go. Her black hair, the whisper in my ear, the way she leaned in and blew on my chip for luck—it all felt too real to be nothing. But Sean was sure. "There was no woman," he'd said. The doubt burrowed in, relentless. A pebble in my shoe, grinding deeper with every step.

Then his phone buzzed. He glanced at the screen, sighing. "Boss." He stood, shrugging into his suit jacket. "Sorry, man, I've got to run. I'll catch you later."

"No problem," I said, waving him off. "Later."

I got in the car and headed toward Bridgeport to see my folks. The drive gave me too much time to think. Too much space for the wrong thoughts to creep in. The woman's face wouldn't leave me alone—black hair, the way she leaned in. Too vivid to dismiss. And then there was Pops. The way I'd left things with him didn't sit right. A face-to-face talk seemed like the only way to fix it. His approval mattered more than I cared to admit, even to myself. I tightened my grip on the wheel, the leather warm under my hands. Maybe seeing him would settle things. Quiet the noise in my head.

I turned onto the old familiar street and killed the engine.

Our house—where I spent the first eighteen years of my life—sat in the heart of Bridgeport, a blue-collar neighborhood in Chicago. A cozy ranch-style place from the '60s, though you wouldn't know it by looking. Pops kept the roof solid, and Mom's obsession with cleaning showed in every corner. The furniture had seen better days—scuffed legs, worn cushions—but it had character, the kind you only get from years of family life. That house held everything: laughter, fights, quiet moments in between. No matter how much time passed, it still felt like home.

I knocked on the door, and Pops opened it almost immediately. He stood there for a second, eyeing me like he was sizing me up, then pulled me into one of his firm hugs. "Glad you dropped by, Son," he said, his voice gruff but warm. "Maybe I can knock some sense into that thick skull of yours. Get in here."

I stepped inside. The smell of Mom's oatmeal cookies hung in the air.

"Your brother Mike ain't around. Off at his girlfriend's place. You know how these kids are. He better not go gettin' all lovestruck and forgettin' to finish high school next year."

We headed into the kitchen. Pops took his usual seat at the table and slid a glass of lemonade in front of me. The ice clinked softly against the glass.

His face bore the marks of thirty years of hard labor, his eyes heavy with the weight of long shifts at the warehouse . . . and maybe a few too many drinks. He'd never made it to my Little League games or school events. But we'd never gone hungry. Never went without clothes on our backs or a roof over our heads. Beneath the rough edges, beneath the unspoken gestures, there was care. The kind that didn't need words.

"I'm glad you swung by, Matt," Pops said. "Your mom and I, we're both happy to see ya. Ain't that right, Diane?"

Mom came over from the sink, wiping her hands on a dish towel. She set a plate of oatmeal cookies in front of me. "Just the way you like them," she said, leaning down to kiss my cheek.

I wasn't hungry, not after lunch, but I picked one up anyway. It was warm, soft in the middle. I took a bite and let the sweetness sit on my tongue.

"We're really happy you stopped by," Mom added. But her smile wavered, and then she said, "but I need to lie down for a bit. My head's been pounding."

I set the cookie down, crumbs scattering on the table. "Is everything okay?" I asked.

She glanced at Pops—quick, barely there, but I caught it. "Everything's fine, dear. Don't worry about me. I've just been a bit tired lately, that's all. Love you."

"I love you, too, Mom," I said. "Go get some rest."

She squeezed my shoulder before heading down the hall to the bedroom. Pops watched her go, his fingers tapping lightly against his mug. Then he exhaled and looked out the window.

"Been one of those weeks," he muttered. "She won't admit it, but she's been feelin' off for a while now."

I frowned. "Did she see a doctor?"

"She says it's just stress." He exhaled sharply, shaking his head. "You know how she is. Stubborn as they come."

I nodded, biting back the obvious. *Just like you, Pops.*

He leaned forward, forearms braced on the table. "You been eatin' enough?" he asked. "You look thinner."

I let out a short laugh. "Yeah, I eat."

"Hmm." He studied me, then nodded. "Alright. Just checkin'."

I traced a crack in the table, a battle scar from when Mike and I used to sword fight with forks. Mom had been furious, but she never replaced it.

My eyes drifted to the framed photo near the kitchen table. Tom and me at high school graduation. Caps in hand, grins wide, laughing like idiots. I tried to remember the joke he'd cracked that day, something about the principal's ridiculous purple suit. It had us doubled over, gasping for air. Back then, we thought the world was ours. Wide open. Waiting. We had no idea what was coming. Pops noticed me staring.

"Matt, you really oughta go see him," he said as he let out a long breath. He rubbed the back of his neck, staring at the photo like it might answer for me. "It's been way too long since the funeral. You haven't set foot in that cemetery since." He leaned back in his chair, the wood creaking under his weight. "Me? I go every month. Just last time, ran into his mom. She ain't doin' so good, truth be told, but we had a few words." He glanced down, tracing the rim of his coffee mug with his thumb. "Tom, well... he was your friend, but he was like a son to me, too." His voice wavered. He straightened up fast, like sitting taller could push it all away. Pops didn't show emotions.

"I'll go when the time's right," I said, though I had no idea when that would actually be.

Pops shook his head and leaned back in his chair again. He folded his arms and looked at me. "Look, kid, I know it hurts," he said in that sturdy, no-bullshit way of his. "That pain ain't gonna just vanish. Life's a sucker punch, and losing Tom? It's a goddamn tragedy. But we can't bring him back." He glanced at the table, his fingers drumming against the edge. "I get it, you want to honor him—and that bar sounds like the ticket. But quitting your job? That ain't the way, Matt."

I exhaled through my nose. *Here we go.*

"I quit, Pops. There's no going back," I said, my jaw tight. My fingers curled around the edge of the table. "I'm opening that bar, with or without your support. This isn't just about Tom—it's about me. I'm not spending the rest of my life miserable. I came here to make you understand. I'm signing that contract the second my realtor calls. I'm putting down the deposit."

His forehead creased, the lines cutting deeper. "So it ain't set in stone yet? Y'got a chance to pull back?"

"Not yet, but it's just a matter of time. The rental deposit's one hundred and fifty grand, and I plan to pay it as soon as possible." I dropped the number deliberately, a pointed reminder of something Pops never had. My hands tightened into fists under the table. Why couldn't he see it? Why couldn't he just say, *I'm proud of you*?

His eyes snapped to mine. He blinked, like he hadn't heard me right. Then his face twisted. "One hundred and fifty grand just for rent?" he asked. "Are ya outta your damn mind, Son? You're actin' like a fool!"

"I'm not a fool," I said sharply. "Rent for a space this size runs about fifty grand a month. So, one-fifty total. It's the city, Dad. Downtown Chicago isn't cheap."

His voice went flat. "Matt, for cryin' out loud, don't go down this road. Don't be so damn stubborn. You ain't got the know-how, and you're about to piss away every cent you got. If you wanna start your own thing, begin small, keep it on the side of your regular gig, find somethin' less costly."

This conversation had hit a wall. Pushing it further would only turn into words we'd regret. Maybe I shouldn't have come at all.

"I thought you, of all people, would get it," I said, standing up. "You've always hated your job. Always talked about how miserable it made you. That's how I felt about mine. If you had this chance, wouldn't you take it?"

He shook his head. "Don't compare your job to mine. Do you work night shifts and scrape by on pennies? Do you sweat it out liftin' heavy crap in some warehouse?"

"No," I said, my voice tight. "I don't haul heavy stuff, but I felt trapped. Every damn day felt like a cage. Honestly, some days I thought a job like yours might've been easier. But I'm chasing my dream—this bar, this building—whether you stand by me or not."

I shut the door behind me. Pops' voice followed. "Don't come beggin' for my help when this whole thing goes belly up."

The screen door slammed. I stepped off the porch, heading for my car.

The drive to prove him wrong burned in me, but it wasn't enough to chase off the hollow ache in my chest. I'd stood my ground, but it felt like losing anyway. *Alone.* That was the word for it. For a second, I thought about turning back, but what was the point? There was nothing left to say.

Halfway to the car, a sudden flurry of wings shattered the stillness. Birds shot into the sky, their movement almost violent—like they were fleeing from something. Or carrying it away.

I stopped and watched as they rose higher, their shapes blurring against the clouds. It felt like nature was trying to tell me something. Like it recognized my sorrow and refused to let me drown in it.

Then, like a cool breeze cutting through the heat, *Alex's face came to mind—her smile, her laugh.* The memory was so clear it stopped me in my tracks. I thought I'd blown my chance. But I had her number now. I could text her. Ask her out. The thought took root in my head, pulling me out of the emptiness I'd been sinking into.

I climbed into the car and turned the key. The engine hummed to life. At the traffic light, I sat for a moment, hands on the wheel. For the first time all day, I felt like I had something solid to hold onto. *Something real. Something worth chasing.*

# ALEXANDRA

As soon as Bruce and I got back from lunch, I threw myself into setting up my new office, racing to get everything just right before Dr. Olivia Jones arrived. The agency buzzed with its usual creative chaos—brainstorming sessions, client meetings, the constant hum of energy that could either light a fire under you or completely fry your brain. My head spun with everything I had to tackle. *Meeting with Dr. Jones soon. The new campaign. Spreading the word about the charity ball. Securing sponsors. Nailing that pitch.* Yeah, I totally got this.

Except... somewhere in the middle of all those to-do lists and deadlines, Matt kept sneaking into my thoughts. What were the odds of running into him today, of all days? Chicago's massive, but somehow today had been a full-blown rollercoaster—starting with the weird lady at the bus stop, the surprise promotion, and now this.

He looked ridiculously good—like, seriously attractive. Faded jeans, snug black tee showing off his muscles, and those blue eyes still had that same spark from two years ago.

But whatever connection spark there might've been back then? That belonged to another lifetime. Seeing him again brought back the hurt, the painful memories. And yet, for some reason I couldn't quite explain, I wanted to talk to him. Not to my mom. Not to Dr. Richardson. To him. Because if anyone could understand, it was Matt.

Not that it mattered. He probably didn't want to talk to me. He'd said it himself—our connection was brief. So why the hell would he reach out now? It was almost funny that Bruce had given him my number. Like he'd actually call.

Still, a tiny, irrational part of me hoped. Even though I knew better. I exhaled sharply, forcing myself back into work mode.

My gaze fell on a bumper sticker I'd slapped onto my desk months ago: "ON MY WAY TO WORK . . . PLEASE KILL ME." I'd crossed out "ME" and replaced it with "LISA." I stared at it for a second, then peeled it off and tossed it in the trash. Lisa was gone. And, let's be real—I didn't even own a car.

With that out of the way, my desk looked almost bare. Just the essentials: a mug, three pencils, an eraser, two pens, a notepad, and my laptop. Oh, and my one and only plant—a tiny pop of green to make the space feel slightly less corporate. Office setup: complete.

I sank into my chair and flipped open the folder I'd prepped for my meeting with Dr. Olivia. This was my chance to make an impact, and there was no way I was messing it up. I'd done my homework—everything from diabetes stats to potential sponsors and fundraising strategies. My notepad was packed with ideas for the charity ball: themes, decorations, guest speakers, entertainment—the works. I'd even mapped out a detailed budget proposal showing exactly how the funds would be allocated to the hospital's diabetes program. This wasn't just another meeting. This was *the* meeting.

Someone knocked on the door.

"Come in," I said.

"Alex, you have a visitor," Janet, my new secretary, said.

I looked past Janet and nearly lost it. Standing in front of me was a tall woman with fiery red hair. *No way. Could it really be her?* The doctor from that coffee shop two years ago? There were three of us hostages who got out, and I definitely remembered the third one being a doctor. Even if her name had slipped my mind, her face? That, I could never forget. What in the actual hell was going on?

My fingers fumbled with my desk drawer, instinctively opening it—though I had no idea what I was even looking for. My eyes landed on the second bus pass inside. The one with "666" and the creepy smiley face. A chill slithered up my spine. Maybe it wasn't just a prank after all. Maybe something was really wrong.

Janet was giving me a weird look, and I knew I had to snap out of it. "Is it still a good time?" she asked.

"Yes," I stammered, forcing my voice steady. "Hi, please come in and take a seat," I added, forcing a smile that felt a little wobbly. Did she recognize me?

"Would you like a cup of coffee or water?" Janet asked.

"No, thanks, I'm good," Dr. Jones replied before turning her attention to me and extending her hand. "Hi, I'm Olivia Jones."

I shook it, doing my best to look composed. "A pleasure to meet you, Olivia. I'm Alex Weisman."

She didn't seem to recognize me. But why would she? It had been two years. We hadn't even spoken that day. Still, I'd watched her in action—tending to an elderly man who'd taken a bad fall. She was incredible. Brave. Confident. Totally unfazed. Even when one of the gunmen had shoved a gun in her face and threatened to kill them both if she didn't shut up, she'd barely flinched. Me? I was a shaking, sobbing, quivering mess.

"I'm really sorry for rescheduling our meeting," she said, flashing me an apologetic smile. "I had a bit of an accident on my way here this morning."

She had this totally put-together, sharp vibe. Sleek, on-point look. Features like a younger Nicole Kidman, with that effortless elegance that made people stop and stare.

But I didn't miss the faint weariness around her eyes. A couple of faint bags. A few fine lines.

"No worries at all," I said. "Mornings can be pretty wild sometimes."

"Yes, they definitely can," she agreed. "I was actually supposed to have a meeting with Lisa, but Janet told me I needed to see you instead.

The short of it is I'm a doctor from Rush Hospital, and we're putting together a fundraising event to support the fight against diabetes," she explained. "We were hoping you could help us plan the charity ball, put together a campaign, and create promotional materials to raise awareness about the event. We'd love your expertise on this."

I pulled out my notebook and nodded, already in full-on work mode. "Absolutely, this is a cause we'd love to support," I replied. "I've already brainstormed some initial ideas, but I'd love to hear your thoughts as well. Could you tell me more about your preferred dates, estimated number of attendees, and any specific themes or goals you have in mind? And do you have any existing branding guidelines we should consider while working on the campaign and promotional materials?"

I kept it professional, knowing how important this account was—not just for the agency but for me, too. This was a cause I genuinely cared about. Sure, the weight of responsibility hung over me, but I was here for it.

Still, no matter how hard I tried to stay focused, my mind kept drifting back to that day two years ago. It was like an itch I couldn't ignore. I wanted to talk to Olivia about the shooting, just like I had with Matt, to see if she felt the same way. Did she ever get scared, like always waiting for something bad to happen? Did loud noises mess with her? Did she have nightmares? The weird stuff I'd been dealing with?

But now wasn't the time to bring that up. I had to focus, prove I could handle this, and show I was the right person for the job. Yet those questions wouldn't stop nagging at me, waiting for the right moment to jump out.

"Thank you, Alex," Dr. Olivia said. "This would be a huge help to us. In terms of dates, we're thinking late summer or early fall—maybe August or September, when the weather is nice. We're aiming for around five hundred to six hundred attendees, but we want the event to feel inclusive and welcoming, so that number is flexible. Our goal is to create an uplifting atmosphere that highlights our commitment to fighting diabetes. A vibrant, energetic theme would be ideal. We also want to raise awareness about prevention, early detection, and management while raising funds to support these efforts."

I jotted everything down, ideas already forming in my head.

"As for branding guidelines," she added, "we'd like to incorporate our hospital's logo and color palette, but we're open to your creative ideas on how to make them shine in the campaign materials."

"Got it," I said, my grip tightening on my pen as my nerves coiled tighter with each passing second. And then—honestly, I don't know what came over me—I just blurted it out. "I was there, you know." My words hung in the air, a confession I couldn't take back.

Her smile faded. "Where?"

"The coffee shop. Two years ago." My voice felt too small, too shaky. "I was one of the survivors. I'm so sorry—I know this isn't the point of our meeting, and I hate to derail it, but I had to tell you. I remember you from that day."

Her entire body stiffened. The warmth in her expression vanished, replaced by something distant. Cold. My stomach twisted as I watched her gather her things. She reached for her purse and stood up so abruptly, her chair scraped against the floor.

"I don't want to talk about that," she said, voice clipped. "I have to go. I have a patient waiting at the hospital."

It was a lie. Our meeting was supposed to last an hour. I'd blown it. "Are we going to reconnect?" I asked, scrambling for some way to fix it. "For the event?"

"Yeah, sure," she said, but the hesitation in her voice told me otherwise.

The door shut behind her. I sank into my chair, staring blankly at my notebook. The neat bullet points mocked me. I buried my head in my hands. *Why the hell did I bring that up?* What was I thinking? It was totally inappropriate, and I should have known better. How could I ever hope to fix this?

I turned to the window, pressing my fingers against the cool glass. Below, Olivia walked briskly, weaving around a couple strolling like they had all the time in the world. At first, it didn't seem like much—just another busy day. But then I saw her.

Oh my god, it was the woman from the bus!

"No way," I whispered, my breath fogging the window. Leaning closer, my suspicion only grew. Same black dress. Same hair. Same build.

She was mimicking Olivia's every move. When Olivia paused to check her purse, she did the same. When Olivia picked up speed, the woman kept pace. At the intersection, Olivia stopped. So did she.

Should I call the cops? What would I even say? "Hey, I think a woman might be following another woman, but I can't be sure if there's any danger." That sounded ridiculous. Maybe I should warn Olivia? But I wasn't even sure if she was really in danger. Then it hit me—I could catch up with her if I ran fast.

Just as I was about to act, a sharp knock at the door startled me.

"How did the meeting go, darling?" Bruce asked.

"Not good," I blurted, waving him off as I grabbed my bag. "I'll explain later. I've got to go."

"Go where?" he asked, eyebrows raised.

"Bruce, I know it might sound weird, but look out the window," I tugged at his sleeve, practically dragging him closer. "There's someone following Dr. Olivia, and I'm worried about her safety. Can you see a woman in black behind the woman with red hair? I think she might be in danger."

Bruce squinted out the window. "Where? I see a woman with the red hair, but there's no one following her."

"What?" My voice shot up as I pressed my forehead to the glass, scanning the street below. Olivia was rounding the corner near the CVS, but the woman was gone. "Someone was following her. I swear it."

"Might you be in dire need of a rejuvenating escape?" Bruce said lightly. "A luxurious day at a spa, perhaps?"

I stared at him, my thoughts spiraling. Was I losing my mind? Maybe it was the PTSD. Maybe it was finally catching up to me, twisting everything into something it wasn't.

Was this it?

Was I crossing the line where I couldn't trust my own mind anymore?

# OLIVIA

By the time I left the hospital, the outside world had surrendered to darkness. All afternoon, I'd avoided the conversation with Charlie's mother, burying myself in work to stay distracted. I pored over patient charts, rechecked upcoming surgeries, even tackled the pile of paperwork I usually let pile up. I chatted with nurses, made my rounds, found a dozen small tasks to keep my hands busy and my thoughts elsewhere. But no amount of distraction could outlast the day. Eventually, I had to admit it was time to call it a night.

The hospital entrance was still alive with motion as I stepped outside. People streamed in and out, some rushing, others dragging their feet, their pace mirroring either urgency or exhaustion. Families gathered in tight clusters, their whispered words lost in the hum of a place that never sleeps. Nurses and doctors moved briskly, their steps sharp and deliberate, like they could outrun the ticking clock if they tried hard enough. It was a race I understood all too well.

A young woman sat on a bench near the door, her head bowed into her hands, her fingers tangled in her hair, gripping tightly, like she could hold herself together if she didn't let go. Nearby, a doctor in wrinkled scrubs slouched against the wall, looking as tired and drained as I felt. He wasn't looking at anything in particular—just the floor, as though it held the answers he couldn't give. The weight of the day pressed down on all of us. Still, we kept moving. Not because we wanted to, but because standing still wasn't an option.

I promised myself I'd talk to Charlie's mother tomorrow. Tonight, I just needed air. Stepping outside, I took a deep breath, letting the warm summer night fill my lungs. I wasn't ready to get on the bus and head home just yet. The truth was, no one was waiting for me there. So, I decided to walk instead.

As I walked, guilt settled in. My conversation with Alex lingered in my mind, especially the way she'd mentioned the coffee shop. It had blindsided me. After the strange encounter with the former police officer, it was one thing too many. Overwhelming, really.

But Alex had been so eager, so invested in making the event a success. Her passion was clear in the way she rattled off plans, asking the right questions within minutes of the meeting. She was young—ambitious in the way only someone still building their career could be, driven by a fire that hadn't yet been dulled by reality. She was beautiful, too—stunning enough to stop you mid-sentence, her energy exhausting to watch but impossible to ignore. At first, I'd doubted her. Too young, I'd thought, to manage something like this. But as she spoke, I saw the depth of her ambition and realized how wrong I'd been to dismiss her.

Our account mattered to her agency, and I didn't want her to face setbacks because of something as cruel as bad timing. Maybe talking to her about that day wouldn't be such a bad idea. The scars from that tragedy ran deep, leaving marks no one could escape. Age didn't make you immune. If anything, younger people like Alex were often more vulnerable, their minds still learning how to process grief and trauma. She'd tried to reach out, and I'd shut her down without a second thought.

Tomorrow, I'd call her office to reschedule. It wouldn't undo the damage, but maybe it would give us both a chance to start again.

"Hey, Olivia, wait up," Daniel called.

I stopped and turned as he jogged to catch up, his worn leather bag bumping against his side.

"Are you going home?" he asked.

"No, not yet. Thought I'd take a walk. The weather's too nice," I said, sidestepping the truth—I just didn't want to go home to an empty apartment.

"Mind some company?" He smiled. "I'm not in a hurry to go home either."

A small, grateful smile tugged at the corners of my lips. "No, I don't mind."

"Did you talk to Charlie's mother?" he asked as we fell into step.

I shook my head, exhaling slowly. "Didn't get the chance. I'll talk to her tomorrow."

It had been exactly a year since Owen left, and the wound still felt as raw as the day it happened. But I wasn't going to think about that now. I just needed the night air to clear my head, to quiet everything for a little while.

"It really is nice out," Daniel said, his voice softer, like he didn't want to disturb the moment. "What if we just kept walking? Pretended the past didn't exist. Started over, right here."

I glanced at him. His life hadn't been easy either—his wife had left him five years ago for someone else. Now, he split custody of their son, juggling work and everything that came with it. Maybe that's why he understood me so well. He never asked too many questions.

"I'd like that," I said.

As we rounded the corner, a warm summer breeze carried the faint scent of asphalt and city life.

A homeless man sat on the sidewalk, his face illuminated by the soft glow of a nearby streetlamp. In his worn hands, he cradled a flute, playing melodies laced with sorrow. The tune was unfamiliar, but it stirred something deep inside me. It wasn't flashy or loud—just quietly beautiful, for anyone who bothered to listen.

I slipped a twenty-dollar bill into the bucket by his feet. Daniel did the same. The man gave a slight nod, his eyes meeting mine briefly as he played on—a silent thank-you.

Laughter from a nearby bench caught my attention. A young couple, hands entwined, leaned into each other, the girl resting her head on the boy's shoulder. They shared a quiet kiss, and something in the sight pulled at me—a reminder of what I'd lost.

The musician shifted into a livelier, jazz-inspired tune. Without warning, Daniel set his bag down and started dancing. Not just swaying—actual dance moves. I laughed as he threw his arms out, spun in place, completely unbothered by the curious glances from passersby. Then, with an exaggerated flourish, he added a dramatic spin, and I laughed even harder.

"Believe it or not, I took dance classes in high school," he said, grinning as he moved to the rhythm. "I was pretty good, honestly."

As the music slowed, Daniel reached for my hand and gently pulled me into a slow dance. Our eyes met, and for a moment, it felt like an invitation to forget—just let the music carry us somewhere else.

"What are you doing?" I asked.

"Let's just dance," he murmured. "The music is beautiful. For a moment, let's forget everything else."

I let him guide me, my steps uncertain at first, then easier. As we moved together, I couldn't help but notice him—his dark curls, the strong line of his shoulders. Daniel was a handsome man, and kind. How had he not found someone in the past five years?

Was I starting to feel something for him? The thought came out of nowhere, and I pushed it aside just as quickly. Daniel was a good friend. Nothing more. Someone who had been there when I needed support. *Nothing more.* But even that thought felt like a betrayal. Guilt pressed in, sharp and insistent, like touching a bruise I hadn't realized was still tender.

I pulled away, putting space between us. "I'm sorry, but it's getting late. I should head home." I motioned across the street. "There's a bus stop over there. I'll catch one."

Daniel's expression flickered, his brows drawing together before softening. He understood. "Sure. Want me to walk you there?"

I forced a small laugh. "No need, Daniel. I'll manage. See you tomorrow. Good night."

"Night, Olivia," he replied, his eyes lingering, like he was searching for something he couldn't quite find.

The bus station was empty, the street illuminated by a few scattered lamps that pooled light unevenly on the pavement. The quiet mirrored the churn of emotions inside me. I stood there, waiting for the bus to take me home, but my mind was fixed elsewhere—on Daniel, and the tangle of feelings he'd left behind.

I told myself it was nothing—just stress, exhaustion twisting my thoughts into something they weren't. But a whisper lingered, persistent and low: *What if this is something more?* And that terrified me.

The stillness of the night only amplified my thoughts, leaving nowhere to hide from them. I wished the bus would come already. I also wished there were more people around. Above me, the streetlight flickered faintly, like it couldn't decide whether to hold on or give up.

Should I have said something different to Daniel? Stayed instead of walking away so quickly? Maybe I was overthinking, letting loneliness twist itself into something easier to carry. Or maybe . . . No. I shook my head. Whatever I thought I saw in his eyes, I was probably imagining it. I crossed my arms over my chest, trying to steady myself, searching for comfort in the emptiness as I waited.

"Bew . . . beware . . . of the lady . . . with black hair!"

The words tore through the night. I flinched, my head snapping toward the sound.

A figure slumped on the sidewalk, half-obscured by shadows. The man sat beneath the dim glow of a streetlight, clutching a bottle of vodka and a tattered McDonald's bag. His shoulders hunched inward, his head drooping forward.

It was Davis. My patient from this morning. Panic rippled through me. What was he doing here?

When he saw me, he stumbled to his feet, nearly toppling forward. "I... I usssed to be Officer Daviss," he slurred, his words slipping and sliding over each other, "but not anymore. Now I'm jussh a bum... I couldn't save 'em all, ya know." His bloodshot eyes widened as they locked onto mine. "I know you! Yer' the doc who got out. 'Member me? Officer Davis. Hostage thing. Ya' must remember. Saw ya this mornin'. Tried to talk, but ya' didn't help me..."

I took a step back, the tremor in my hands impossible to stop.

"I tole ya she'sh always followin' me," he slurred, taking another swig of vodka. He wiped his mouth with the back of his hand, his bloodshot eyes darting wildly. "An' she . . . she got this long black hair, her face all like a mask." His voice cracked, then rose, each word sharper than the last. "She'll ruin yer life!"

Long black hair. A mask-like face. His words landed hard. The woman from the coffee shop surfaced in my mind—her black hair, the overdone makeup, the way she'd smiled, wished me good luck. Could it possibly be the same woman? No. It couldn't be. My breath came short and fast, like I couldn't get enough air. Davis was unwell, drunk, drowning in his own delusions. That's all it was. That's all it could be.

"Look . . . look over there." Officer Davis rasped, jabbing a trembling finger toward the street.

A low rumble broke the stillness, and I turned just in time to see the bus. My chest tightened as the number came into view: 666.

The bus slowed as the headlights swept over the cracked pavement. Shadows stretched and shifted like they were alive. My gaze flicked to the windows, scanning the faces, and then—there she was. The woman from the coffee shop.

She sat in the back, perfectly still, her dark hair framing a face plastered with thick, exaggerated makeup—just as I remembered from the coffee shop. But she wasn't watching the road. She wasn't watching the other passengers. She was watching me.

"There she is!" Officer Davis shouted. "See, she's followin' me again. It's like she's tryin' to drive me insane. Punishin' me... but I don't even know what for..." His words came faster now, tripping over themselves, spilling out like water from a broken pipe. "Tried to find out, but there's nothin'. Nothin' to prove she's real."

I stared at her, unblinking, my feet rooted to the ground.

And then she waved.

Slow. Almost casual. Like greeting an old friend. The bus rumbled on, its red taillights fading into the darkness, but her gaze didn't leave me. It lingered, etched into the air, into me, long after she was gone.

"Oh my god," I whispered. "It's her."

"You can see her too?" Davis grabbed my elbow. I wrenched free, stumbling back, my breath catching in my throat. Before I could think, my legs were moving, feet pounding against the ground. The streetlights blurred around me, my body moving faster than my thoughts could keep up. None of this was real. It couldn't be real.

My legs felt weak, like I might give out any second. The hospital came into view, and relief hit so hard I nearly collapsed. The glowing entrance felt like salvation, like safety. I was just steps from the door when a hand grabbed my arm and yanked me back. I twisted hard, kicking out, my breath coming in sharp bursts.

"Olivia! Olivia! It's me. It's Owen."

The name stopped me cold. My leg hovered mid-kick as I turned, and there he was—my husband. The man I hadn't seen in a year. His eyes, filled with concern and worry, met mine. There was scruff along his jaw, like he'd let a few shaves slip. His white T-shirt was wrinkled, his faded jeans were creased with wear, and his hair stuck up in messy waves, just a little too long, as if overdue for a cut. And yet, somehow, standing there, he looked more handsome than I remembered. Or maybe it was just that I had spent every single day missing him.

"Are you okay?" he asked, his voice urgent. His hands came up, cupping my face, his thumbs brushing over my cheeks like he was afraid I'd disappear. "What happened? You're shaking. Talk to me."

The words jammed in my throat, tangled in the storm of emotions rushing through me—fear, relief, disbelief. I tried to focus. To find the right ones. To explain.

"There was a man," I finally choked out. "Down there . . . and a woman. She had black hair. She . . . she waved at me." My voice cracked. "He grabbed me. He was shouting. She was on the bus."

Owen's brow furrowed, concern deepening. "The guy down the street? He's just a drunk. Said a bunch of nonsense to me too. Something about surviving trauma. Kept pointing and screaming, 'There she is.' He's clearly been through a lot."

I took a deep breath. Held it. Let it out slowly. "I guess it was just... unsettling," I admitted, my voice still shaking. "He seemed so unstable, and today's been... one thing after another."

God, I was exhausted. Maybe I didn't really see the same woman. Maybe I was just too tired. The thought hovered, fragile at first, but then it settled. Steadied me.

And then it hit me, sharp and sudden, cutting through the fog in my mind: Owen. Here. With me.

I stared at him and asked, "What are you doing here, Owen?"

His eyes flickered down, then back up. "I missed you." His voice wavered just slightly. "It's been a year since we... parted, and I couldn't stop thinking about you. I wanted to see you. I thought about going to your apartment, but I figured you'd be here."

"You did?" The words barely slipped out, more breath than sound.

I wanted to reach out. To push his hair back from his face. To touch him. To feel the closeness we'd lost.

He nodded slowly. "I did. I can't imagine my life without you, Olivia. Leaving was a mistake. I'm so sorry. Can we try again?"

I didn't answer. I couldn't. Instead, I stepped forward and wrapped my arms around him, holding on like I'd never let go. For a moment, neither of us moved. Then his arms came up around me, pulling me closer, anchoring me. I pressed my face into his shoulder. His scent—warm, familiar—pulled me back to a time when everything felt whole.

"Olivia," he murmured, his hand brushing softly through my hair. "Why are you crying?"

"Because you're here," I whispered. "Because I thought I'd lost you."

He wiped my tears with his thumbs and kissed me softly. "I'm never leaving again, I promise," he said, his forehead resting against mine. "Now, can we go home?"

# MATT

They say cemeteries feel different at night, like that's when the ghosts come out to play. But ghost stories never scared me. I was the kid who'd watch the scariest movies in the dark without blinking. Same with Tom. On Halloween, we'd race through haunted houses, laughing and jumping out to scare other kids instead. Ghosts didn't give me chills. The real hits came from the living—from life itself. The twists that blindsided you, knocked the air out of your lungs when you thought you were standing steady.

It was ten at night, and I was standing at Tom's grave, my flashlight slicing through the dark. I'd left my folks' place a couple of hours ago when Lucas called to say he'd sent the signed contract to the landlord. "You're good to go," he'd said. I didn't hesitate. I wired the deposit right away. A few hours later, Lucas's text came through:

*We're good to go. The landlord confirmed the deposit, and the building is officially yours. Congrats! I'll get you the key this week so you can start the remodeling.*

Pops was right about one thing. It was time to visit Tom. I needed to tell him the news that "Tom's Bar" was about to become a reality. Maybe the name wasn't flashy or clever, but it was the only one that felt right. It was the name his dad had wanted, and I'd promised to make it happen. Plus, it was my way of honoring my brother.

The cemetery was empty, not a single soul in sight, which suited me just fine. The only sounds were the hum of traffic in the distance and the rustle of leaves shifting in the breeze. The moon hung low, pale and weary, stretching shadows long and thin over the gravestones. It had been two long years since I last came here. I stayed away because the pain cut too deep, too raw to face.

The funeral still lingered, clear as yesterday. The packed crowd, the muffled sobs, the choking grief that clung to the air like smoke. My breath had reeked of vodka that day, my legs unsteady, but I didn't bother hiding it. Not from Sean, not from our friends, not even from Tom's family. Pops was furious. "I didn't raise you to be like this, Son. You can't show up to a funeral drunk," he said, his eyes burning with disappointment that stung worse than anything he could say. But I couldn't help it. I thought the vodka would dull the edges, take the sting out of it all. It didn't.

It made everything worse—grief sharper, guilt heavier, the emptiness unbearable. Tom's mom sat there, staring at nothing, her face hollow. His dad stood next to her, pretending to hold it together, wiping at his face when he thought no one was watching. Tom's little brother sat on the grass, his knees pulled to his chest, his face streaked and swollen. Then they started lowering the coffin. The chains rattled against the wood, and something cracked open deep inside me.

"Don't bury him! If you do, he'll be gone!" The words tore out of me before I could stop them. I stumbled forward, my legs too weak to carry me. I went down hard, hands digging into the dirt. "If you do, he'll be gone!" I said it again, louder, desperate, my voice breaking apart.

No one said anything. I just felt Pops hands on my shoulders, dragging me back. The coffin sank lower, swallowed by the earth. And then it was gone. He was gone. Really gone. Forever out of reach.

Standing here now, staring at the tombstone, the loss hit me all over again. My hands stayed jammed in my pockets, the words catching in my throat before I finally let them out.

"We made it, bro," I said quietly. "The bar's happening, just like we planned. I wish you were here to see it."

The wind stirred, brushing against my face. I shifted, kicking at a loose stone near my foot, watching it skitter away. "Oh, and you'll never guess," I said, forcing a smile that didn't quite land. "Remember that girl from the coffee shop? The one you said I didn't have a shot with? Yeah, ran into her today. Crazy, right? I'm planning to text her tomorrow. I didn't do it today—didn't want to look too desperate."

I let out a slow breath and took a step back.

"Miss you, Tom," I said. "More than I can even say."

A rustling sound came from somewhere behind me.

I swung my flashlight toward the noise. A flock of pigeons burst from the ground, wings beating hard, frantic. I flinched as two of them swooped low, close enough that I ducked. Their cries were sharp and panicked, cutting through the quiet like a warning.

But it wasn't just the birds. It was the darkness behind them—thick, unbroken, stretching over the cemetery like it meant to *hide* something.

Out of the corner of my eye, I saw movement. A figure, cloaked in shadow, her hair loose and caught in the wind. My flashlight jerked toward her, but when the light hit—nothing. Just empty space. I swung the light wider, scanning the cemetery. The tombstones stood quiet. The trees shifted faintly. The shadows swallowed everything else.

"Shadows," I muttered. "Just shadows."

I turned back toward Tom's grave—and froze. Three pigeons were perched on top, their beady eyes locked on me. They didn't move. Didn't blink.

One of the pigeons took off into the air, wings flapping hard before it dropped straight to the ground. I shone my flashlight on it. It was dead. My breath caught in my throat.

Then—soft as breath against my ear—I swore I heard it.

"Six."

I stepped back, my pulse hammering. Again, barely more than a whisper.

"Six."

Another pigeon fluttered its wings, tilting its head like it was *listening*. One last time, softer now, like something pressing inside my skull.

"Six."

I turned and walked—fast—out of the cemetery. By the time I reached the car, my hands were shaking. I yanked the door open, slid inside, and slammed it shut. The dull thud echoed in my ears.

"Pull yourself together," I muttered, gripping the wheel. "Just birds." The words felt flat, hollow. I glanced at my reflection in the window. My face was pale, my eyes wide.

*Get it together. Think about normal things. Do normal things.* I inhaled deep, held it, let it out slow.

"Like asking that girl out," I said. Her face popped into my mind— her smile, her laugh. That was better. That was something real.

I gripped the wheel tighter, grounding myself. "Just focus on her."

# ALEXANDRA

*Oh my god. This was bad. Really bad.* My fingers twitched at my sides, searching for something—anything—to hold onto. The hallway was too dark. Too cold. The kind of cold that seeped past skin, twisting deep in my gut. The walls pressed closer, the air thick and unmoving. The space ahead stretched endlessly, impossibly narrow.

My brain screamed, *Run!* But there was nowhere to go. I spun around—only to find a solid wall where there'd been open space seconds ago. Forward. That's the only way out.

And then, footsteps. Slow. Deliberate. Getting closer.

A door appeared at the end of the hall. The lights flickered—shadows stretched and recoiled. My breath came sharp and uneven.

I looked down. Blood. It streaked my hands, soaked my sleeves.

The door creaked open. She was there. The woman from the bus stop. Her black hair fell across her face as she smiled, head tilting, watching me like a cat watching a mouse. A knife glinted in her hand.

"This way, Alex."

My heart lurched. My voice barely came out, shaking like the rest of me. "Who are you?"

Her smile widened, teeth too white, too perfect. "You already know." She lunged. Steel fingers crushed my arm, the blade flashing—

I screamed.

"Alex, wake up! Wake up!" My eyes flew open, and I gasped for air, my chest rising and falling like I'd just surfaced from underwater. My roommate Jessica was beside me, her face tight with concern. "You were screaming," she said, sitting on the edge of my bed. "You had a bad dream."

My throat burned. The dream clung to me, thick and sticky. "It was just a dream?"

"Yeah." She studied me, still wary. "Just a bad dream."

I rubbed my clammy forehead, my hand trembling. "Thank god."

Jessica leaned closer. "Was it the coffee shop again?"

"No," I whispered. "Something different."

The woman. The bus stop. The blood. I thought about telling her. But instead, I shook my head. "It's nothing. Just a stupid dream. I'll be fine." I swung my legs over the side of the bed. The cold floor grounded me. "I just need to use the bathroom."

Jessica sighed, her concern fading into exhaustion. "Well, it's two in the morning, and I've got nursing class tomorrow. You know where I am if you need me." She yawned and shuffled back to her room.

I slipped into the bathroom and turned on the sink, splashing cold water on my face. The nightmare should've faded, but it didn't. I stared at my reflection, rubbing my tired eyes. "How much longer can I keep going like this?"

Something shifted in the mirror. My breath caught. Something on the right side of the mirror caught my eye. On the right side of the glass, a single word was scrawled in bright red lipstick. *Lucky.*

But it wasn't just there. It gleamed. The edges still wet, still fresh. Like it had been written seconds ago.

Ice shot through my veins. I spun, scanning the bathroom. Nothing.

I turned back. The word hadn't smudged, hadn't faded. I swiped at it with my hand. It didn't move.

Like it wanted to stay.

Something snapped inside me. Then, before I could stop myself, my fist slammed into the glass. The mirror fractured with a sharp, splintering crack. The word stayed.

"Alex, what the hell?"

Jessica's voice was sharp as she burst through the door. Her eyes went wide. "Oh my god, you're bleeding!"

I looked down. Blood pooled in the lines of my palm, dripping onto the counter.

She grabbed a towel and pressed it against my hand. "What happened?"

"Look at the mirror," I said, barely able to glance at it again. "There's a message."

She frowned, stepping closer. Her fingers brushed the cracked glass. "There's nothing here, Alex. Just a broken mirror."

The room spun. Tears burned my eyes. "No. It was there. It was right there."

Jessica hesitated. She wanted to believe me. But she didn't. "Are you sure? Maybe it was a trick of the light."

"I'm not imagining this!" My voice cracked. "It was there. I swear it was there."

"I think—" She hesitated, glancing between me and the mirror. "You've been through a lot. I know stress doesn't just disappear overnight. But I thought the nightmares would be the worst of it." Her voice softened when she saw my eyes well up. "Let me see your hand again." She unwrapped the towel, her fingers careful as she examined the wound. "Luckily, it's not too deep," she murmured. "Didn't hit any veins. You'll be fine, but I need to bandage it properly." She wrapped the towel back around my hand. "Stay here—I'll grab the medical kit."

Once she finished bandaging my hand, I forced myself to return to my room, but my chest was tight, and my thoughts wouldn't settle. I climbed into bed, but I couldn't stop glancing at the bathroom door. *Was something still in there?*

My fingers hovered over the bandages, tracing the gauze, but my thoughts spiraled. *It wasn't real. It couldn't be real.* But the crack in the mirror was real. The blood on my hand was real. The way my heart was still racing—it was all real.

I stared at the ceiling, trying to steady my breath. *No message. No woman following Olivia. Nothing. Just my brain, twisting reality into something unrecognizable.*

My throat felt dry as the weight of it all settled over me. *It's the PTSD,* I told myself. *It has to be.* But even as I tried to reason with myself, the unease refused to fade. The image of the cracked mirror and that single word—Lucky—burned in my mind, an afterimage I couldn't blink away.

I turned onto my side, curling my fingers into the sheets. *Don't look. Don't check again. Just close your eyes.*

But my gaze kept drifting back to the bathroom door. Had it always been open that much?

*Waiting.*

\*\*\*

Sunlight sliced through Dr. Richardson's window, aiming straight at my eyes. I squinted and shifted my chair, dodging the spotlight. Across from me, he sat calm as ever, notebook open, pen poised. He'd carved out time before his first patient, probably because my 6 a.m. call made me sound like I was about to lose it.

I zeroed in on the peace lily on his desk. Usually, its crisp white blooms radiated that sterile, therapy-office calm. But today? It looked wrong. Like something had soured beneath its neat little facade. Something festering. Or maybe I just needed more sleep.

"Good morning, Alex." Dr. Richardson said. "Let's delve into how you're feeling today."

I fidgeted with the lid of my coffee cup. "Honestly? Not great. I hardly slept," I admitted. "Dr. Richardson, something feels off. I keep telling myself it's just the PTSD, like you said, but—" I hesitated, biting the inside of my cheek. "I think it's more than that."

He tilted his head slightly, the calm patience of someone who'd heard it all before. "Take a deep breath. Start from the beginning.

What's been happening since yesterday?" His eyes flicked to my bandaged hand. "And what happened there?"

I glanced down at my hand, the gauze rough under my fingertips. "I, uh, broke a mirror," I said, avoiding his gaze. "I thought I saw something on it—written in red lipstick. The word 'Lucky.'"

His pen hovered over his notebook. "How did you break it?"

My thumb traced the cardboard sleeve of my cup, softening it under the pressure. "I had another nightmare last night," I said. "Jessica—my roommate—woke me up because I was screaming. I went to the bathroom to calm down, and that's when I saw it. The writing on the mirror." My voice dropped. "But when Jessica came in, it was gone."

Dr. Richardson leaned back slightly, tapping his pen against the notebook's edge. "So you didn't see it again?"

"No, it just… vanished." I rubbed at a spot on the side of my cup. "I know it sounds nuts, but I swear it was there. Bright red. 'Lucky.' It felt like it was taunting me."

His pen stilled. "What was the nightmare about? Was it Charlie again?"

I hesitated. "No," I said. "It was about the strange woman I told you about. The one from the bus stop." I hesitated again, then added, "I saw her again later in the afternoon. She was following Dr. Olivia after she left my office. Or… at least I think she was. When I pointed her out to Bruce, he didn't see anyone. And when I checked again, she was gone."

Dr. Richardson's brow furrowed slightly. "So you're not entirely sure if you actually saw her?"

I exhaled sharply. "Well… no. I mean, yes. I saw her." A beat passed. "I think." I ran a hand through my hair. "She was following Dr. Olivia. But then Bruce didn't see her. And in my nightmare… she had a knife. She was going to hurt me."

I hated how my voice cracked at the end. Hated how, the more I explained, the more I sounded like I was unraveling. Dr. Richardson's expression didn't change. His fingers drummed lightly against his notebook—a small, deliberate movement that made my stomach twist.

"Is Dr. Olivia just a client?" he asked, shifting gears.

I blinked. "Well, it's complicated. She's technically a client, but she's also a survivor from the shooting two years ago." I let out a humorless laugh. "Crazy, right? I didn't even recognize her until she walked into my office. And before that, I bumped into Matt—remember him? The other survivor? It's just... too many weird coincidences in one day."

Dr. Richardson nodded thoughtfully. "It's unusual, no doubt. But life has a way of throwing unexpected things our way."

I crossed my arms, feeling a flicker of relief. "Right? What do you think it means? Is this some kind of sign?"

"These coincidences can definitely be unsettling," he said. "But overanalyzing them might make things harder for you. They could be triggering your PTSD, making you more susceptible to seeing things— like the writing on the mirror or the woman from the bus stop."

"But they felt so real." My fingers dug into the edge of my chair.

"I'm sure they did. The mind is capable of incredibly vivid experiences," he said. "Here's what I suggest: I'll prescribe something to help you sleep. And maybe consider reaching out to Matt or Dr. Olivia. Connecting with others who've been through the same thing could help."

I nodded, even though doubt gnawed at me. I hadn't heard from Matt since yesterday. And after that disaster of a meeting, I doubted I'd hear from Dr. Olivia again either. But I didn't say any of that to Dr. Richardson. Instead, I gave him a tight smile and said, "Okay."

I stepped out of his office, letting the door click shut behind me. The hallway was quiet. Inside, my mind was anything but. Talking through everything—again—left me feeling more drained than relieved. My head buzzed like static, exhaustion settling over me like a heavy coat I couldn't take off. The session hadn't helped. If anything, I was unraveling faster.

By the time I reached the elevator, my thoughts had already jumped to Kyle. How the hell was I supposed to explain that train wreck of a meeting with Dr. Olivia? Maybe I should call her office. Come up with some polite excuse to check on her. Casually work in a reschedule. Apologize for being completely unprofessional, obviously.

My phone buzzed, cutting through my spiraling thoughts. I pulled it out and saw a new text message.

*Hey, Alex, it's Matt. I wanted to ask if you'd be up for grabbing a drink this Thursday.*

# OLIVIA

The morning light filtered through the curtains as I opened my eyes. Eight o'clock. I rarely slept this late. Had I forgotten to set my alarm? I reached for my phone. No missed calls. No urgent messages.

I exhaled and looked around the room. Clothes were scattered across the floor. Last night came back in flashes. Owen waiting for me by the hospital door. The drive home—too fast, too hungry. When we stepped inside, we couldn't keep our hands off each other. The need to reconnect was overwhelming. I'd almost forgotten what it felt like to have him here, to have him at all.

I stared at the ceiling, letting the moment settle. Owen was back, and I finally felt like I could breathe.

Though the bedroom door was closed, I heard him in the kitchen, humming to himself as he cooked. A few minutes later, he appeared, tray in hand—fluffy pancakes, crispy bacon, steaming coffee. Still in his navy boxers and the white shirt from last night.

"Breakfast in bed for my beautiful wife," he said, setting the tray down beside me.

*Wife.* He said the word *wife.* The word settled between us, as if to confirm this was real.

I swallowed hard, then laughed, a soft sound. "You're spoiling me."

"Only because you deserve it," he replied.

"That's so sweet of you," I said, slipping out of bed. I grabbed my robe from the chair, draping it around myself before walking over to him. "I can't believe you came back."

He stepped closer. "I can't believe I ever left," he said. "This past year has been torture without you, Olivia. I've regretted every moment."

I didn't want to go there. I kissed him quickly, cutting off the words. "Let's not talk about that," I said, pulling back just enough to look at him. "Actually..." I trailed off, wrapping my arms around him. "I've got time today. Breakfast isn't what I'm craving."

He raised an eyebrow, a smile tugging at the corner of his mouth. "No?"

"No," I murmured, brushing my lips against his neck.

His hand slid down my back. "Are you sure we have enough time?" he whispered, his voice thick with desire.

"We have plenty of time," I assured him, pulling him back into a kiss, slow and deep.

He scooped me up and carried me to the bed, lips still locked to mine. He laid me down gently, removing my robe, his hands moving over me with tenderness, as if he were learning every part of me all over again. A soft moan escaped me as his fingers traced the curve of my thighs.

He pulled back, his eyes meeting mine. "I love you, Olivia. I love you so much."

"I love you too."

We kissed again and again. Time seemed to stretch. I wanted to hold on to it all—love, longing, the sense of us becoming one. Our past had been difficult, filled with heartache, but this moment was ours. I wasn't going to lose it. The arguments, the misunderstandings, the loneliness—they seemed like distant memories now. We held each other close, the outside world fading. In his arms, I felt whole again. The future felt bright, full of possibilities. I didn't want to let go of this feeling.

But then, a faint thought crept in, a shadow in the midst of my happiness. The words of Officer Davis echoed in my mind:

*Beware of the lady with black hair. It was like she offered me the world, only to snatch it back.*

\*\*\*

My day at the hospital began as soon as I stepped inside. The usual routine—patient check-ins, medical rounds—took over. I had scheduled Charlie as my last stop, partly to avoid running into her mother. The conversation about life support was coming, but I had no idea how to begin.

"Dr. Jones!"

The voice echoed down the corridor. Bella, the little girl I'd treated, ran toward me, her eyes shining.

"Look at my arm," she said, holding it up, beaming. "It's all better now! I can play softball again. Thank you so much!"

A warm rush spread through me as I hugged her. "I'm so glad to hear that, sweetie."

Bella's mother approached, smiling. "Thank you, Dr. Jones."

"It was my pleasure," I said, feeling a familiar sense of satisfaction settle in.

It wasn't the only good news I'd had today. Earlier, still in bed with Owen, I got a call—Richard, one of my patients, had finally found a kidney donor after a long wait. Moments like that always made everything worth it.

As I continued my rounds, I tried to push Officer Davis's unsettling words to the back of my mind. *It was nonsense*, I told myself. Owen's return was what mattered now. That was where I wanted to focus—on him and my patients, not some lingering doubt.

I passed George, the security officer, as I made my way through the hospital. He was sitting by the entrance, sipping his coffee.

"You seem happy today," he observed.

"And why shouldn't I be?" I replied. "A lot of my patients are making progress, and I'm feeling hopeful. It's a good day."

Being a surgeon is tough, but moments like this make it worthwhile. My grandmother, a surgeon herself, had told me that the rewards came from those quiet moments with patients and families who truly understood the impact.

I still remember the day a neighbor knocked on our door, tears in her eyes, and hugged my grandmother like she never wanted to let go. "You saved my son," she said. "I don't know how to thank you."

I watched from the doorway, barely breathing. The meaning of those words and the power to make a difference changed me. That was the moment I knew—I wanted to be a doctor.

But I also remembered her caution. When I told her my plans, she smiled, but her eyes turned distant. "You can't save everyone," she'd said. "Luck often plays a part."

"Well, who controls luck, Grandma? Is it God?"

She'd placed a hand on my shoulder. "I'm not sure. But whoever holds that power, it's far greater than mine."

"I still want to be a doctor," I had said. "I'll do my best."

Now, standing outside Charlie's room, my hand hovered over the door handle. Through the glass, I saw Ms. Moretti, her face a mixture of love and exhaustion as she gently brushed Charlie's hair. Charlie lay still, just as she had for two years. Her mother looked worn out, her eyes dark with sleepless nights. She carried the weight of the world on her shoulders.

Daniel's words came back to me. *Every day brings false hope, and it's tearing her family apart. That boy in there. And you, too, Olivia.*

I watched them, and as much as I wanted to delay it, I knew this moment couldn't be put off any longer. It was time.

I knocked softly and entered. Ms. Moretti didn't look up. Her eyes stayed locked on Charlie, her hand holding her daughter's with a grip so tight, it hurt to watch. I began my examination, aware of her gaze following my every move. When I finished, I asked, "How are you holding up, Ms. Moretti?"

Her eyes lifted, tired and red from lack of sleep. She wore a worn sweater over her faded factory uniform, the fabric thinning from long hours. "I . . . I'm trying, Doctor," she whispered, her voice a little cracked. "It's just so hard seeing her like this. She's my baby, you know? She's all I've got."

"I know it's difficult," I said, grounding myself in the role I had to play. The words felt distant, but I said them anyway. "Charlie's been fighting for so long, and your care and love have been unwavering."

Ms. Moretti tightened her grip on Charlie's hand, her face softening despite the tears. "She's a fighter. I know she'll get through this."

I took a deep breath. "Ms. Moretti, I know this is agonizing, but we need to talk about Charlie's quality of life." I spoke slowly. "She's been on life support for two years now, with no improvement. It might be time to talk about letting her go peacefully."

I felt like I was splitting in two—part of me, the doctor, saying what needed to be said. But deep down, another part of me wanted to scream, "No, please don't let this happen!"

Ms. Moretti's face crumpled. Her hands rose to cover her mouth, tears spilling over. "You want to take her off life support? Are you giving up on her?"

I shook my head. "I want you to understand, it's not about giving up. It's about giving her the peace she deserves."

She shook her head, her tears coming faster. "I can't... I can't let her go. She's all I have left."

"I know, Ms. Moretti," I said gently, reaching for her shoulder. She pulled away. "This is the hardest decision a parent could face," I said softly. "We'll be here to support you every step of the way. You don't have to make this decision today. Take your time, talk to your family. We'll discuss it when you're ready."

"There's no other family. I'm all she's got. And she's all I've got."

"I understand," I said quietly. "But keeping her here, unable to move, won't bring her comfort. It might only prolong false hope."

Ms. Moretti wiped her tears with the back of her hand and glanced back at Charlie. "I'll think about it, Doctor. It's just so hard."

Then the monitor beeped—sharp, urgent. Charlie's heart rate had dipped. A profoundly concerning sign that her already fragile condition was rapidly deteriorating.

"I'm sorry, Ms. Moretti, but you need to step out of the room now," I said firmly.

Her eyes widened with panic. "What's happening? Is something wrong? What's happening to her?"

I had no time for gentle reassurances. "Please, step out now."

I pressed the emergency button. Nurses and doctors rushed in. Resuscitation began immediately.

Amid the chaos, Ms. Moretti's cries rang out.

"Get her out!" Daniel yelled, and the two male nurses swiftly led her away.

Sweat beaded on our foreheads as we worked—chest compressions, treatments, doing what we could to bring Charlie back. The room was filled with a tense energy —a battle between life and uncertainty—and none of us knew how it would end.

And in the midst of it all, a question lingered: Was bringing Charlie back the right thing to do?

# CHARLIE

Just when I thought things couldn't get worse, they did. I lay there in that sterile, suffocating stillness, my body hooked up to machines, unable to move or speak. But I could hear. I could hear Mammina and Dr. Olivia Jones talking, discussing taking me off life support, plotting my death sentence.

*Dr. Jones, you left me there in that coffee shop, taking my place and leaving me behind. And now you're really talking about pulling the plug? And Mammina... you said you'd think about it? How could you do that? Wasn't I your only child? Haven't you promised to fight for me?*

"Charlie, Charlie, you gotta stay calm. The monitors are showing warning signs, that's why all these medical professionals are swarming like bees."

Her again. That voice. Whispering to me.

Fear locked around me, cold and unrelenting. I tried to shut it out, to push her words aside, but they wouldn't let go.

"I'm here to help you. I understand that you can't see it now, but you will. The doctors won't let you slip away. And I won't allow your mind to shut down, no matter how hard you resist."

*How was this possible? How could she be standing there, talking to me, yet no one else seemed to notice? They'd made Mammina leave.* The room around me hummed with the sounds of doctors and nurses, moving, working. Yet none of them reacted to her. This woman. Standing there. Whispering to me.

"Got a tiny clue for you, dear Charlie. I get to pick who gets to see me and hear me and when," she whispered. "But don't get too excited—that's all you're getting for now. Everything will roll out when the time is right. You just have to be patient. Now, let's take a stroll down memory lane. What pops up after Daddy said bye-bye?"

I tried to push it back, tried to block the memories, but it was like trying to stop the ocean with my hands.

And then, I was there again. Back in time, just months after Daddy left. Everything played out like a movie I couldn't stop watching—Mammina and our neighbor Susan, deep in conversation.

"Can you watch Charlie for a bit?" Mammina asked Susan.

I loved Susan. Her long black hair was so pretty, and her eyes sparkled like dark chocolate. I always thought she looked just like Pocahontas from TV! She even flipped her hair just like Pocahontas!

"I've got a job interview at the factory. It won't take long, just a few hours," Mammina added.

"Of course, anytime, Isabella. I hope you find a job soon," Susan replied.

Mammina sighed. "No luck yet, but I'm still hopeful. Maybe this one will work out. But they need someone for the evening shift. Charlie's only five, and I wish my parents were still here to help."

"Don't you worry, I'll help you out," Susan reassured. "Any word from, you know, him?"

"No, not a peep," Mammina answered. "He's gone, just like that. Left us high and dry. I don't know what to do. Money's running out, and I couldn't even pay last month's mortgage. We might lose the house. I can't afford a lawyer for child support, and who knows if he'll ever send anything."

"We gonna lose our house?" I piped up, my voice shaky and scared. "I don't wanna lose our house. I love our house!"

Mammina seemed lost in thought for a moment, then she pulled me close. "No, sweetheart, that won't happen. I'll fight tooth and nail to keep our home."

"Really, really, really?" I asked, hugging my teddy bear tight.

"Have I ever lied to you, baby?"

"No," I whispered, feeling reassured by her words.

"I have to go now, honey, but I'll be back in time to read you a bedtime story. You're my everything, my precious baby. You mean the world to me."

And with that, she was out the door, leaving me with Susan, who smiled at me with that sweet Susan-smile I loved, her dimple showing as she placed her warm hand on my shoulder, making me feel safe and loved.

"So, do you have many friends in kindergarten?"

"Nuh-uh, not really," I said. "I like playing with just my teddy bear. And you."

"And I love playing with you," she said, smiling. "You're my absolute best friend."

"You're mine too!" I exclaimed just before my tummy rumbled.

"Hungry?" Susan asked. "How about we grab some pizza?"

I nodded eagerly. "Yes, yes! Pizza sounds yummy!" But then I hesitated. "Susan, can I ask you something?"

"Of course. You can ask me anything."

"Do you think we'll lose our house?" I asked.

She shook her head. "No way! Your mom would never, ever lie to you."

But then, a chilling whisper slid into my ear, jerking me back to the present.

"But Mammina did lie to you. You lost the house. What else was a lie?"

Mammina did get the job that night, which meant most evenings were spent with Susan. Mornings became a struggle—her exhaustion seeping into everything as she got me ready. I could hear it in her voice, the frustration creeping in, sharp and bitter. She blamed Daddy for everything, but sometimes I wondered if she blamed me too. If she ever wished for an easier life without me in the way.

Then, when our old home became unaffordable, we had no choice but to move. That's how we ended up in Rogers Park, in the small apartment we've stayed in ever since. Mammina hired an older woman named Beth to take care of me, but she wasn't like Susan. Where Susan had kindness, Beth had only coldness and demands. She asked for too much money and gave nothing in return.

When I didn't follow Beth's instructions, she hurled words like "stupid" and "worthless" at me. Told me I'd never amount to anything. That I'd end up marrying a loser like my mama. Beth was manipulative, her cruelty hidden behind a careful mask. Then Jason came into my life, and everything seemed to get better. I spent more time at his house. Less time with Beth. Eventually, Mammina decided she didn't need Beth anymore.

"See? See? Your Mammina wasn't so great at being a mama, was she?" the voice hissed, its words laced with a cold thread of truth.

My anger toward Mammina burned. *How could she abandon me when I needed her the most?* She did it again just now—saying she'd think about taking me off life support, when she should have said, *"No, that's out of the question."*

Lying there, hurt and betrayed, I wondered if her love had always been this fragile. *Had I ever truly been her priority? Had she fought for me when Daddy left? Had she fought for me when Beth's words didn't add up?* And now, with Dr. Olivia, she was ready to let me go. She should've fought for me. Her only child.

"Our progress is remarkable," the voice sneered. "Monitors stable. Doctors leaving. Ah, your Mammina's coming back. I must go too, but worry not—I'll be back."

I didn't want Mammina near me. The thought was strange, unsettling. A painful truth settled in my chest—*sometimes the deepest hurt isn't the kind that comes from the outside.* It comes from the people closest to you.

*The ones you thought would never hurt you.*

# ALEXANDRA

My attempts to reschedule the meeting with Olivia were a disaster. After what felt like hours of mind-numbing hold music, I gave up and dropped my forehead against the desk.

"Ugh," I groaned. Could this day get any worse?

Desperate for a reset, I dove into the Berrylicious Smoothies campaign. A new start-up selling organic, healthy smoothies that practically screamed, *Drink me and transform your life.* My job? Make those bottles look like the key to happiness, health, and everything in between. The problem? A market overflowing with brands promising the exact same thing. Sticky notes and half-formed ideas cluttered my desk, but no matter how hard I tried, I couldn't block everything else out.

"How did the meeting with Dr. Olivia Jones go?"

Kyle's voice snapped me back. He leaned against the doorframe, crisp suit, white shirt—like a stock image for corporate perfection.

I opened my mouth, scrambling for a response that didn't sound like *I completely blew it*, when Janet appeared behind him. "Sorry to interrupt," she said, glancing between us. "Dr. Olivia Jones's office just called. Her receptionist, Kate, said she'd like to reschedule for next week."

Relief hit, sharp and sudden. She'd requested it this morning. That meant she was okay. Maybe I'd imagined the whole thing—the eerie feeling, the woman following her—after all.

"Oh, that's great," I said too quickly. "I'm really glad—uh, I mean, glad she rescheduled."

Kyle's eyebrow lifted at my flustered tone.

I scrambled to clarify. "She had to cut the last meeting short. There was a hospital emergency, but she seemed eager to work with us."

"Excellent, Weisman," Kyle said with a nod. "Keep up the good work." He turned, stepping aside as Bruce sauntered in. "Hey, Bruce."

Bruce grinned as Kyle walked away, then flopped into the chair across from me.

"Come and knock on our door..." he sang with theatrical delight. "Oh wait, don't. We're far too busy being wildly successful."

I rolled my eyes, but a laugh slipped out. "Is this your way of forgiving me for stealing the promotion?"

"Darling, I am far too evolved to hold grudges," Bruce said, adjusting his tie like a politician at a press conference. "Besides, success means nothing if you can't share it with the ones you love." He gestured at my desk. "Look at you, all busy and important. You're finally living the glamorous life you were always meant for."

A lump formed in my throat. *Glamorous?* If barely holding it together counted as glamorous, then sure, I was winning. The fear still lurked, gnawing at the edges, but Bruce didn't need to see that.

"I can't even put into words how much your support means to me," I said. "We work so well together—it's not about titles; it's about collaboration. We're equals, and I truly appreciate you. . ."

Suddenly, Bruce's eyes widened. "What happened to your hand?"

I glanced at my bandaged fingers. "Oh, it's nothing. Just an accident."

"Alex." His tone sharpened.

I exhaled. "I broke a mirror. And—bad luck of all bad luck—a shard got stuck in my hand."

Bruce gasped, clutching his chest like I'd told him I sacrificed a kitten to the dark arts. "A mirror? Oh no. That's seven years of misfortune." Then, catching my expression, he waved a dismissive hand. "No, no, don't look so tragic. We're banishing those naughty thoughts immediately." He snapped his fingers. "Forget superstitions. Nothing bad is coming your way."

Before I could answer, his eyes sparkled with fresh gossip. "Oh! Guess who I bumped into in the elevator this morning?" He held up a hand. "Wait—no need to guess. I can tell from your face you *already* know." He grinned. "Yes, Matt."

My stomach tensed.

Bruce grinned. "He mentioned he had to rush off, but I couldn't help noticing your name at the top of his texts. So. Spill. Did he ask you out?"

I nodded. "Yeah. I said yes." Earlier, I'd hovered over Matt's text, second-guessing if it was the right move. But Dr. Richardson had said reconnecting could help, so… why not? I'd finally typed back, *Sounds good*. After a few back-and-forth messages, we locked in the day and time.

Bruce clasped his hands together, delighted. "That's wonderful! When?"

"Thursday."

"You'll be fabulous. I need a full debrief after, obviously." He stood, smoothing his blazer. "And on that note, I must dash. Clients await. But Thursday, Alex—you're going to shine."

I forced a smile. "Sure," I said.

But the truth was, I wasn't sure at all.

*What if seeing Matt stirred up everything I'd been trying so hard to push down? What if it shoved me closer to the edge I was already teetering on?*

Then again, maybe grabbing a drink with him was exactly what I needed—a small break from the chaos. It wouldn't fix the nightmares. It wouldn't erase the fear. But it was something.

And right now, I'd take anything to keep from unraveling.

# OLIVIA

Daniel was pouring himself a cup of coffee in the hospital's kitchen area when I finally made my way there after Charlie's code. Steam rose from his cup as he took a sip, his tired eyes meeting mine, concern clear in them.

It was already six in the evening, and I had promised Owen I'd be home for dinner. I needed to leave soon. I couldn't let myself slip back into the old habits—putting the hospital and Charlie first. Those habits had pushed Owen away before.

"What an evening, huh?" Daniel sighed heavily. "I can't wrap my head around what's happening with Charlie. Her brain activity has been a rollercoaster these past few days. It's like there's a storm inside her head. Today, I was so sure . . . I thought this was it, the end."

"I know—I don't understand either," I said. "I spoke to her mother today about taking Charlie off life support. It was the hardest conversation I've ever had. And I still don't know if it's the right decision."

"We'll never know, Olivia. But I just can't see her improving," he said, his expression somber. "My heart breaks for her and her mother. Sometimes I wonder why I chose this profession. We've seen so much pain and loss... it's hard not to question if it's all worth it."

I felt utterly drained. "I have to go, Daniel," I said. "Owen is back, and I promised him I'd be home for dinner."

He blinked, surprise flashing in his eyes. "Your husband, Owen? The one who left you a year ago?" he asked. I nodded. "And just like that, you took him back?"

"Yes, Daniel," I replied, my voice tight. "Owen is back. He's my husband, and I love him. It's complicated, I know, but we're working through it. It's not for anyone else to judge or understand."

Daniel raised an eyebrow. "Have you asked him why?"

I crossed my arms over my chest. "Yes, he said that he missed me."

"I hope it's not just because things didn't work out with someone else. He left you once, Olivia. What makes you think he won't do it again?"

His words cut deep, and for a second, something unsettled me. A thought I didn't want to entertain. I shoved it down. "He left because I was too focused on the hospital. It was never about anyone else."

"Are you sure?" he asked, pressing.

My face flushed. "Honestly, Daniel, it's none of your business. Focus on your own life. Find your own happiness, for god's sake. Your wife left you five years ago for another man, and you still can't move on?"

I saw it land. He took a breath, stepping closer, our faces nearly touching.

"Maybe I have moved on," he said. "Maybe I have feelings for someone... someone incredible, who can't see how much better she deserves. She's too good to take back a man who walked away."

So, he did have feelings for me. For a moment, something stirred in my chest, like a bird that couldn't quite settle. It was the same feeling I'd had when we danced yesterday. Was there really something more between us? His face was so close now, lips inches from mine, so familiar, so full of things unsaid. No. It couldn't be. I had Owen. He was back.

"I have to go, Daniel. Like I told you, Owen is back, and I'm happy. Really happy."

He nodded, but I saw a flicker of sadness in his eyes.

I walked away, the knot in my chest tightening. Despite the tension, I couldn't ignore the fact that Daniel and I had always shared something deeper—more than just colleagues, more than just friends. He had always been there for me, in ways no one else had. Would this past year have been different if I'd known how he felt?

Strangely, I found myself at a loss for an answer. Were my feelings for Daniel more complex than simple companionship? I had no idea. It was all so confusing. But it didn't matter—Owen was back in my life, and my heart belonged to him. I couldn't give Daniel what he wanted.

And yet, somewhere deep inside, an unbearable ache whispered of the fear of losing Daniel, of our friendship fading because of these unspoken feelings. The thought made my stomach churn.

As I walked outside, I couldn't shake the feeling that I was leaving something unresolved—like a door left slightly ajar that might never fully close.

***

The smell of garlic and herbs greeted me as I stepped into the house. Only then did I realize how hungry I was. I hung my jacket on the hook by the door, exhaling slowly, letting the weight of the day slip from my shoulders.

"Hey, sweetie," Owen called from the living room.

He was stretched out on the couch, flipping through a hardcover copy of *The Trusted Advisor*—the book he always swore would change my life, though I still hadn't gotten around to reading it.

"You tired?" he asked, looking up with a smile.

"Not too tired for you," I said, stepping toward him. It felt good to be home, to have him here. I'd missed this. I'd missed him. "And thank you for making dinner."

"I love cooking for you," he said. "How was your day?"

I dropped my purse and keys on the table, then walked over and wrapped my arms around his neck. Resting my head on his shoulder, I let the tension in my muscles slowly dissolve. "I missed you today," I said.

"I missed you more," he replied, kissing my hand.

His words were enough to push Daniel's accusations to the back of my mind. The mention of another woman felt distant now. Owen was back. That was enough.

I started to sit next to him, but without a word, he pulled me onto his lap. His lips met mine instantly—fast, hungry. My body responded before my mind caught up. His hands slid beneath my blouse, fingers tracing my skin, and I melted into him.

"You're already so wet," he whispered in my ear, slipping his finger inside me.

"You do this to me," I murmured, my voice breathless. "Don't stop . . ."

But then—a flicker of movement. A shadow outside the window.

My pulse stumbled. I stilled, breath catching in my throat.

"What's wrong?" Owen asked, his grip loosening as he pulled back. "Did I do something wrong?"

"Did you hear something?" My voice barely registered as my own.

"Like what?"

"I thought I saw someone outside," I said, glancing toward the window. Just the stillness of late evening.

"It's probably just the wind," he reassured me. "Want me to close the blinds?"

"No, you're right," I replied, swallowing hard. "Probably nothing."

*Just the wind.* But something in the room felt off. Like we weren't alone, like we were being watched.

"You look like you've seen a ghost," Owen said, his hand resting on my shoulder as he gently moved me off his lap. "I'll close the blinds anyway, just to ease your mind."

I exhaled, trying to shake the feeling. Then, just as I was starting to regain my sense of calm, the sound of a text message coming through on Owen's phone broke the silence.

"Who's it from?" I asked, my curiosity piqued.

"No one. Just work," Owen said, flipping his phone over a little too fast.

The words Daniel had spoken—*another woman*—slithered back into my mind. Why was he being so secretive about a simple work message?

"Oh, is it Ryan, your boss?" I asked casually.

His expression faltered, a flicker of something behind his eyes. Then he forced a smile, brushing it off. "No, it's a client. Nobody you'd know," he replied. "So, where were we?" he added with a suggestive smile.

I tried to smile back, but the air between us had thickened. "How about we eat now? I'm starving, and the food smells amazing," I said.

A flicker of disappointment. Then, his expression smoothed over too quickly. "Yes, of course, honey." Then, with a playful waggle of his eyebrows, he added, "We can save this for dessert."

Owen headed into the kitchen, leaving his phone on the table. The temptation to sneak a peek at the message clawed at me. Should I? My fingertips brushed against the screen, but then his phone beeped again, making me jerk my hand back.

"Honey, can you please bring me my phone?" Owen called out from the kitchen. "I need to see who it is. Actually, I'll get it myself."

He reappeared, sliding the phone into his pocket. "Let's go eat," he said.

"Sure," I said, my smile barely holding.

# ALEXANDRA

Matt studied the laminated drink menu like it held the secrets of the universe. Meanwhile, I soaked in the vibe of this adorable spot called *Sea's the Day*. The walls, painted seafoam green and lively azure blue, were covered in nautical art and marine-life pictures, making it feel like we were dining inside a stylish aquarium.

The décor balanced rustic charm and coastal elegance, with distressed wooden tables, softly glowing glass lanterns, and shell-shaped lights twinkling overhead. The air carried the buttery, briny scent of fresh seafood, and my mouth watered.

For a Thursday night in the city, the place was surprisingly quiet. A few couples lingered at nearby tables, their low voices blending with the soft clink of silverware. The whole scene should have felt intimate. Romantic, even.

But tonight, romance wasn't on the menu.

Matt looked... good. The kind of good that seemed effortless—black shirt, well-fitted jeans, hair slightly tousled like he'd run a hand through it five minutes ago and hadn't thought about it since. Meanwhile, girls like me spent hours trying to pull off even a fraction of that kind of casual perfection. In my pre-shooting life, sitting across from a guy like him would've given me butterflies the size of pterodactyls.

That was then.

This wasn't a hot date. Instead of swooning, my brain was in overdrive, searching for a way to steer the conversation where I needed it to go.

How do you even start that kind of conversation? *So, have you noticed anything... strange lately?* Yeah. That wouldn't be awkward at all. The last time I'd tried this with Dr. Olivia Jones, it had backfired spectacularly. But I had to know—was Matt seeing the same things I was? Feeling the same unraveling? Maybe together, we'd make sense of it all.

A waiter approached, a polite smile on his face. "Can I start you off with some drinks?"

Matt finally set down the menu and glanced at me. "What are you having, Alex?"

"I'll have a glass of Kim Crawford wine," I said, even though my nerves whispered that maybe a whole bottle wouldn't be the worst idea. Liquid courage might be exactly what I needed tonight.

"I'll have the same," Matt said, then looked at the waiter and added, "Actually, let's just get a bottle." Like he'd read my mind.

The waiter nodded and stepped away, leaving us in the kind of quiet that felt too loud.

Matt's fingers tapped a slow rhythm against the table, his eyes skimming over me, searching for what to say. The silence stretched just long enough to feel awkward.

"It's a cute name—Alex," he said eventually, like he'd grabbed the first thing that came to mind. "Is it short for Alexandra?"

"Yeah, but I prefer Alex," I replied. "Alexandra just sounds way too formal, like I should be hosting royal tea parties or something. My mom only used it when I was in trouble."

Matt huffed out a small laugh. "Did you get in trouble a lot?"

"Depends who you ask," I said, managing a smile. His eyes flicked over my pink dress, lingering just a second too long, like this was some casual first date.

But it wasn't. While he laughed without a care, my thoughts spiraled back to everything that had happened—the shooting, his friend who didn't make it. I remembered reading about him in the news. How could Matt sit there, so at ease, when I felt like my insides were splintering? I forced myself to hold his gaze, willing my hands not to fidget, trying to match his calm when all I wanted was to ask him what I really needed to know.

"So . . ." Matt leaned forward slightly, his hands resting on the table. "Bruce mentioned you both work at the ad agency. Do you like it?"

"Yeah, I do," I said, but my mind was already racing ahead. I couldn't keep skating on the surface of this conversation. "How about you? How do you feel about your job?"

"I'm fully focused on getting my bar up and running. Honestly? It's going pretty great," he said, his face lighting up. "The lease is signed, and now it's all about construction and vendors. Spent this morning in meetings, shaking hands and writing checks. It's chaos, but I love it." A flicker of uncertainty crossed his face. "Fingers crossed it all works out, though. It's a big investment."

"Very cool," I replied, trying to sound interested even as my nerves churned. "Got a name for the place yet?"

Matt hesitated, his smile slipping. "Uh, it's called Tom's Bar," he said, his voice quieter. "After my friend . . ."

"Tom," I said softly, finishing for him.

He nodded, looking down. "Yeah. Tom. Naming the bar after him felt right, like a way to honor him."

I couldn't hold it back any longer. "Matt, why did you want to go out with me?" My voice wavered. "Aren't I just a painful reminder of everything that happened? I read about Tom, and I'm really sorry for your loss. I can't imagine what that was like for you."

His eyes met mine, steady, sincere. "I'm done running, Alex," he said finally. "For two years, I've been avoiding the pain, but it never went away. Then I saw you again, and it felt like fate was giving me a nudge. Even back in the café, that morning when I first saw you, I told Tom I was going to ask you out."

"Oh, really?" I said, a smile breaking through despite my tears.

"Yeah." He smiled, just a little. "You've got this way of bringing light into a room, even on the darkest days. I guess it's time I stopped ignoring that."

The waiter arrived with a bottle of wine and two elegant glasses, setting the tray down with practiced ease. I dabbed at my eyes with a napkin, trying to erase any evidence of tears, and leaned back as the waiter poured a small taste into one of the glasses, placing it in front of Matt.

"Let's get a connoisseur's verdict," Matt said with a slight grin, sliding the glass toward me.

I swirled the wine like I knew what I was doing, pretending I wasn't internally debating if I should just chug it. Taking a slow sip, I tilted my head thoughtfully. "Positively exquisite," I declared, channeling a British aristocrat. "Excellent choice, Matthew."

He chuckled, and for a moment, things felt lighter. The waiter filled our glasses and set the bottle on the table. "Are you ready to place your orders?" he asked politely, pen poised.

I realized I hadn't even glanced at the menu. Scrambling, I flipped it open and skimmed. "Salmon sounds great," I said, relieved to have made a quick decision.

"Excellent choice. And for you, sir?" the waiter asked.

"I'll go with the white fish," Matt replied, then turned to me and asked, "Do you like oysters?"

"Yes, love them!" I said, surprised by my enthusiasm.

"Perfect. We'll start with oysters too," he added, nodding to the waiter, who smiled and disappeared toward the kitchen.

As soon as he was gone, the lightness between us dimmed. I took a breath, forcing myself to say what I'd been holding back. "I'm really glad you asked me out," I began, forcing the words out before I could second-guess them. "Because, honestly? It's been tough for me too. Even after two years, I still have nightmares. And then there's all these... strange things that keep happening. PTSD, I guess, but still." I glanced up, unsure if I'd said too much.

His hand slid across the table, resting gently on mine. "I get it," he said softly. "It was a nightmare for all of us. We all went through something that changed us. And honestly? I'm still figuring it out too. Sometimes... it's hard to know what's real."

"Same here," I admitted, my thumb tracing the edge of my glass. "It's gotten worse since this woman with black hair at the bus stop wished me good luck."

His hand stilled. "Wait, what?" He slowly pulled back, his brows knitting together. "You met a woman with black hair who wished you good luck?"

I nodded, hesitant. "Yeah, and I know how weird it sounds."

"That's the thing—it doesn't sound weird," he said, running a hand through his hair. "I met someone just like that. Afterward, I won a huge chunk of money, enough to help me open the bar. But Sean—my buddy—swore he didn't see her." He paused, his eyes narrowing. "What did she look like? Just so we're sure it's the same person?"

I swallowed, trying to steady my voice. "She had long black hair, almost unnaturally straight, and this long, black dress. Her makeup was heavy—like, too heavy—purple eyeshadow that made her look... off. And she had this aura, like she wasn't quite . . . human." My grip tightened on my glass as I pushed the words out. "After she wished me luck, my boss—who was a total nightmare—got fired. Then I got this promotion out of nowhere. It was everything I'd wished for, but that's when all the strange things started happening."

Matt sat back, staring at me like I'd just handed him the missing piece of a puzzle he wasn't sure he wanted to solve. "That's her," he said finally, his voice quiet. "It's the same woman. But why couldn't Sean see her? And why us? We both got what we wanted after meeting her. Do you think she's behind all of this?"

"I don't know, Matt. I'm trying to make sense of it too," I said, my mind spinning. "There's just too many weird coincidences. Why both of us? And then Dr. Olivia Jones shows up at my office on the same day."

His brow furrowed deeper. "Wait, that name sounds familiar." He reached into his pocket and pulled out a business card. "Holy crap, it's the doctor that I rescued from the cab that same day I ran into you. Do you know her?"

My stomach twisted. "Yeah, Matt... she's the third survivor from the coffee shop." The color drained from his face. His grip on the card tightened like a vice.

"No wonder she looked familiar," he said, exhaling sharply. "But I've never gone through the news of that day. I couldn't look at any photos. The thought of seeing Tom's face among the victims..." He trailed off, his voice cracking slightly.

"This is all seriously bizarre," I said, leaning forward, my elbows on the table. "What's even weirder is that I thought I saw Dr. Olivia being followed by the black-haired woman after she left my office. But when I pointed her out to Bruce, he didn't see anyone. And that same night, I went to the bathroom and saw a message on the mirror—'lucky' written in red. That's how I hurt my hand. I freaked out and smashed the glass, trying to erase it. But when my roommate Jessica came in, the message was gone." I shook my head, the memory making my skin crawl. "I don't know what's happening, Matt. Either I'm losing it, or there's something seriously strange going on. And honestly, I'm leaning toward the latter since you saw her too. Have you had any other weird experiences?"

For a moment, I thought I'd said too much, but Matt didn't look away. His eyes stayed on mine, his expression thoughtful.

"No, not really," he said at last. Then, after a beat, he added, "Have you thought about talking to Dr. Olivia Jones about this?"

I shook my head, too quickly. "No. I already freaked her out once. She's an important client, and I can't risk making things worse."

"Okay," Matt said, nodding slowly. "Then I'll reach out to her. I won't mention your name."

When our food arrived, neither of us touched it. The oysters sat untouched on their bed of ice, the once-mouthwatering seafood smell now feeling like it belonged at someone else's table.

"I'm really scared, Matt," I confessed. "I'm scared I'll never be okay again. That my mind is broken forever."

He reached across the table, his hand covering mine. "You're not alone in this, Alex. We'll figure it out together. And honestly? If we see her again, let's just ask her what she wants. Whatever's going on, we'll face it head-on."

"Okay," I said, nodding. I wanted to believe him. "Thanks, Matt. I'm glad you're back in my life, even if everything feels... weird."

Later, as I climbed into the cab, I realized I didn't want the night to end. I wished we could keep talking, but tomorrow was a workday.

"Text me when you get home," Matt said. "I'll call you tomorrow."

As the cab started moving, I allowed myself to think that maybe I was starting to turn a corner. Maybe things could get better. Maybe this connection with Matt could help me find my way back to normal.

A black cat darted across the road, vanishing into the darkness. The driver muttered, "Damn. Bad luck."

# OLIVIA

The sharp beeping of the alarm clock pulled me from sleep. I blinked, my vision adjusting to the dim light filtering through the window. Owen's arms wrapped around me—strong, warm, familiar. His chest rose and fell against my back, his breath soft against my ear. He was here. I had him back. I loved him. So why did it still feel… off? Someone had sent him texts. Who? If it was work, why the secrecy? Owen had never kept things from me before.

I thought about what Daniel had said yesterday—about another woman. How I should've known better than to take back the man who'd walked away from me in the first place. I hadn't even asked Owen what he'd been doing for the year he'd been gone. Had he been as lonely as I was? Or had he been seeing other people? The thought of those messages kept tugging at me, the questions unanswered, stirring up something I wasn't ready to face. I wanted to ask, to clear the air—but something held me back. I didn't want to complicate things, not when everything was finally starting to feel normal again.

I shifted, pulling away just enough to sit up, ready to start the day. But before I could fully pull away, his grip tightened slightly, drawing me back toward him. His voice, thick with sleep, rumbled against my ear.

"I love you," he murmured, pressing closer. "Let's try for a baby again—like we always talked about. What do you think?"

*What did I think?* I wanted that more than anything. "Yes," I said softly. "But right now, I have to go to the hospital. I have patients to see."

"Maybe we can be quick," Owen murmured, his lips trailing heat down my neck. He shifted over me, slipping my sleep shirt off with a touch that was both tender and urgent.

"Yes," I whispered, my breath catching as heat curled through me.

His lips found mine, then drifted lower. Thoughts dissolved. Nothing existed beyond this, beyond him. The heat of his skin against mine, the hunger in his touch— it consumed me, pulling me under. I felt his breath on my neck, his hands tracing over me with a need that made my heart race. In that moment, everything else fell away. He pulled me closer, and I let go, lost in the rush, in him, in us.

Then— a ripple in the reflection. A flicker in the mirror. A broken heart. An arrow piercing through it. A smear of red—there, then gone.

"I love you so much," Owen whispered, pressing a final, tender kiss to my skin before rolling onto his back.

"Me too," I whispered, but my thoughts stayed on what I'd seen. *Had it even been real?* I forced a smile and slipped out of bed. "I really should get to work. But first, a shower."

The hot water poured over me, and I soaped myself absently, trying to wash away the lingering doubt that clung to my mind.

\*\*\*

Two hours later, the elevator doors opened, and I spotted Daniel talking to someone. My first instinct was to slip past him, to avoid yesterday's tension. But before I could duck into a lab, he saw me.

"Olivia, wait," he said, stepping toward me. "I just need a moment."

"I really need to go," I said, my voice calm, but my thoughts were already racing. What was he going to say? What did he want now?

"Please," he said. "I owe you an apology. I had no right to interfere. You were right, Olivia. It's none of my business. I just want you to be happy."

"I am happy, Daniel," I said, the words coming out sharper than I meant. Why did I feel like I had to say that? Like I owed him an explanation when I didn't?

Daniel's lips softened into a smile. "I'm glad to hear that. Truly. And you were right about me needing to move on. Actually, I've got a dinner date this weekend."

I stilled. A date? My stomach twisted. That shouldn't have mattered—but it did. Why? Was I really still holding on to something I shouldn't? No. I was happy with Owen.

"Oh, that's great, Daniel. Who's the lucky person, if you don't mind me asking?"

"It's a blind date my sister set up," he said. "She's been pestering me about a single woman from her work. Finally gave in."

"That's wonderful, Daniel," I said, curving my lips into something close to a smile. "I hope it goes well. You deserve happiness, too."

Before he could respond, a rush of nurses swept past, their voices tense and urgent.

"Gene, what's going on?" Daniel called out to one of the nurses.

"It's the girl's mother," Gene shouted back. "She's having a panic attack."

Instinct took over. We sprinted toward Charlie's room.

# MATT

Two months before the coffee shop incident flipped my world upside down, I went on a date with a girl who didn't hold back. She asked point-blank why I wasn't tied down with a serious girlfriend. I gave her the usual line: I just hadn't found the right person yet.

But in my head, I thought: *Why settle for one girl when I could meet plenty?* Maybe that makes me sound like a jerk, but I'd tried the whole boyfriend-girlfriend thing—once in high school, once in college. It was fine. Just… never enough.

Then there was Alex. She was different. I felt different around her. Hard to explain, but she got under my skin like no one else ever had. It wasn't just about attraction, even though that was definitely there. It felt deeper, like she could see past the walls I'd put up. She'd gotten into my head and stayed there, and I already wanted to see her again. I also had this instinct to protect her. That's why, when she asked if anything strange had happened, I kept my mouth shut about the birds I saw at the cemetery. No point in freaking her out more than she already was.

My thoughts circled back to the coincidences, looping like a scratched record. Why did our paths keep crossing? And who the hell was that woman? Later, I'd call Dr. Olivia Jones—see if she'd spotted her too.

"Hey, Matt, sorry for being late," Lucas's voice snapped me out of my head. "Thanks for meeting me this morning. Sorry for the short notice," he added, sliding into the booth across from me. He had messaged me at six a.m., wanting to talk in person. I'd picked the breakfast joint across the street from my place.

"No problem. How're you holding up?" I asked, nudging a menu toward him. "If you're hungry, this place does killer breakfast. You won't regret it."

He shook his head, barely glancing at the menu. "Thanks, I already ate. Just need coffee." His fingers tapped impatiently on the table. He looked like hell. Scruffy, dark circles under his eyes. A completely different guy from the sharp, put-together one I'd met before.

The waitress came over, ready to take our order.

"Two coffees," I told her, and she nodded before walking off. I leaned forward. "So? Why'd you hit me up so early?"

Lucas rubbed the back of his neck. His eyes dropped to the table, refusing to meet mine. "The money's gone, Matt."

At first, I thought I'd misheard him. "What money?"

"Your money, Matt. The rent money you put up—it's gone."

I ran a hand across my damp forehead. My brain scrambled for an explanation that made sense. *Gone? No. That's not possible.* The word didn't belong here, didn't belong in my life.

"Gone? What the fuck do you mean, gone? That was everything, Lucas!" My voice shot up, sharp and unfiltered. Heads turned. I didn't care. I smacked the edge of the table harder than I meant to. Glass tipped. Crashed. Water spread fast, shards scattering everywhere.

The waitress hurried over, her brows knit, lips thin, eyes darting between me and the shattered glass.

"Sir, you need to calm down or we'll have to ask you to leave." She warned.

*Calm down?* I almost laughed. This wasn't the kind of problem you could calm down from. I forced a slow breath through my teeth and muttered, "I'm sorry. It's just been a shitty morning."

"We all have our problems," she said flatly, motioning to the busboy to clean up the mess.

"Look, Matt," Lucas said, his hands up like he was surrendering. "I know it's hard to believe, but it's not my fault. And I feel terrible about the whole situation..."

"Feel terrible?" I snapped. "You feel terrible? What about me, Lucas? What the hell happened? I trusted you."

"The building's in foreclosure," he said, rubbing a hand over his face. "The landlord got in deep. Debt collectors, bad deals—you name it. Your rent money? He used it to cover his ass, then filed for bankruptcy. Now the bank owns the building."

I stared at him, the words landing like punches. *Foreclosure. Bankruptcy. The bank owns it now.* None of it made sense.

"Why didn't you check his credit before this?"

"Credit checks are for tenants, not landlords," Lucas said.

"But I still have the space, don't I? I still have the rental contract?"

Lucas sighed. "The bank owns it now, and your contract with the previous landlord doesn't hold up. You could try legal options, but that would take time and money."

*Time and money.* Two things I didn't have. I leaned back in the booth, staring past Lucas, past the diner walls, to the future I'd just watched collapse.

"I quit my job," I muttered, the words hitting different now. Like they finally meant something. Like they were a death sentence. "Most of my savings are gone. Nonrefundable deposits for remodeling. I don't have the money or the time to deal with lawyers, Lucas. What the hell am I supposed to do now?"

Lucas didn't answer right away. His eyes drifted to the door, like he was already halfway out. "I'm sorry, Matt. I wish I had better news. If I had the money, I'd lend it to you."

"Even if you did, I couldn't pay you back," I said, my voice flat. I kept my eyes on the table, tracing the faint scratches in the surface.

He stood up, pushing his hands into his pockets. "I have to go, Matt. I'm truly sorry once again." He walked out, the bell above the door jingling behind him, leaving me alone with nothing but wrecked plans.

The waitress returned with two cups of coffee. She set them down without a word.

"Thanks," I murmured, not bothering to look up. The steam curled into the air, but I didn't touch the coffee.

My phone buzzed, and a message from Dad lit up the screen. *Son, I've been chewin' on our talk. I figure I didn't handle it the right way. I wanna be there for you and your bar, show my support. How 'bout swingin' by for dinner? Your ma and I been missin' ya. Love ya.*

I stared at the message until the words blurred. I could already see Dad's face when I told him. The disappointment. I'd failed him, just like I'd failed Tom. Just like I'd failed myself.

The booth felt too small. Too close. I stood and stepped outside. A couple of guys leaned against the wall, puffing on cigarettes. Smoke drifted in lazy spirals above their heads. I wasn't a regular smoker, but I craved a cigarette now.

"Hey, man," I said. "Mind if I bum a smoke?"

"Sure thing," one of them said, pulling out a beat-up pack of Marlboro Reds. He handed me a cigarette and lit it for me.

"Thanks," I said, taking a drag. The first hit burned my throat, but it settled me.

I stared at the street. People passed by, caught in their own lives. Cars honked. A dog barked. Life kept moving, like it always does. But my world? It had been flipped upside down again.

That's the thing—life doesn't stop. It doesn't care about your pain or your failure. Not mine, not anyone's. Seconds dragged into minutes as I stood there, the cigarette burning down to the filter. No job. No cash. No bar. No plan. Everything I'd worked for was gone, leaving me feeling lost.

And then I saw her—the same black-haired woman from Las Vegas. This time, I was sure. She stood in front of Panera Bread, locking eyes with me across the street. Her hand rose in a small, almost mocking wave.

I crushed my cigarette under my shoe and stepped off the curb, weaving through cars without waiting for the light. Horns blared. I didn't care.

She didn't move. Just stood there, her smirk steady, like she knew I'd come.

"Well, hello there, Matt. Fancy seeing you again," she said.

"Who are you? What's your game in Chicago? Are you following me?" I fired questions at her. "And how do you even know my name?"

She chuckled, low and throaty, like she was in on a joke I couldn't understand. "Wow, all the questions at once." She paused, tilting her head slightly, her eyes drilling into mine. "But it looks like luck isn't exactly smiling on you today. Oops."

"How do you know about the money?" The words came out sharp. There was something off about her eyes—too bright, shifting colors in a way that didn't seem natural. I recalled what Alex said. *And she had this aura, like she wasn't quite . . . human.*

Then it clicked. She was the one who brought the luck—and now she'd taken it back. Just like with Alex. Soon, maybe even now, she'd strip it all away. Everything. And Dr. Olivia Jones? She wouldn't be spared either.

"Did you cause me to lose my money?" I demanded.

"Perhaps," she said, her tone playful, almost bored. "Or maybe not. But think about it—didn't I help you get that money in the first place? In a way, wasn't it mine to reclaim?"

"How?" I pressed. "How the hell do you have this kind of power?"

She laughed, sharp and jagged, like glass breaking in the quiet. "Time, my dear Matt. Time holds the answers, and you'll know when the moment's right."

"What does that mean?" I shouted.

People started glancing my way, their faces full of something between concern and irritation. A man with a coffee cup stopped and tapped me on the shoulder. "Hey, man, you all right? You're just shouting at nothing," he said, giving me a weird look.

"What do you mean?" I asked, baffled. "Can't you see her?" I gestured toward the woman.

The man rolled his eyes and shook his head. "See who? You're talking to air, dude." He muttered something under his breath and walked off.

I turned to a woman passing by. "Do you see her?" I asked, my voice edged with desperation.

The woman glanced quickly at where I was pointing, then hurried off, her shoulders stiff. "No," she called over her shoulder.

It hit me then. To them, I was talking to no one. But she was there, staring back at me, solid and real. That's why Sean had insisted he couldn't see her. He literally couldn't. So who else could? Was it just me, Alex, and Dr. Olivia Jones? And why us?

"What do you want from me?" I asked, stepping closer. "What do you want from Alex and Dr. Olivia Jones?"

Her smirk didn't waver. "Nothing is for nothing, Matt."

"What the hell does that mean?"

"Dig into your memories, Matt," she said, her voice slow and deliberate. "You left something behind that day in the coffee shop. And it's waiting for you."

My throat tightened. "Who are you?" I asked. "I was a victim in that coffee shop. I didn't do anything wrong."

Her smile widened. "You already know who I am," she said calmly.

"How could I possibly know that?"

"I was there," she replied, her voice steady as her form flickered— just for a second, like a glitch in a bad video feed.

My stomach twisted. "Wait, hold on . . . you were there? Are you a ghost of one of the victims?"

She tilted her head, her smile hardening. "I can't reveal all my cards today, Matt. That wouldn't be any fun." Her voice turned colder. "The game isn't over. Next time you see me, I'll be out for blood. Don't try to stop me. You'll lose. Tell the others the same."

And then she was gone.

But she wasn't. Not really. I could still feel her—a presence lurking at the edges of my mind.

She had underestimated me. She didn't know what happens when someone has nothing left to lose. I'd track her down, find out who she really was, and end this.

First, I had to find Alex and Dr. Olivia Jones. Before she did.

# ALEXANDRA

"Ever wonder what it feels like to have a coffee shop stormed by ghosts?"

I stopped mid-step, the question snagging my attention. A guy slouched at the bus stop, wild Einstein hair and a death grip on a bottle. Drunk. Totally.

But then he mumbled something else, words so garbled they shouldn't have made sense—but they did. *Coffee shop. Ghosts.*

My stomach dipped. Could he actually be talking about *that* place? No, impossible. Just a random drunk, spewing nonsense. Shoving the weird thought aside, I kept walking, dragging my focus back to the here and now.

Up ahead, the Fictive Creative building gleamed like it had been plucked straight out of an architecture magazine—sleek glass, razor-sharp lines, and an air of *look but don't touch*. Somehow, its modern facade fit seamlessly into downtown Chicago's chaotic charm—like it belonged but knew it was better than everything around it. The street was alive with the morning rush—suits speed-walking to power meetings, tourists juggling shopping bags and selfies, and a street performer in a tilted black hat strumming a moody tune. Life rolled on, business as usual.

It was the kind of morning that felt hopeful, like the universe was rooting for you. The flowers lining the sidewalk practically glowed in the sunlight, the sky was postcard-perfect blue, and the air hummed with possibility. For the first time in forever, I actually felt good.

Last night had been... something. Reconnecting with Matt felt like the tiniest crack of sunlight breaking through storm clouds. I couldn't stop replaying our conversation, analyzing every look, every word. Was this the universe finally throwing me a bone?

"Hey, buddy," the man slurred behind me, waving his bottle at the empty space next to him. "Did I ever tell you about the coffee shop? Blood everywhere, bodies piled up. You should've seen it."

My steps faltered. *Blood? Bodies?*

His hollow laugh cut through the air, too loud, too wrong. "No one answers," he croaked. "No one ever does."

I turned, the words pulling me back. He wiped a tear with the back of his hand, smearing dirt across his face. "Why won't anyone talk to me? Why am I always alone?"

As I got closer, his bloodshot eyes locked onto mine, and he started screaming. "I used to be someone! Officer Davis! Now I'm just a broken man! Haunted by the past! Shunned by the present!" He staggered forward, nearly collapsing. "Beware of the lady with black hair! She'll ruin your life! She'll bring you nothing but bad luck!"

My chest clenched. *The woman with black hair. Could he mean... her?* And what did he mean, "ruin your life"?

I opened my mouth to ask, but two officers appeared before I could get the words out. "Move along," one of them barked, grabbing the man's arm. "No public drinking. We see you again, you're spending the night in a cell."

One officer pulled the man to his feet. He gave them a sad look and shuffled off.

"Wait," I called after him, turning to the police. "I want to ask him something."

One of the officers shook his head, barely sparing me a glance. "Don't bother, lady. He's just a drunk. Crazy as they come."

I watched as the man disappeared around the corner, shoulders hunched like the weight of the world was dragging him down. *Could he actually know something? The coffee shop? The woman with black hair?* The thought twisted in my gut. Should I run after him?

I took a deep breath, forcing my feet to stay planted. What would I even get from him? The guy could barely string a sentence together, let alone drop any life-changing truths. Chasing down a rambling drunk wasn't going to get me the answers I needed. Dr. Richardson's voice echoed in my head: *Focus on the positives, Alex.*

I turned back toward Fictive Creative, the morning sun trailing behind me as I stepped through the revolving doors.

Inside, the lobby pulsed with its usual rhythm—colleagues zigzagging between meetings, coffee cups in hand, their chatter blending into a hum of deadlines and big ideas. I nodded at a few familiar faces, doing my best to look like I had it all together, but that guy's words clung to me like gum on the bottom of my shoe.

As the elevator doors slid shut, I caught my reflection in the gleaming surface. A young woman stared back, her eyes still clouded by whatever weirdness had wormed its way into my morning. I straightened my shoulders and took a breath, forcing the tension out of my jaw. *This is your life,* I reminded myself. *You're good at what you do, and you belong here.* Whatever doubts or fears had crept in earlier, I shoved them to the back of my mind. There were goals to crush, clients to impress, and dreams to chase. And as the elevator dinged to a stop, I stepped out, ready to face the day.

\*\*\*

A knock on my office door pulled me out of the client file I'd been buried in. I'd barely had time to claim my desk this morning before diving straight into work. GreenStyle Couture, a high-end, eco-friendly fashion brand, was rolling out a new line of sustainable clothing, and our ad campaign had to be nothing short of perfect. No pressure or anything.

Bruce popped his head in. "So . . . spill the tea! How did last night go? Dish the deets!"

"It was great. He's honestly such a great guy," I said, aiming for casual, but the warmth creeping up my cheeks totally gave me away.

Bruce dropped into the chair across from me, smirking like he'd just won a bet. "Oh, girl, I see that blush!" he teased. "You're totally smitten."

I rolled my eyes, but a grin broke through anyway. "Fine, you got me. I like him. A lot."

"Don't forget me when you two are walking down the aisle so I can claim matchmaking credit."

I laughed, waving him off. "Okay, let's not get ahead of ourselves. But speaking of weird stuff..." I hesitated, unsure how to phrase it. "What's your take on superstitions? You know, like breaking a mirror or a black cat crossing your path?"

He raised an eyebrow. "Superstitions? Darling, that's quite the leap from wedding bells. Do tell, why the sudden curiosity?"

I twirled the pen in my hand, the memory of this morning nudging its way back into my thoughts. "I don't know, it's just been on my mind. Someone today was ranting about bad luck, and it got under my skin. I mean, I broke a mirror. Then a black cat ran straight in front of my cab last night."

He shook his head. "Darling, luck is what we make it. And bad luck? That's just an excuse for not showing up fabulous enough. Let me tell you—"

Before he could launch into a full pep talk, a sudden interruption threw us off. The door slowly opened. It was Lisa. "What's the matter, Bruce?" she said. "You don't seem thrilled to see me."

Bruce stiffened, his playful smirk replaced with something closer to a grimace. "Lisa..."

"Lisa, what are you doing here?" I blurted, mirroring his confusion. As far as we knew, she'd been fired. How did she even get past security?

Lisa stepped further into the room, her smile widening, eyes locking on me like a predator zeroing in on prey. "Guess what? I'm back."

I blinked, trying to process. "Back? What are you talking about?"

Lisa's voice dripped venom, sweet as honey. "Ran into Kyle yesterday, had a little chat," she said, brushing imaginary lint off her blazer. "We're not besties or anything, but it's a start. Long story short, I'm reinstated. So here I am." She spread her arms, like she was expecting applause. "Isn't it just fabulous?"

"Fabulous" wasn't the word I'd use. "Dreadful" was closer. Bruce shot me a look—half reassuring, half "don't lose it"—but it was impossible to stay calm. This was hell, and Lisa was dragging me deeper with every word.

"Where's Kyle?" I managed. "And shouldn't HR be handling something like this?"

Lisa leaned closer, her tone silky with condescension. "Kyle thought it would be more... personal if I delivered the news myself." Her smile sharpened. "Here's the deal: I'm back in my old role. And to make room? We've had to make some cost-cutting decisions. Effective immediately, Alex—your position has been eliminated."

The room tilted. "What?"

Lisa's smile didn't falter. Her voice stayed honeyed, but every word landed like a punch to the gut. "Eliminated. Budget cuts, you understand. And let's not forget your little... *mishap* with Dr. Jones. Rescheduled? Really? None of my clients ever needed to reschedule. But feel free to run to Kyle—he'll probably spin it nicely for you. As for HR, Cindy will be in touch to finalize things. You'll have your chance to, I don't know, share your feelings."

I gripped the edge of my desk, trying to keep my voice steady. "This is insane. I've poured everything into this job, and you're just cutting me loose? You think I'm just going to accept this?"

Lisa's smile widened. "Oh, Alex. Accept it, fight it—makes no difference to me. Either way, you're done here. Now, please pack up your things. You've got ten minutes. If you're not out by then, I'll have security escort you."

"Security? Are you serious?" I asked, my voice tight. Could she make this any more humiliating?

"Serious as a heart attack," she said, then checked her watch, the picture of smug efficiency.

Bruce looked like he wanted to jump to my defense, but I held up a hand, stopping him. Lisa wanted a show—tears, shouting, a scene she could gloat about later. Not today. Instead, I grabbed my bag and headed for the door. Just before stepping out, I let myself imagine the ceiling giving way, collapsing onto her smug, satisfied face. But real life doesn't hand out fairy tale endings like that.

I slammed the door behind me, the sound echoing in the hallway. A few people glanced up from their desks, their curiosity like tiny pinpricks against my skin. I didn't slow down, didn't stop. Head high, I muttered under my breath, "Guess my plans went to hell."

Out of sight, I took a steadying breath and kept moving toward the elevator. My pulse hammered, anger and humiliation knotting tight in my chest, but at least I'd made it out without giving Lisa the meltdown she wanted.

Inside the elevator, I jabbed the button for Kyle's floor. Nothing happened. I pressed it again. Still nothing. Panic curled its way into my ribs as I grabbed my phone. No signal.

"Damn it!" I shouted, the sound bouncing back at me like a cruel echo. I pounded on the doors, my fists hitting uselessly. "Hello? Anyone?"

Silence.

The space seemed to shrink around me. My breathing sped up, shallow and ragged, the walls inching closer by the second.

"Deep breaths, Alex," I murmured, my voice barely steady. "In. Out. Just breathe."

I repeated Dr. Richardson's advice, forcing each breath in, each breath out, the way he taught me to handle my claustrophobia, but the elevator felt more like a cage, the air growing thinner by the second. My chest tightened as the walls seemed to close in. Dizziness pressed against my temples, the floor threatening to tip me over. I gripped the rail, squeezed my eyes shut, and whispered, "Slow and easy. Slow and easy," like a mantra that might keep me grounded. It wasn't working.

*Someone will notice soon.* A fragile lifeline I clung to. But what if "soon" turned into hours? There were six elevators in this building—five others humming along just fine. Would anyone even think to check this one? My chest tightened as the thought spiraled. *Woman Suffocates in Stuck Elevator after Being Fired.* What a headline. Truly the perfect cherry on top of this disaster!

Lisa wouldn't check. She was probably busy planning a "Finally Rid of Alex" party, while Janet packed up my things. No way would she lift a finger to help.

But Bruce—yes, Bruce. He'd notice. He'd text. He'd worry. Except my phone wasn't working, and his concern couldn't reach me here.

I let out a heavy sigh and sank to the floor, the cold metal pressing into my back. My brain tried to logic its way out of the panic, but it didn't stand a chance against the suffocating quiet.

A sharp squeak jolted me upright. The elevator shuddered, then jerked to a stop. Relief surged. Finally. *Finally.*

The sixth-floor light blinked on, but the doors didn't move. I pressed the open button, harder than necessary. Nothing.

"Come on," I muttered. "Don't do this."

And then I heard it. A whisper.

"Help me, Alex. Please, help me."

My breath snagged, caught somewhere between my lungs and my throat. It was faint, like a stray thought—there, then gone.

I squeezed my eyes shut. *No. Just panic. Just my brain playing tricks.*

Louder now. Closer. And it was coming from above me.

"Please, help me."

"No," I whispered, dread coiling in my throat as I recognized the voice. *No, no, no.*

"Who's there?" I demanded, even though I already knew.

"It's Charlie. You know me, right? I'm in trouble, I need your help."

The voice slipped in and out of sync with itself, words folding over each other like a broken recording.

*It's not possible.*

Charlie was in a coma. Charlie was nowhere near here. And this time, I wasn't dreaming—I was awake.

I pressed myself against the wall, every muscle locking tight. "Where are you?"

"Above you. On top of the elevator."

My chest squeezed as the words slid through the cracks in the elevator, curling around me like smoke. She was just beyond the ceiling panel. Watching. Waiting.

"Go away," I choked out, clamping my hands over my ears like that would stop it. "You're not real! None of this is real!"

"Please, Alex."

The voice bent again, glitching, distorting—like two Charlies speaking at once.

"Time is running out. I'm trapped. Something terrible is coming."

A pause. A shift. Then, more deliberate. Too calm.

"You need to know the truth about the coffee shop shooting."

A second voice. Overlapping. Echoing the same words, half a second too late.

"Your luck has already run out."

A metallic creak sliced through the silence. Then another.

Above me.

The elevator lurched. A snap. Then another. The cables gave way, one by one, sharp cracks shuddering through the shaft. The walls warped. The floor dropped out beneath me. A scream ripped through the air—maybe mine, maybe Charlie's.

Then nothing. Blackness swallowed everything.

And in that last, fleeting second before it all disappeared, I swear—I felt Charlie there with me.

# CHARLIE

"I swear, she woke up and said, 'Leave!' But Charlie wouldn't be mean like that. She wouldn't tell me to go away."

Mammina kept repeating it, over and over.

"She wouldn't be mean. Never."

Dr. Olivia and Dr. Daniel spoke to her in calm, measured voices, trying to soothe her. "Please calm down, Ms. Moretti."

"We're here to monitor Charlie now."

But Mammina just kept crying.

Somehow, I managed to open my eyes. My tongue felt dry and heavy, but I forced out a whisper. "Leave." That was when Mammina started screaming. The medics rushed in, but I was already slipping back. The coma pulled me under, dragging me back to that endless dark.

But I could still hear them. I could still listen.

My anger at Mammina hadn't faded. If anything, it had only grown, like a storm that refused to pass. She was still my Mammina, but right now, warmth felt impossible. I tried to reason with myself, to remember she was struggling too. I should understand that. But it felt like the good between us was shrinking, while the bad was getting bigger. And now, a question I'd never dared ask before crept in: *Was she the reason Daddy left?*

I remembered how Daddy's face would twist with frustration, how Mammina's voice would rise, louder and louder. I couldn't even remember the days when we laughed together, when things felt normal. Those moments seemed like they belonged to a different family, as if they'd never really happened at all. And Mammina—she would yell, always yell.

"I'm very sorry to tell you, but your daughter had another 'coma arousal event,'" Dr. Daniel explained. "She's still in a coma. We just checked her. She's also on life support. She's intubated and on a ventilator, so saying anything would be difficult."

Mammina sobbed, and for a moment, pity crept in. And then—

"Oh, poor Mammina, crying her eyes out, feeling so sad. And to make it worse, nobody believes her." The whisper curled around my thoughts. Cold, slick, creeping in where it didn't belong. "Don't feel sorry for her, Charlie. That's exactly how you felt when you were all alone. Hurt and abandoned. With that awful babysitter."

I wondered how long she'd been there, quietly watching She was slipping into my mind, winding through my thoughts like ivy—slow, insidious, impossible to stop. Her words seeped in, taking hold where doubt had already begun to grow.

And just like that, I found myself agreeing.

*Why should I feel sorry for Mammina? She never felt sorry for me.*

Her influence unsettled me—but it also soothed me. Like she understood my pain in a way no one else could. A dark validation settled inside me, a twisted comfort that fed my growing resentment.

"Good, good, Charlie," the voice whispered. "Let's stop being such a good girl. Stop feeling sorry for everyone else. You are what matters. Others should get what they deserve."

The words rooted themselves deep.

*Others should get what they deserve.*

I heard Mammina talking again. "She said, 'leave,' and . . . and I also heard her say, 'I have her now. She'll protect me.'"

"Her?" Dr. Olivia asked. "Was there anyone else in the room with you when all this was happening?"

"No," Mammina said. "I was alone. I don't know who she was talking about—I was wondering the same thing. But it wasn't Charlie speaking. It was like…someone else had taken control. That's not my sweet girl at all."

She was right.

I couldn't stop what was happening inside me. The voice. The strange feelings taking over.

"Could she be hallucinating? It hurts to see her suffer. Worst of all, she doesn't want to see me."

A long pause. Then, gently, Dr. Daniel said, "We don't really know what's happening in Charlie's head." He hesitated before continuing. "Stress can make you imagine things that aren't real. Hard times can do that. Olivia, why are you looking at me like that?"

"It's nothing, Daniel," Dr. Olivia said quickly. "Ms. Moretti, I've been through times when stress made me see things that weren't there. I know it's tough, but… maybe you should take a break? A day or two away from Charlie? Take care of yourself."

"Maybe," Mammina murmured.

Suddenly, there was a loud beep.

"Daniel," Dr. Olivia said urgently, "I'll have to step out for about an hour soon. Can you cover for me?"

"Of course," he replied. "Is everything all right? You seem rattled."

"Yes, uh…" she replied, her voice tinged with unease. "It's just—I received a message from someone I recently met. There's an urgent matter. Could you cover for me?"

"Sure thing," Dr. Daniel said. "All right, Ms. Moretti, let's all step out of Charlie's room for now and let her rest."

The room fell silent.

And then the voice whispered, "Soon, all this will be over. And you'll wake up."

*Soon? For who?*

And then—nothing.

# OLIVIA

Matt reeked of cigarette smoke, and his eyes kept darting over his shoulder, like he was expecting someone to follow him.

I suggested we meet at the Daily Grind—it was close to the hospital, and I wanted to get back as quickly as possible. Charlie and her mother were still on my mind. I couldn't make sense of it. How could her mother think Charlie had woken up? Spoken to her? Was there some truth to it? *No, that was impossible.*

The coffee shop was busy. Nearby, a couple of young women laughed too loudly, and the TV on the wall showed breaking news from Chicago.

I pushed away thoughts of Charlie to focus on Matt. He sucked in a shuddering breath, eyes still skimming the room before settling on me. "Is it okay if I sit down? Can we still talk?"

I nodded toward the empty chair across from me. "Of course, please sit down."

"Thanks for meeting me," he said, trying for a smile, but the tension in his face didn't quite match it. "I was going to ask if you wanted anything, but I see you already got some coffee."

"Yes, thank you," I replied. "I got here a few minutes early, and there was no line. So, Matt, your message said this was urgent." I leaned in, lowering my voice. "You mentioned meeting a woman with black hair who poses a threat. Can we talk about that?"

Matt rubbed his hands together, his eyes briefly flicking to the window before returning to me. "Honestly, if I'd known this was Gio's old coffee shop, I might've picked somewhere else. Haven't stepped foot in here since the shooting. Why do you keep coming here?" His voice dropped. "You were a survivor, just like me. And like Alex. She was also—"

"I know who she is," I cut him off. "She works at the ad agency. I've met her."

I watched his face carefully as he sat back, his posture rigid. I recognized him now. The courageous young man who had tried to protect Gio that day. His best friend had died.

"I work nearby, so it's convenient," I said, keeping it simple. "And while the past is painful, I've learned to focus on the present."

He sighed deeply. "Yeah, I wish I could do that. But it just... it stays with me." He shook his head, then got to the point. "Listen. The reason I called you here—the woman with black hair. I saw her again. So did Alex," he said. "From her description, it sounds like the same woman. You told me you met someone like that too. If it's her, you're in trouble. She's bad news."

*Beware of the lady with black hair. She'll ruin your life.*

Was Officer Davis not as crazy as I'd thought?

"Did she wear a lot of makeup?" I asked, my throat dry. His nod made my heart tighten. "How do you know she's bad news?"

"This woman sat next to me at a roulette table in a Vegas casino. She asked if she could blow on my chips for good luck. Then she moved them and picked a number for me. You won't believe it, but on that exact turn, I hit the jackpot—raked in a substantial amount of money. It felt like my big break, you know? Like I could finally open that bar Tom and I always talked about," he said. "At first, I brushed it off as a damn coincidence. But then I saw her again this morning in Chicago, right after I lost all of it." He slammed his fist on the table. "All of it."

The girls at the next table shot us curious glances, one of them twirling a finger around her temple.

"I believe she had something to do with my loss," he continued. "I'm telling you, she's been following me, deliberately trying to ruin my life. And if it's the same woman, she'll do the same to you."

Memories of the bus with the number 666 flashed through my mind. I'd dismissed it all as stress or anxiety, a trick of my imagination. But now? Now, I wasn't so sure. Two people couldn't possibly be making this up. Why were we all crossing paths with the same woman? And what troubled me the most—the thing I couldn't shake—was the thought that Owen's return, my most cherished dream, might be tied to this. . . *No, there had to be a rational explanation for what Matt was telling me.*

"But how could she possibly make you win money just by blowing on your chips?" I asked.

Matt ran his fingers through his hair. "I don't know. But when I confronted her this morning, she didn't even try to hide or make it seem like a game," he said. "She validated everything. Told me 'nothing is for nothing' and that she's seeking justice. I'm at a loss, Olivia. I don't know what she meant by that. And she even claimed to be at the coffee shop the day of the shooting." He paused, then added, "So, are we talking about the same woman? Did the woman you met have long black hair and wear too much makeup, like a clown?"

I nodded. "The woman you're describing sounds like the one I saw. But what kind of justice could she want?"

He sighed, rubbing his temples. "I don't know. I tried searching for answers this morning, but came up empty. It sounds insane, but here's the thing—I don't think she's human."

I set my coffee down so quickly I almost spilled it. "Hold on—did you just say you don't think she's human?

He nodded, steady in his belief. "Yeah, I'm pretty sure she's not. Humans don't vanish into thin air like that. And we're the only ones who can see her."

The girls at the next table exchanged nervous glances, then got up and hurried away, shooting us a few uneasy looks as they passed.

"Can you keep it down?" I whispered, leaning in closer. "Matt, I don't really buy into the idea of aliens or supernatural stuff. She's just a regular person. That's all." I met his gaze squarely, hoping he'd hear me. "Look, we've been through a lot. It's understandable if we're seeing things, but we shouldn't jump to conclusions. I'm sure there's a logical explanation for all of this."

Matt slid his phone across the table, directing my attention to an article. *Officer Claims He Witnessed the Supernatural.*

"Have you seen this?" he asked. "Officer Davis was the one leading the rescue operation during the coffee shop incident."

I took the phone from him and zoomed in on the photo at the center of the article. Officer Davis looked nothing like the disheveled man I remembered. In this picture, his white hair was neatly trimmed, his clean-shaven face projecting authority. His crisp uniform was a sharp contrast to the chaos of that day. As I scrolled through the article, his words stood out. *She just vanished right before my eyes*, he recounted. *Just like that.*

The reality hit harder than I expected. I hadn't believed him then, but now, the truth seemed undeniable. I set the phone down slowly, trying to steady my hands. I'd turned him away when he'd needed someone to believe him the most.

"It's true," I said, my voice barely audible. "Everything I saw, it was real. I thought I was losing my mind."

"We're not losing our minds," Matt replied. "There's something happening here, something we don't understand. I'm telling you—she's not human. I watched her vanish before my eyes, just like Officer Davis did. For reasons I can't explain, she's after us. She can see right into us, take what we care about most, and rip it away at the worst moment." He leaned closer, eyes locking onto mine. "Think back to when you first met her, Olivia. Did she wish you good luck? And did your life change after that?"

My heart sank. "Yes," I whispered, "Owen, my husband. We were apart, and then he returned to me from out of nowhere. It felt like a dream come true."

The sound of the TV anchor's voice snapped me back to the present. "In a shocking incident today, Officer Joe Davis, celebrated for his bravery during the coffee shop rescue two years ago, was struck by a bus and is now in critical condition."

"Oh my god," Matt gasped.

I felt the breath leave my lungs. The coffee cup slipped from my fingers, shattering on the floor. Just like that cup, my heart cracked into a thousand pieces.

# ALEXANDRA

"Hello? Can you hear me, lady? Lady, can you hear me? I'm a firefighter, and we're here to help you," a man's voice called out.

I blinked into the blackness, the floor beneath me cold and hard. My head throbbed in sync with my heartbeat, each pulse hammering Charlie's warning deeper into my mind: *Your luck has already run out.* I tried to inhale, but my breath came shallow, uneven, like my lungs had forgotten how to work. How long had I been lying here?

"Yes! I'm here!" I yelled, my voice cracking. "I'm stuck in the elevator! Please, don't leave me!"

"We've got you, don't worry," the firefighter said, his tone firm, calm—like he was holding all my panic for me. "We're working on the door. Are you hurt?"

I pressed a hand to my temple and winced. "My head... it hurts."

"Can you move?"

"I think so," I said, forcing myself upright. The floor seemed to shift beneath me—or maybe my balance was failing. Pain flared behind my eyes, making my vision blur. I steadied myself with a hand on the wall, the cool metal grounding me.

"Okay, stay still," the firefighter instructed. "We're forcing the door. Hang tight—we've got you."

Time dragged, each second stretching thinner as I strained to hear something—anything—beyond the elevator's creaks and groans. Then, finally, a metallic screech tore through the silence, and a sliver of light sliced into the dark. I exhaled shakily, the breath trembling out of me as I swiped at the sweat beading on my forehead. I blinked, forcing myself to believe I wasn't alone in here anymore.

"All right, here's the plan," the firefighter said, his voice clipped, no room for questions. "We'll guide you out slowly. Take it easy, and we'll get you to safety."

Another firefighter stepped closer, urgency clear in the tilt of his flashlight as he directed it into the shaft. "John, we gotta move! Now!" His light flicked downward, illuminating the floor below, which tilted at an unnatural angle. "This thing's not holding much longer."

The urge to look down fought with the knot in my stomach. I didn't need to see it to know how close I was to falling through.

"I'll go in and help her," John said, already leaning toward me, his hand reaching out.

The other firefighter grabbed his arm, stopping him. "Not a good idea. That thing won't hold both of you. Just pull her out by the hand. Need a second pair?"

"No, I got it," John said, his hand still extended. "Come on, grab my hand."

"Are you sure?" I asked, my voice wobbling as my eyes darted to the slanting floor. Another groan echoed from below, long and grinding, like metal taking its final breath. "That guy said this thing could give way any second."

"We don't have time to debate this," John urged, his voice sharp now. "Let's move."

I stared at his outstretched hand, my fingers hovering just shy of his. The words were right there—*I'm scared, I can't.* But they died in my throat. I lunged for his hand, but then I saw her. She was there. Right behind him. Her black hair fell over one shoulder as she flipped it back, her eyes drilling into me.

"Behind you," I blurted, yanking my hand back. "She's right behind you."

John spun, his flashlight slicing through the space behind him. "What? There's no one there."

"She must've hit her head harder than we thought," the other firefighter muttered. "Let's just get her out and have her checked."

"She's right there!" I yelled.

"Don't be crazy, girl, and give me your hand," John snapped, his hand still outstretched. "The elevator can go down any second."

But I couldn't. Because she was talking.

"He can't see me or hear me. Neither can the other one," she murmured, her fingers brushing against John's back like a breeze he never noticed. "Only you can." Her tone was calm, almost amused, and it made my skin crawl. "See? He doesn't feel a thing. Only you can. Just like at the bus stop—pouring your heart out while that boy and the old man thought you'd lost it." She tilted her head, her laugh low and sharp.

"Why? Why just me?" My throat tightened as I forced the words out. "Who are you? What do you want?"

"Who are you talking to?" John shouted, his eyes darting around.

"Stop babbling nonsense," the other firefighter snapped. "Take John's hand. Now."

But she leaned closer, her face so near I could see the cracks in her lipstick, the dry flakes curling at the corners of her mouth. "You really don't recognize me?" she whispered, her voice a needle slipping beneath my skin. Her smile twisted wider, colder. "We've met before. And since then, I've been right here, watching. Always closer than you'd imagine. But you can only see me when I let you."

"I don't get it!" I said, my voice shaking. "Why won't you just give me a straight answer?"

Her smile deepened, all teeth and malice. "So many questions. You're just like Matt. You both have a knack for that."

"Matt?" My heart kicked against my ribs. "You know Matt?"

She nodded slowly, savoring the moment. "Yes, and Olivia too. Think back, Alex. Go back to that day at the coffee shop. You might find some clues there."

Suddenly, her voice fractured into a swarm of others.

"*Next!*" *the gunman yelled.* "*What's your number?*"

"Six, six, six," the voices echoed, a chilling, discordant chant.

"*Move to the side!*" *the gunman commanded.* "*You're free to go! Lucky you!*"

"Lucky, lucky, lucky," the voices droned, the sound burrowing into my head.

I clamped my hands over my ears, desperate for the torment to stop. "No!" I shouted. "Stop it! Please, make it stop!"

"I have to go in there!" John's voice cut through the din. "She's losing it!"

But the woman only stepped closer, her cracked smile curving wider, twisting into something that made my stomach lurch. "Nothing is for nothing, Alex," she hissed, her tone razor-sharp, slicing through my last shred of sanity. Then louder, harsher: "*Nothing is for nothing!*"

"What does that mean?" I begged, my voice breaking, trembling. "I don't understand."

Her laugh rolled out, sinking into my bones, twisting tight around my spine. "You'll find out soon enough. Everything will be revealed. But for now, take his hand. It's not your time yet. The game's far from over."

"You want me dead?" I yelled. But she was already gone.

John grabbed me and pulled me out just as the elevator dropped with a sound so violent it could've torn the building apart. A deafening screech of metal ripped through the shaft, a gut-wrenching explosion of destruction that made my ears ring. My legs buckled, but I clung to his arm, gulping air like I'd forgotten how to breathe. We were safe—I should've felt relieved—but my brain wasn't having it. All I could think about was her. She wasn't done with me. And the next time she showed up, I might not have John there to pull me out.

"Gosh, lady, you scared the hell outta me," John said, glancing back as we moved toward safety. "And seriously, you gotta stop all that crazy talk. People might start thinking something's really wrong with you."

*If only he knew.*

# MATT

Olivia was clearly rattled. Her foot tapped against the floor, her gaze flicking to the door like she was ready to leave. And yeah, maybe I felt bad for unloading on her. But that wasn't on me. I was helping her. Someone had to wake her up. That woman was tearing everything apart—her life, my life, all of it. And I wasn't about to let that happen.

News of Officer Davis getting hit by a bus knocked the air out of me. I'd pinned my hopes on him, thinking he might have answers about the woman pulling the strings. Now that hope was gone.

Alex worried me, too. I'd texted her a dozen times before coming here, but still no reply. I checked my phone again, half-hoping, half-dreading. Still nothing. Maybe she was busy. Or maybe she wasn't as into me as I'd thought. But what if it was worse? What if she was already in danger?

The soft scrape of a broom pulled me back. One of the baristas swept up the shards of Olivia's mug. The coffee spill was gone, but jagged pieces still littered the floor.

"I'm really sorry about the mess," Olivia said, her voice distant.

"No problem," the worker said, leaning on his broom. "These things happen. Want me to get you a fresh coffee?"

She shook her head. "No, thank you."

I checked my phone again. Still nothing. I called Alex again, but it went straight to voicemail.

"I can't believe this is happening," Olivia muttered, more to herself than to me. Her hands pressed together, fingers stiff and trembling. "Officer Davis was in my office," she said, her voice halting. "Then, later, I saw him at the bus stop."

"He was in your office?" I asked. "Was he one of your patients?"

"No," she said, lowering her hands. Her voice steadied, but just barely. "I had never seen him before in my life. I didn't even recognize him from the shooting day. He just showed up, said he needed help. He thought he was going insane. Said he was seeing a woman who was ruining his life, like what you're telling me now. I didn't believe him."

"Damn it," I muttered, leaning back in my chair. "So, Davis was caught up in this too? I thought she was only after survivors. But no—she's pulling the strings, making us cross paths. She wants us chasing her. It's a game to her. She's out to ruin us. Just look what happened to Davis."

Olivia's fists clenched on the table, her knuckles bone-white. "For heaven's sake, I don't need this right now. I finally felt like my life was coming back together again. I don't need another mess."

I reached over and rested my hand on hers, more to steady her than anything else. "Look, I get it. This is all kinds of messed up, but we've got this. We'll handle it—and her. Together."

"Thanks, Matt," Olivia said, brushing a tear off her cheek with the back of her hand. "Usually, I'm the one giving comfort, you know? But right now, I just feel so helpless. I don't even know what we're supposed to do next. Have you found anything? Anything at all?"

"Not much on her," I admitted. "But I did come across something strange."

I pulled out my phone and brought up a photo of two young men, almost boys, grinning at the edge of a dock, fishing poles in hand.

"These are Jimmy and Billy Miller, brothers," I said, turning the phone toward her. "Jimmy's the older one, Billy's the younger. They're the ones who did the coffee shop shooting."

Olivia's face twisted in anger and disgust. "Why are you showing me this? I don't need to know anything about them."

I got it. I really did. But this mattered. I pressed on. "Listen, I get it," I said. "But this is important. Two years before the coffee shop shooting, they were in a bad car crash on I-90—Jimmy driving, Billy in the passenger seat. The article says they were critically injured, but they were the only ones who made it out alive." I turned the phone toward her, showing the wreckage of their red Honda. "Check the license plate—last three numbers? Six-six-six. And this happened exactly two years before the shooting."

Olivia hesitated, then took the phone, her eyes narrowing as she studied the photo. "They were just twisted," she said, her voice sharp. "This doesn't tell us anything new."

I shook my head. "I don't think they were satanists before the accident," I argued. "That six-six-six? Maybe it's a coincidence. But something changed after the crash. Look at this." I scrolled to another article and handed her the phone again. "Read what their mom said after the shooting."

She skimmed the text, her brow furrowing. "What am I supposed to see here?"

"Their mom said they changed after the accident. Got withdrawn. Aggressive. Like something flipped inside them. Before that, they were church kids—volunteering, good grades, all that. It's not just her; neighbors, friends, everyone said the same thing."

Olivia's face softened. "So, you think the accident turned them into what they became?"

"I don't know for sure," I admitted. "But there's more to this than we realize. We need to talk to their mom. I've got her address—she's in Woodstock. It's about two hours, depending on traffic. I'd ask Alex to come, but she's not answering. Honestly? I'm worried. I don't even know where she is right now."

"I know where she works," Olivia said, pulling out a business card from her purse. "Here—this is Kyle's card, her boss." Her phone buzzed, and she glanced at it before tucking it away. "I can come with you, but I need to stop by the hospital first. I've got patients to check on, plus I need to see Charlie. She might be on this woman's radar too."

"Charlie? Why would she be a target?" I asked.

"She's one of the survivors," Olivia explained. "She was shot that day, but she's been in a coma for the last two years. She's at my hospital."

"Two years in a coma?" I said, shaking my head. "Is that even possible?"

"Yes." Olivia sighed, brushing a strand of hair behind her ear.

"Damn." I rubbed my face, trying to process it. "Okay, first things first—I've got to make sure Alex is safe. Once I track her down, we'll swing by the hospital to grab you. But please, Olivia—stay safe."

"I will," she said quietly. "You take care too."

As soon as she left, I hit redial on Alex's number. The phone rang forever. No answer. I pulled up her office's address on my GPS. Ten minutes away.

Then the TV in the coffee shop cut through the background noise: "Elevator on verge of collapse in a downtown Chicago skyscraper, a young woman trapped inside."

I shot to my feet and headed for the door. I didn't need more details. It was Alex. It had to be. She was next on that damn woman's list.

I ran like hell. The streets were packed, the sun pounding down, but none of it mattered. Time was slipping away too fast. I was afraid I was too late. What if she didn't make it? But I couldn't stop. I had to get to her. No matter what.

Somewhere between the panic and the pounding of my feet, it hit me—I was falling for Alex. I barely knew her. It didn't matter. From the first time I saw her, something shifted. She wasn't like anyone else. The lost money, the bar—all of it blurred into the background. None of it mattered anymore. Only her.

I pushed harder, legs burning, sweat stinging my eyes. *C'mon, just let her be okay.* I wasn't the praying type, but hell, I'd try anything. Every step felt heavier, like fear was pulling me down, trying to slow me. And then, as crazy as it sounds, I felt him—Tom. Running beside me. It wasn't just a memory. It felt real, like he was there, pushing me forward. I glanced over, and there he was—dimples, that stupid grin, like nothing had changed. "Come on, bro. You've got this," he said, laughing like we were kids again.

I ran harder. Right then, I made a promise: *If Alex was alive, I'd be ready for whatever came next.* Love wasn't just some soft, pretty thing people wrote songs about. It was grit. It was the thing that dragged you through hell and kept you moving. I wasn't just running for Alex anymore. I was running for Tom, for the life he didn't get to finish. Saving Alex felt like saving a part of what we lost.

When I got to Alex's building, it was a nightmare. Emergency vehicles clogged the street, lights flashing everywhere. The elevator was a mangled wreck at the bottom of the shaft. I pushed through the crowd, desperate to find her.

"Is there a young woman named Alex Weisman here?" I asked, out of breath.

A rescue worker nodded. "Yeah, she's with the medical team over there."

He pointed, and there she was—by the ambulance, wrapped in a blanket.

"Alex!" I called, running toward her. She looked up, and I pulled her into a hug so tight I thought I might crush her. She didn't let go, her face buried in my neck, her tears soaking into my shirt.

"It's okay. You're safe now," I said. My hand brushed her hair as I held her close.

The rest of the world—the noise, the flashing lights—faded. It was just us.

"I saw her, Matt," Alex said. "That woman we've been talking about. She was there, right before the elevator... She tried to kill me. She won't stop. She's after all of us."

I pulled her closer, my voice steady even though my gut was in knots. "I'm here," I said. "We'll figure it out. She's done. She's not touching you again."

# OLIVIA

As I headed back to the hospital, my mind churned with questions I couldn't answer. How do you fight a threat you don't understand? And what about Charlie? Had she become a target too? She couldn't speak, couldn't signal if something was wrong. What if I was missing something? Overlooking subtle signs while she silently suffered?

My thoughts drifted to Owen. I couldn't shake the worry, especially with the nagging sense that my luck was about to change. I pulled out my phone and dialed his office.

"Good morning, this is Stacey. How may I help you?"

Stacey had been Owen's receptionist for as long as he'd been with the firm—eight years. Mid-thirties, divorced, two kids. Always polished. Always smiling. And always just a little too close. I'd long suspected she had a crush on him—the way she leaned in at holiday parties, gaze locked on him like no one else existed. Like I didn't exist. But I never let it bother me. Owen had never given me a reason to feel jealous.

"Hi, Stacey, it's Olivia. Can I talk to Owen, please?"

"Olivia?" Stacey's surprised tone made it clear she wasn't expecting my call. "As in his ex-wife?"

"His *wife*," I corrected her. "We're back together."

"Hmm, interesting," she mused, "Owen never said anything. How are you, Olivia?"

"I'm good," I said quickly, wanting to end the conversation as soon as possible. "Thank you for asking. Can I please talk to Owen?"

"He's in a meeting with a client," she said. "Can he call you later?"

"Does he have any meetings after that?" I asked.

"Let me check," she said, and I heard her fingers tapping on the keyboard. "Oh yes, his whole day is packed."

"Then I can't wait," I blurted. "Can you please ask him to step out for a minute?"

"Oh." There was a pause before Stacey answered. "Olivia, you know I can't interrupt him—he hates that. You know how important these meetings are."

"I know," I said. "But this is important."

A slight throat clear. "Okay. I'll be right back."

Two minutes later, his voice cut through the line. "Stacey, I'll take the call in my office!" A door clicked shut. Then, finally—"Olivia, is everything okay?"

"Hi, Owen. Yeah. I just wanted to check in, um... Are you okay?" The words fell flat the second they left my mouth.

"Honey, what's wrong?" His voice tightened.

"No, nothing's wrong," I hurried to reassure him.

"Then why are you asking if I'm all right?"

I paused. This was it. The moment I had to say something, but how? Where do I even begin?

"Owen, there's something... a situation." I trailed off, unsure how to explain.

"What situation?" he pressed.

"I, uh, I just missed you, that's all," I said quickly, deciding it was better not to unload everything. I didn't want to burden him with my worries—or worse, have him dismiss them. What if he thought I was unraveling, like I had with Officer Davis? I had no solid proof, just a string of strange occurrences, too easy to write off as stress.

"Oh, honey," His voice softened, and I could almost hear the smile behind it. "I miss you too. But listen, I need to get back to my meeting. I'll tell you something, though. That text I didn't want to tell you about?

Well... I've been planning something special. I want us to renew our vows. I'll explain everything when I get home tonight."

I wasn't expecting that. "Really?"

"Yes, really," he chuckled. "I love you, Olivia. Now I really have to run."

"I love you too," I said. "Just one more thing before you hang up. I might be heading to Woodstock today."

"Woodstock?" he asked. "What's going on there?"

"Just some event the hospital is organizing. But I should be back home in time."

"All right, honey. I'll see you soon," he said.

"See you soon," I replied, ending the call.

As I lowered my phone, someone bumped into me, knocking it from my grasp. It clattered onto the pavement.

A blur of black hair. My stomach plummeted. *No. Not her. It can't be.*

Heart racing, I spun around, shielding my eyes from the sun, bracing for the impossible. The woman who'd bumped me paused, removed her sunglasses. Relief hit so fast it left me lightheaded. *Not her. Just a stranger.*

I let out a shaky breath, willing my pulse to slow. Was this my new reality? Always on edge, flinching at every dark-haired woman, second-guessing every glance? Would I ever stop looking over my shoulder?

"I'm so sorry," she said. "Are you okay? Did I hurt you?"

"No, it's fine." I bent down, picked up my phone. The screen was cracked but still working.

"Did I break your phone?" she asked.

"No, it's still working. Don't worry about it."

She gave me a small, apologetic smile before walking away, disappearing into the crowd.

I started to shake off the tension—then a thought struck me. I remembered Charlie's mother's words:

*Charlie wouldn't be mean like that. She wouldn't tell me to go away.*

What if Charlie hadn't experienced a coma arousal event at all? What if she had truly awakened, and we hadn't recognized it for what it was? The recent strange occurrences started to take on a new shape in my mind. Could they somehow be connected to the woman? A scenario began to form: what if the woman was communicating with Charlie? And what if, in her own way, Charlie could hear her— triggering her brain to respond?

Fifteen minutes later, I arrived at Charlie's room. The door was slightly ajar, and through the crack, I saw her mother sitting on the edge of the bed, a book resting in her lap. Exhaustion weighed on her, her shoulders slumped, her face lined with fatigue. It didn't surprise me that she hadn't gone home, hadn't taken a break.

As I stepped inside, she looked up, her red-rimmed eyes meeting mine. "Dr. Olivia," Ms. Moretti said. "I'm glad you're here. I just couldn't leave her alone."

I nodded. "How is she doing?"

She closed the book carefully, her fingers marking the page. "She hasn't woken up again." Her voice was thin, brittle. "Doctor, I don't know how much longer I can hold on to hope." A tear spilled over, and she swiped at it with trembling hands. "I'm starting to lose faith. I—I don't know if I'll ever get my daughter back. I've been thinking about what you said. About taking Charlie off life support."

Her voice broke. A sob shuddered through her.

I handed her a tissue. She clutched it tightly, pressing it to her face. As I listened, I couldn't help but feel conflicted. Removing Charlie from life support no longer felt like the right decision—not when her brain was responding to something. Someone. But how could I prove that?

"It's crazy," she whispered, "but I keep thinking—what if she's already gone? What if what I saw was just... her spirit, trying to tell me to move on?" She swallowed hard. "I believe in the afterlife. I do. But..." Her breath hitched. "Would it be easier if I just... let go?" Her whole body shook. "I don't know if I can. I'm not ready to say goodbye to my daughter."

I rubbed the back of my neck, overwhelmed by the uncertainty. I was at a loss, completely unsure of what to do or say. I had a hunch, but a hunch wasn't enough. Should I spend all my time in Charlie's room, waiting for the mysterious woman to return? But what about my other patients? I couldn't abandon them.

"I know this is incredibly difficult," I said gently. "It's natural to have fears and doubts, especially with so much uncertainty. But we don't need to rush into any decisions just yet. Let's take more time." I gestured toward the monitors. "Charlie is still very much alive. Hear that steady beep? That's her heartbeat. Every heartbeat is significant. Every moment offers her a chance to heal."

*And in that time, maybe I can figure out the truth.*

She exhaled unsteadily, nodding. "Thank you for being so kind," she said. "Dealing with all this is just so hard. I'm holding onto hope for a miracle." She paused, then opened the book in her lap, revealing a painting. "Our family is Italian, and I find healing in our culture. This painting, *The Healing of the Cripple and Raising of Tabitha* by Caravaggio, is one of the most famous ones. Have you seen it?"

"Yes," I said, recognizing the image immediately. "It's from the *Acts of the Apostles.* Peter, the apostle, is in the background raising a woman named Tabitha from the dead."

Her fingers traced the edges of the page. "I keep looking at their faces. The disbelief. The shock. The hope." Her voice cracked. "I'm praying for the same for Charlie. Every day, I hold her hand, I talk to her, I pray out loud... hoping she hears me." She wiped at her eyes. "She's such a good girl. So kind. So bright. She never gave me trouble." A fresh wave of grief wracked her. "But it's hard. So hard. To keep holding on." She pressed a kiss to her fingers, then touched Charlie's hand. "I love you so much."

I reached for another tissue, but just as I did, a movement caught my eye. Charlie twitched. Ever so slightly.

Every muscle in me went rigid. Could she hear us? Had she been listening all this time? And if she had... then maybe that woman had been speaking to her, too. And what if she wasn't just speaking to

Charlie, but influencing her mind—tampering with her brain activity in ways we couldn't begin to understand? Like she was accessing Charlie's cerebral cortex directly, bypassing words altogether. If so, we were running out of time.

We had to reach Charlie. Make her realize she wasn't alone. But how? How could we be sure she heard us?

I moved to the other side of the bed, leaning in close to Charlie's ear, feigning an examination. Keeping my voice low, I made sure Ms. Moretti couldn't hear me.

"Charlie, I don't know if you can hear me, but if you hear the voice of a strange woman, don't listen to her. Try to block her out of your mind. She's dangerous. She wants to hurt you." I gripped her hand, willing my words to reach her. "Please, stay strong. Don't believe anything she says. We're here to protect you."

A faint, nearly imperceptible movement of her finger stirred a surge of hope inside me. It was so slight, so subtle, that anyone else might have missed it—but I knew it had happened. It felt like a sign. A quiet reassurance that she was listening. That my words had reached her.

But the clock was ticking, and whatever time we had left was slipping away. We needed to act—*now*.

Ms. Moretti was still lost in the painting. Peter was kneeling, his prayer a desperate plea for Tabitha's return.

"Keep praying, Ms. Moretti," I said, more firmly now. "Pray aloud. I have to step out for a few hours, but I'll be back later. If anything seems off, call me immediately."

I took one last look at Charlie. Her chest rose and fell, steady but unmoving.

I shut the door behind me with a soft click. Then, in the emptiness of the hallway, I said, "I won't give up without a fight. I've let you down before, Charlie. I won't do it again."

# CHARLIE

*Dangerous. Trying to hurt you. Stay strong. Don't believe anything she says.*

Dr. Olivia's words echoed in my mind, looping like a warning siren. But a new fear crept in. Could she hear the voice too? Did she know where it was coming from? And if she did, why warn me now?

The voice had gone silent, but I wasn't fooled. I knew it was still out there. Watching. Waiting.

All I could hear now was Mammina's voice—her prayers spilling out like a broken record. Over and over, the same words.

*Heavenly Father, I come before you with a heart full of hope and trust, seeking your divine healing touch upon Charlie Moretti. Please help my daughter heal.*

If I could, I would turn away. Would shut it all out. But I couldn't. I was trapped inside my own body, unable to speak, unable to move.

Why wouldn't she just go home like the doctors told her? Why couldn't she understand that I needed space—to think, to figure this out?

But then... something about the way she said it got to me.

*Please help my daughter heal.*

Her voice, so full of hope. Like she still believed in prayer. Still believed in goodness. Had I lost that? It made me wonder if I'd lost that faith—if I had stopped seeing the best in people. The voice had messed with my head, made me turn against her when she was only trying to help. She had done everything for me. Worked so hard. Sacrificed so much. All so I could have the life she dreamed for me. And all this time, she'd been alone, holding it together as best she could. I should have seen that. I should have understood.

I thought back to the day I got my college acceptance email.

"Go on, open the email," Mammina urged, leaning over my shoulder, her excitement barely contained. "Let's read it."

"I'm scared, Mammina. What if I didn't get in?"

"I'm sure you did," Jason said, his voice full of confidence. "Okay, I can't know for sure, but I have a feeling it's good news."

I took a deep breath. My heart raced. "Okay, okay—oh my god, I'm so nervous. Here we go. Mammina, Jason, oh my god, I got in. I got in! I can't believe it—I got into Northwestern!" I jumped up and down. "And they're giving me a swimming scholarship."

Mammina wrapped her arms around me. "Congratulations, honey!"

Jason's grin was so wide it nearly split his face. He scooped me up and spun me around in the air. "Congratulations, babe. I knew you'd get in."

I laughed, breathless, the world spinning around me—full, happy, safe. Then doubt crept in. "Jason, how are we going to survive a long-distance relationship? You'll go to Indiana University and forget all about me."

"Never. I love you too much."

"And then what happened?" The voice slipped into my thoughts, giddy, almost amused. "Did you conquer the world? Did you achieve all your dreams?"

*No.* A sharp pain twisted inside me. Where was Jason? He hadn't visited me. Not in the last few days. My heart ached for him. I just wanted him here. Needed him close. But all I had was this emptiness.

"Or did Dr. Olivia take your spot and leave you to get shot?" The words coiled around me, tightening, squeezing.

The memory surfaced, slow and merciless. Dr. Olivia, walking free. Me, left behind. Gunshots. Cracks slicing through the air. Screams. Giovanni's eyes—something unsaid, something final. The fire in my back, tearing through me. And then—darkness.

"See?" the voice murmured." It's Dr. Olivia who's evil, not me. She took your place, she took your dreams away. Not me. I'm here to help you."

Mammina's voice cut in. "Charlie, my dear. I'll have to leave you alone for a couple of minutes. Just going to grab a cup of coffee, and I'll be right back. I love you, my sweetie."

The voice sighed, almost pleased.

"Don't worry, Mammina," it whispered. "She's not alone. Someone else is lurking in this room, silently watching her. A true friend, she comes every day. You can't see her, you can't hear her, but she's smiling. Oh, how she's smiling, for she's ready to execute her chilling plan . . ."

# ALEXANDRA

We were leaving downtown Chicago behind, heading toward the quieter suburb of Woodstock, Illinois. Matt had the wheel, and I was riding shotgun, the sun turning the highway into a ribbon of gold. Dr. Olivia sat in the backseat, looking more exhausted than the last time I saw her—deeper shadows under her eyes, every movement slower, like the day had wrung her out. The second she slid into the car, she peeled off her badge and white coat, folding them like she hoped the day's stress would stay behind with them.

The skyscrapers dissolved into sporadic trees, the open highway stretching endlessly ahead. Billboards popped up along the roadside, pushing greasy diners and quirky tourist traps. Cars zipped past, each carrying its own story. A family minivan stuffed with luggage and kids making faces at us in the rearview mirror. A lone trucker in a faded cap, eyes heavy with miles. And a shiny red convertible, its driver singing her heart out, her hair whipping wild in the wind.

The motion of the road tugged at old memories, unspooling summer road trips with my parents. Every year without fail, we'd pack up and hit the highway. I'd sit in the back, pointing out anything that caught my eye: a license plate from a faraway state, a cloud shaped like a dragon, a water tower in the middle of nowhere. Their voices wrapped around me like a favorite song, blending with the soft crackle of 80s hits on the radio.

Dad loved telling jokes, most of them corny enough to make you groan. "Why did the scarecrow become a successful neurosurgeon?" he'd ask, pausing for maximum suspense, his grin already giving away the punchline. "Because he was outstanding in his field!" Mom and I would laugh, partly because it was easier than not laughing and partly because he loved it so much.

But it wasn't just jokes. On those long drives, we'd talk about everything—about the little things we passed on the road and the bigger things that shaped us. Mom told stories about my great-grandparents, how they escaped pogroms in Eastern Europe with nothing but courage and a stubborn hope for something better. She'd tell it with this quiet reverence, her voice steady but proud. I used to wonder if I could ever be that brave. Sitting there in the backseat, everything seemed simple and safe, like the world outside couldn't touch us. Now? That kind of safety felt like a lifetime ago.

Matt had just finished walking me through everything he'd dug up, and somehow, I felt even more nervous—because apparently, that was possible. What exactly were we going to find in Woodstock? And would the shooters' mom even talk to us? I mean, we're total strangers showing up unannounced at her door. Would you open up to us? And even if she did, did I really want to have that conversation? Her sons had taken innocent lives.

I glanced at Matt, and he squeezed my hand, like he could see every doubt spinning through my head. All I wanted in that moment was to press pause on reality—bury myself in his arms, forget about losing my job, and pretend the creepy woman shadowing us wasn't real.

"So Matt has filled you in on everything?" Olivia asked from the back seat.

I nodded. "Yeah. And apparently, I'm not the only one she's been stalking. For a while, I thought I was losing it."

"I'm sorry I didn't recognize you earlier," she said. Her eyes flicked to the rearview mirror, meeting mine for a moment. "The only person I clearly remember from that day is Charlie. We were standing next to each other when they made us line up." She hesitated. "She's the patient I'm looking after now."

"Charlie and I chatted in line just before everything turned into a nightmare," I said. "But I totally remember you. Seriously, you were unbelievably brave."

Olivia shook her head. "I was terrified. I just tried not to show it." She paused, her voice dropping slightly. "And I'm sorry about leaving your meeting, Alex. I thought if I could just... avoid it, I might be able to leave it behind. But clearly, I was wrong." She let out a quiet sigh. "I was actually looking forward to our next meeting."

"There won't be another meeting," I admitted, the words sitting bitter in my mouth. Saying it out loud made it real, and real was harder to swallow. "At least not with me. I got fired."

Her eyes widened. "Fired? Why? When?"

"This morning. Lisa—my boss from hell—told me Kyle gave her back her old job, and apparently, that meant mine had to go."

"Alex, I'm so sorry," she said.

"Thanks," I said, the word more sigh than gratitude. "But maybe it's for the best. Lisa was awful, and if Kyle and HR backed her on this... well, they're just as bad."

Lisa always did have a sixth sense for showing up at the worst times, always about as welcome as a bee at a picnic. Before we left to pick up Olivia, she had sauntered over to where Matt and I were standing by the ambulance.

Bruce got to me first. He rushed over and threw his arms around me, nearly lifting me off the ground.

"Oh, thank God!" he exclaimed, squeezing me so tight I thought I might actually suffocate. "Darling, you scared the life out of me! Are you okay? I mean, really okay? Look at you—you're a vision of survival, but I need to hear it straight from you!"

"I'm okay, Bruce. A little banged up, but alive," I said, patting his back as I tried to catch my breath.

Lisa stepped closer, raising a hand to silence him. "Oh, spare me, Bruce. She's fine. She's standing here, isn't she?" Her gaze flicked to me, icy and dismissive. "Let's not pretend this is a reunion scene from a soap opera."

"Hi, Lisa," I replied, though my teeth were clenched.

"Well," she said, her arms crossed, "I'm glad you survived. But just so we're clear—you're still fired. Life moves on. Isn't that right?" She gave me a tight smile, as if daring me to challenge her.

It was almost impressive how heartless she could be. But I'd had enough. She'd already fired me—what more could she take? My patience snapped like a worn thread.

"Lisa," I said, my voice sharper now, "there's something I've been dying to say for a while."

Her eyes lit up with interest. "Oh? This should be good."

"You're an awful human being," I said, letting the words hit like a slap. "So awful I'm shocked the entire world hasn't just washed its hands of you. I'm done with your bullying. So do me a favor—go fuck yourself."

For a split second, her mask cracked—just enough for me to see the hit land. Then, just as quickly, she stitched it back together, straightening her shoulders like I was nothing more than a bug on her windshield. Behind her, Bruce shot me a quick thumbs-up and a proud grin, which only made it sweeter.

"We're here," Matt said, pulling me back as he pulled into the driveway of what could generously be called a house.

The place looked like it had given up years ago. Peeling paint clung to the siding in stubborn patches, refusing to let go completely. The windows were cracked or boarded up, depending on how many storms had bullied them, and a sagging picket fence limped around the yard, more decoration than defense. Weeds had claimed everything, snaking up the house like they were planning to pull it under. The roof sagged in uneven spots, shingles missing here and there, like someone had started patching it and just... stopped. The porch steps leaned so badly I half expected them to crumble out of pure exhaustion. And then there was the swing set in the yard—rusted chains dangling lifelessly, like it was still waiting for kids who'd outgrown it years ago. The crickets chirping in the distance didn't help, either. If anything, they made the place feel even emptier, like it had been forgotten by everyone except them.

"Maybe no one lives here," I said, half hoping I was right.

Matt shrugged. "Only one way to find out." He opened his door and stepped out like this wasn't the opening scene of a bad decision.

"We probably should've brought something for protection," Olivia muttered from the back seat. Her unease wasn't exactly helping mine.

I stepped out of the car, grabbing Matt's hand as the summer air turned colder than it should have.

Matt rang the bell. Nothing. He tried again. Still nothing. Knocking this time, he called out, "Hello?" but the silence refused to budge.

"I don't think anyone's home," Olivia whispered behind us. "Maybe we should—"

Before she could finish, Matt reached for the doorknob. It turned without resistance, and the door creaked open like it had been waiting for us. We exchanged looks, none of us entirely sure whether to go in or run back to the car.

"Matt, look," I stammered, pointing toward the window.

Out of the shadows inside, the barrel of a rifle slowly emerged, aimed directly at us.

# OLIVIA

"Get out of my house!" The voice slammed down from above. I snapped my head up—a woman stood at the window, rifle aimed dead at us. "Or I pull the damn trigger."

My eyes locked on the barrel. And just like that, I was back there. Another gun. Another moment. The same paralyzing weight of it, the same lung-tightening certainty that this was it—as I crouched beside an elderly man, his ankle twisted in pain. The same cold fear poured into my gut. My brain did what it always did—it ran straight to Owen. Just like last time. Would she pull the trigger? Would I ever see him again?

Matt stepped in front of Alex, shielding her. She pressed in closer, tucking herself against him.

"Stand behind me, Olivia," he instructed me.

"Matt, I really don't think this was a good idea," I replied. "Maybe we should just go back to the car and leave."

But Matt didn't budge. He kept his eyes locked on the window, shaking his head. "No. We can't just walk away. We need her, and without her, we're out of options. We have to make her talk."

Alex's voice trembled. "But how, Matt?"

Matt raised his hands in a non-threatening gesture, trying to soften the tension. "Ma'am, we're not here to cause any trouble. We just want to talk. I'm Jimmy's friend, and I have something important to share, something he wanted you to know."

"What friend?" The voice came back, dripping with suspicion. "I know all of my boys' friends. Why are you coming now?"

Matt called up again, "I'm sorry for the confusion. I'm a friend he made at the hospital after the accident. I was—"

"He was one of the nurses who attended Jimmy," I stepped in. "And I'm his sister. Jimmy told us something important at the hospital, something he wanted you to know. We really need to talk."

A long silence. Then, heavy footsteps echoed from the stairs. She appeared at the door moments later. She looked to be in her early fifties—deep lines etched into her face, streaks of gray cutting through her unkempt hair. The heavy scent of cigarettes hit me first, followed by the sharp sting of whiskey. She took a long drag from her cigarette and exhaled slowly, her eyes scanning us with a cold, unflinching gaze. A cynical laugh escaped her, sharp and dry.

"You're not Jimmy's friends," she said, bitterness curling in her voice. "You're the three who survived." Her eyes flicked over us. "I've seen all your faces. Read every damn story. So, why are you here? To tell me what a terrible mother I am? Save your breath. I've got reporters hounding me, death threats piling up, and the whole damn neighborhood hoping I'd just drop dead."

She started to close the door, but Matt quickly wedged his foot in to stop it.

"No, ma'am. Please don't close the door on us," he said, his voice steady but urgent. "We're not here to judge you. We just need to talk about something else."

"We're in trouble," Alex added, shifting her weight from one foot to the other, her hands fidgeting with the hem of her blouse. "There's a dangerous woman with black hair who's after us. We think she might have had something to do with your sons, too."

"A dangerous woman with black hair?" she repeated, her eyes narrowing as we nodded. She studied us for what felt like an eternity before stepping aside. "All right, come in if you want to talk. And don't worry, I'm not going to shoot you," she added, as though it were a joke.

"Believe it or not, I didn't raise my boys to be killers. I wasn't going to shoot you, just scare you a bit."

We exchanged glances and then cautiously stepped inside. The stench of rotten food hit my nose, and I had to swallow hard to keep from gagging. Alex didn't fare much better, visibly recoiling, her face scrunching in disgust. The small living room was cluttered with piles of clothes, and I could see the kitchen sink from where I stood, overflowing with dirty dishes.

I expected to see pictures of her sons everywhere, some hint of their lives, but there was nothing. No family photos, no mementos. Not a single sign they existed at all. The walls were bare, the paint chipped and yellowed with age, contributing to the grim atmosphere. The room was dim, the shades drawn tight, blocking out any light or hope.

She gestured toward the worn couch near a table littered with overflowing ashtrays. "Sit down. I'm Becky, the mother," she said, her voice flat, a dullness that matched the room. "The mother of Jimmy and Billy. I've got whiskey or water. Take your pick."

"We're fine, thank you, Becky," Alex replied, settling onto the couch. Matt and I followed, the cushions sagging beneath us.

"Well, I need a refill. Just give me a minute," Becky said, disappearing into the kitchen.

As we sat there, I couldn't help but think about the two boys—once just kids. Had this house always been in such disarray, or had it fallen apart after everything happened? Matt had said they used to be different. I tried to picture them as little boys—laughing on the old swing set, the rusted chains creaking with each push. Now, all I could see was the dark reality of who they had become.

Becky's face was hard to read, but the weariness in her eyes said everything. The house, the brokenness, the alcohol—it was all a consequence of years of pain. Where was their father through all of this? But the bigger question still lingered: what had twisted them so badly? What turned those kids into killers?

Alex leaned in, her voice barely a whisper, "Why do you think she let us in? Do you think she's seen the woman too?"

Matt's gaze lingered on the kitchen doorway. "I don't know," he said, quiet, thoughtful. "But I was wondering the same thing."

Becky appeared with a fresh drink in one hand and a sketchbook in the other. She took a long drag from her cigarette, exhaling slowly. Settling into a chair, she sighed, her eyes never meeting ours. When she spoke, her words seemed to drag behind her, as if stuck behind a wall she could barely push through.

"I didn't raise my boys to be killers," she said. "Neither did their father. He passed last year... couldn't handle it anymore." She took a long drink, her eyes lost in the depths of her glass for a moment. "And here I am, still stuck in this mess. I wish I could join him, but I'm still here. Fate, I guess." A hollow laugh escaped her, dry and without humor. "We used to have a good life. The house didn't always look like this. Everything started falling apart after that coffee shop... but even before that, it all started with the car accident. You know about it?"

"Yes," Matt answered. "I read about it. The accident left your sons in a coma. The only survivors."

Becky's gaze grew distant, her focus shifting to something far beyond us. "They were in the last car, at the end of the line. When I saw the wreckage, I didn't even understand what I was looking at. But I was thankful. My boys were alive. I stayed with them, day and night, praying they'd wake up." She took another sip of whiskey, fingers tightening around the glass, the cigarette ash falling in a careless trail onto the overflowing ashtray. She didn't seem to care. "They were in a coma for six months. Billy woke up first. Then, Jimmy—just the next day. But..." She faltered.

"But what?" Alex prompted softly.

"They weren't the same," she murmured, her voice cracking on the last word. "Not the same sweet boys I knew. They didn't want to see me or their father. At first, I thought it was trauma. But it never passed. It only got worse. They still lived with us, but locked themselves in Jimmy's room, whispering." Her hands shook as she spoke, her memory clearly painful.

"What would they whisper?" I asked.

"They said they had her now," Becky replied, meeting my gaze for the first time, as though confessing a secret. "That she'd protect them. And that they served the devil." She shuddered, clearly reliving the memory. "I'll never forget it—Jimmy screaming at Billy, telling him he had no choice. That something terrible would happen if he didn't do it. Two days later, the coffee shop..." She paused to take a shaky breath. "I've been haunted by it ever since. Wondering who this woman was and why my boys did what they did." She opened the sketchbook on her lap. "Jimmy was the artist. Every page is filled with drawings of her. I couldn't understand why she looked so terrifying." She flipped the page. "Is this the woman you're talking about?"

There she was. The woman, staring back at us from the page. We exchanged silent, fearful glances.

"Yes," I said. "Have you ever met her?"

"No," Becky replied, shaking her head slowly. "I don't know who she is. Never seen her before. My boys were good kids. But after the coma, they changed. I tried to find answers, but all I could find were these drawings."

She flipped to the next page. A sketch of Jimmy, lying in a hospital bed. The woman hovered over him, hand extended like she was casting a spell. At the bottom of the page were the numbers "666," boldly underlined.

She looked at the drawing, her lips barely moving as she whispered. "I don't know what this means."

A cold knot tightened, then sank. The sickening realization settled in. The answers I'd been chasing, grasping at like loose threads, finally snapped into place. The pattern was clear. Clearer than I could stomach. I heard Charlie's mother again.

*She woke up and said 'leave'. Charlie wouldn't be mean like that. She wouldn't tell me to go away. Yes, I heard her talk. She said, 'leave' and . . . and I also heard her say 'I have her now. She'll protect me.'*

That was it. The proof I'd been searching for. The same dark influence that had consumed Jimmy and Billy was coming for Charlie.

This woman—whoever or whatever she was— didn't just break people. She burrowed inside them. Twisted them up from the inside until nothing was left but something cold. Something rotten. Something evil. She'd done it to those boys. And now, she was coming for Charlie. Even if Charlie woke up, she wouldn't be Charlie anymore.

I jumped to my feet. "Oh god, Charlie's in danger!" I shouted. "We need to get to the hospital. Now."

"What?" Matt shot up beside me. "What's going on?"

I could barely catch my breath. "This woman transformed Jimmy and Billy. And now—now she's coming for Charlie."

Matt's eyes narrowed. "How can you be sure?"

"Charlie's mother said today that she saw Charlie wake up and say, 'I have her now. She'll protect me.' It's the same thing the boys said before. Don't you see the pattern? I know Charlie can hear us. She responded to my voice today. I can feel something is happening."

Becky stared at me, her eyes clouded with disbelief. "You think… she somehow changed my boys?"

"There's something supernatural going on, Becky," Alex said, rising to her feet. "This woman is dangerous. We don't know who she is, but she's not human. Olivia thinks she's after Charlie now—just like she was after your sons. And if she gets to her, she'll change her too."

"She'll twist her, just like she did with your sons, using her for some terrible purpose," Matt added.

I dragged a hand down my face, like I could wipe away the sick feeling crawling under my skin. We were about to lose Charlie. Not just her life—her. Everything that made her Charlie. We had to move. Now. I moved toward the door, but then—

A floorboard creaked above us. A rustling sound. "Is someone else here?" I asked Becky.

She shook her head. "No, and I left my gun upstairs."

Matt looked toward the stairs. "You all stay here," he said. "I'll go check."

"I'm coming with you," Alex said, moving to follow him.

"Shouldn't we all go?" Becky asked.

Matt shook his head before saying, "No, please stay here."

He made his way up the stairs, each step slow, careful. Alex stayed at the bottom, her eyes locked on the stairs, biting her lips with enough force that I could almost hear her thoughts.

Then, a creak from above. A door slammed shut.

"I can't take this anymore," Alex muttered, but just as she was about to move, Matt's voice called down.

"It's okay. It's just a pigeon. Window's open. Damn thing flew in. I've been seeing these birds everywhere lately."

Then, he opened the door. The pigeon darted out, landing on the stair rail.

The tension loosened, but not enough. That pigeon—something about it felt off. Too smooth, too intentional, like it had been placed there. A detail that didn't belong. I couldn't shake it. It meant something. And whatever it meant, it wasn't good.

"You're all crazy," Becky said, her voice frayed, teetering between anger and exhaustion. "Do you even hear yourselves?" She exhaled hard, shaking her head. "Get out. I don't need this. I don't need more pain." Her fingers tightened around the glass in her hand. "I've got nothing left." Her eyes flicked to the pigeon, lingering, like it was a thing that had just now started to matter. "In some cultures, pigeons are symbols of peace and good luck, if you believe in that kind of thing." A dry, humorless smile. "Maybe this one finally brought me some."

Then it moved.

The bird shot up, swooping over Matt's head, landing hard on Becky's shoulder. Then, just as fast, it lurched forward, slipping off her shoulder and hitting the floor with a heavy thud. She went still. For half a second, she just stared at it, her chest rising and falling like she wasn't sure if she'd just been attacked or blessed or cursed.

Then, her eyes widened. She dropped to her knees, hands hovering over the bird, reaching—but not touching. Too late.

Silence slid into the room. The pigeon was dead.

# ALEXANDRA

On the drive back, the silence felt like it was squeezing the air out of the car. Matt's foot pressed hard on the gas, his jaw clenched tight, like he thought speeding might somehow outrun what we'd just heard. His eyes stayed locked on the road, but I could tell his mind was miles away, tangled in Dr. Olivia's words. Whatever she'd dropped on us felt like a live grenade, and I couldn't tell if it was about to save us or blow everything apart.

In the backseat, Dr. Olivia stared out the window, her brow furrowed like she was trying to piece together a puzzle only she could see. Her fingers twisted the strap of her bag, tightening with every bump in the road. Every so often, her gaze flicked toward us, like she was gauging if we were holding it together any better than she was.

I stared down at my phone, my mind spinning in circles. Every "what if" hit harder than the last, and none of them led anywhere good. I needed an anchor, something to keep me from spiraling completely. Without thinking, I dialed the one person who could always make things feel less impossible.

"Hey, sweetheart," my mom answered, her voice warm, like an instant hug I desperately needed. "Aren't you usually drowning in meetings right about now?"

"Not today, Mom," I said, trying to sound casual. "Actually, I need to tell you something..."

I hesitated. She didn't know about the elevator, the firing, or the woman stalking me. Part of me wanted to keep it that way—protect her from all of it. If I told her, she'd drop everything, rush over, and try to fix what couldn't be fixed. But I called anyway. Maybe I just needed her voice, the calm she always carried, like everything would be okay just because she said so.

"What's going on?" she asked, her voice still warm but immediately suspicious.

"I got fired today," I said, cutting straight to it. "All those late nights, all the coffee... and for what?"

"Oh, honey. That's it? I thought it was something *serious*!" she said, relief clear in her voice. "Honestly, this might be the best thing that could've happened. That boss of yours? She sounded like she was one unkind woman. You're free of her now! And you know what? Good riddance." A pause. Then, a smirk in her voice. "I bet her houseplants don't even like her."

"She doesn't have any houseplants," I sighed loudly, surprised I could find humor in this moment. "She's not exactly the nurturing type."

"Well, if she did, they'd hate her," Mom said. "And you, honey, deserve so much better. This is your chance to find something that makes you happy. Somewhere they appreciate how brilliant you are. You're stronger than you think, Alex. Setbacks don't define you—it's how you bounce back."

I wanted to believe her. Really, I did. But every time she called me strong, it felt like she was talking about someone else entirely. I'd nod and smile when she said things like that, pretending it resonated. Deep down, though? Not so much. Especially now, when it felt like my whole world was tilting off its axis.

But as I listened to her, something flickered—a tiny spark of the strength she swore I had. Maybe this was my chance to prove her right, to show her that her belief in me wasn't misplaced. Sure, it wasn't superhero-level strength, but it was something. And no matter what came next, I wouldn't be facing it alone.

"I'll remember that," I said. "I love you, Mom. So much."

"Love you more, honey," she said. "Are you coming home this weekend?"

"I'm not sure," I replied. "I hope so."

"Well, I better see you next weekend, then. We'll light the Shabbat candles—it's been too long."

"Okay, Mom. I love you. Tell Dad I love him too, okay? I'll call you soon." I hung up just as we pulled into the hospital parking lot.

As we stepped out of the car, Matt's phone rang. His shoulders stiffened, and his brows pulled together as he glanced at the screen before answering. Olivia, already in a hurry, rushed past us. "I'm going to go check on Charlie. I'll see you inside once Matt's done with his call," she called over her shoulder before breaking into a run.

I tilted my head back, eyes catching on the sky. The sunset stretched wide, colors bleeding into each other—pink smudging into orange, orange swallowing purple. Too soft for how I felt, too perfect for the kind of day I'd had. I took a slow breath. Let it settle me. Ground me. Why didn't I do this more often? Just stop. Just look. Life was always a dead sprint, all forward motion, never a second to take anything in. The best moments slipped past like missed exits on a highway—realized too late, already gone.

"Hey, Dad. Yeah, I'm kinda tied up right now," Matt said, his voice sharper than usual as he answered the call. His free hand raked through his hair, and he turned slightly away from me. "What's going on? ...Okay. Yeah, I'll head over now." He ended the call and let out a heavy breath and dragged his hands down his face. "Alex, something's wrong with my mom. Dad says her blood pressure's through the roof, she's got killer headaches, and now she's struggling to breathe. I need to go."

My stomach dropped, and a hundred worst-case scenarios sprinted through my head. "Now? Why now? It feels... strange."

"I know. It feels off," Matt said, his voice low. "But she wasn't doing great the last time I saw her, and if something happens and I'm not there..." He trailed off, shoving his phone into his pocket. "I have to go, Alex."

"I just—" I hesitated, the words catching. "I'm worried something's going to happen to you."

He stepped closer, brushing his thumb along my cheek, then tracing my lips, like he was trying to calm both of us down. "Hey," His voice was quiet, solid. "We'll get through this. I'm not letting anything happen to us. If nothing else, at least something good came out of this—meeting you again." He laced his fingers with mine, giving my hand a squeeze. "You make me believe things can still be okay."

"Really?" I asked, whispering.

He nodded. "Absolutely. It might sound crazy, but…" He faltered, his voice dipping. "I don't know—I just feel something with you. Something real. Haven't felt that in a long time. I'm just glad I got another shot."

And just like that, my heart ignored every ounce of rational thought. "I feel the same," I admitted, a small smile breaking free. When our lips met, it wasn't some perfect movie moment—it was quiet, unsure, like we both knew what we were doing but couldn't tell if it was enough.

When he pulled back, his gaze locked on mine. "We'll figure this out, Alex. We'll turn the tables, outsmart her. And we're not alone—Dr. Olivia's with us. But right now, I need to be with my mom."

"Of course," I said, forcing my voice to sound calm, even though worry was doing cartwheels in my chest. "I hope she's okay."

"Thanks," he said, pulling me in for a quick hug. "Stay safe, all right? I'll be back soon."

As I watched him drive away, headlights fading into the distance, a knot twisted in my stomach. The timing felt too perfect, too… convenient. I wanted to believe everything would be fine, that Matt would come back. But as the taillights disappeared, that nagging voice in my head got louder. What if he didn't?

I turned toward the hospital. The sunset's warmth was already slipping away as I stepped into whatever storm waited inside.

# OLIVIA

Owen called just as I was hurrying toward Charlie's room. I hesitated, my phone buzzing in my hand, knowing I didn't have time to stop. But still, there it was—that tug, the urge to hear his voice, to feel a connection, even for a second.

I worried about losing him. Matt had lost all his money, and Alex just told me she'd lost her job. It felt like I was the only one left holding onto any semblance of a dream, the last one with something steady to cling to. But how much longer could that last? With each step, I couldn't shake the feeling that my turn was coming, that the cracks in my own life were just waiting to show.

"Hello, honey, I wanted to let you know that I'll be running quite late tonight. The clients from New York are here, and I can't pass up this dinner opportunity with them," he said.

I reassured him, saying, "No problem, I understand. Enjoy your dinner." My shoulders relaxed slightly at the thought of having more time to figure things out with Charlie.

"You sound a bit off," he observed. "Is everything all right?"

I paused, weighing how much to say, before settling on a half-hearted reply. "Yes, everything's fine. Just got a bunch of work to tackle. Love you."

"Love you too," he replied. "By the way, we should discuss that surprise I mentioned. I'm really excited about renewing our vows."

Trying to sound enthusiastic, I replied, "Sounds wonderful. Can't wait," before quickly ending the call.

Renewing vows, having a baby, even something as simple as sharing a quiet dinner with Owen felt like distant dreams—beautiful, but completely out of reach. I envied the people walking past me, their lives seemingly untouched by fear. No shadows hanging over their shoulders, no constant dread clouding their thoughts. Every carefree laugh I overheard felt like a sharp reminder of what I might never have again.

When I reached Charlie's room, Ms. Moretti was still sitting by her bed, her lips moving softly in prayer. Charlie lay as still as ever, unchanged. A thousand questions circled in my mind. Had she already been taken over? Was there still time to save her, or had that window closed?

I couldn't just open her skull and look inside.

"How is she, Ms. Moretti?" I asked.

She looked up from her prayer. "She's the same," she said. "I've been praying for her, but she's not responding."

I reached out, brushing Charlie's cool hand with my fingers. Seeing her so vulnerable, so still, pulled something tight in my chest.

We had to get her away from whatever this was, but I couldn't do that with Ms. Moretti watching over her.

"You should go home," I suggested, my voice gentle but firm. "I'm here now, and I promise to stay with her all night if necessary. Please, go home and get some rest."

Ms. Moretti hesitated, looking torn. But she was exhausted, and I could see it in the way her shoulders slumped, the way her eyes sagged.

"Please," I said again. "Charlie needs you to be strong. We won't give up on her."

Ms. Moretti gave a slow nod, her face drawn with fatigue. "You're right," she said, pushing herself out of the chair. "I'll go. I'll be back in the morning."

After Ms. Moretti finally left, I settled into the chair beside Charlie's bed and gently took her hand, hoping for even the faintest sign of life beyond her stillness. Her hand remained limp in mine, and her serene face showed no trace of awareness.

"Charlie," I said, leaning closer. "Has anyone been talking to you? Has a woman been visiting you? Someone whose voice you didn't recognize?" I studied her face for any sign of movement—anything at all.

But nothing. She lay there completely still, the silence thick around us. I leaned in a little closer, trying to soften my voice even more, like somehow that would help. "If you can hear me, Charlie, please give me a sign. Blink once if you've seen that woman. Blink if you can hear me."

I held my breath, hoping for a response, watching for the smallest hint that she was breaking through. But the room remained quiet, the steady hum of the machines the only sound.

I sighed, finally letting go of her hand. The quiet between us felt like a barrier I couldn't break. For now, it seemed, I wasn't going to reach her.

I didn't realize how lost in thought I was until Daniel's voice broke through. I looked up to find him standing in the doorway, pen and notepad in hand.

"Mind if I come in for a moment? No lectures this time, I promise."

I looked up and managed a small smile. "Of course, Daniel. And thank you for covering my other patients. I know it was a lot."

He waved it off, like it was no big deal. "You don't have to explain, Olivia," he said. "I've noticed something's been bothering you. I'm not here to pry, but I want you to know I'm around if you need to talk. No pressure."

I swallowed the lump in my throat. Daniel had been kind to me, and I couldn't help but feel a twinge of guilt for how I'd snapped at him earlier. "Thank you, Daniel. I really appreciate it. Life sure knows how to throw curveballs."

He nodded, a far-off look in his eyes. "It does. Full of ups and downs. And as doctors, we get to see it all—the victories and the losses. Not easy, but all we can do is try to give people that chance," he said.

"In the end, we don't have a choice but to make the best of it. We've chosen a difficult path, but it's our job to keep fighting for our patients."

"I know," I said quietly. "But sometimes... what if there's nothing left to save?"

Daniel looked at me, and the silence stretched between us. Then, quietly, he spoke. "There's always something. There has to be. But we need to give her more time."

My brow furrowed. "That's different from what you said before. You don't think she should be taken off life support now?"

Daniel straightened, eyes narrowing. "While you were gone, I checked on her a few times. And something's been nagging at me all day. When her mother said she thought Charlie woke up, it stuck with me. You remember—I thought I saw her wake up too. Two incidents like that, so close together? Maybe it's not just another 'coma arousal' event. Maybe I was too quick to give up. And there's something else. When I passed by her room not too long ago, I swear I saw her move again."

"You did?" Hope flared in my chest.

"I'm sure of it," he said. "As her mother was reading, I could've sworn I saw her hand twitch."

I nodded slowly. "I noticed it too. Makes me wonder if she's responding to voices."

"You were right," Daniel said. "I let my emotions cloud my judgment. But we need to give her more time. I believe now that she'll wake up. We have to hold on to that hope." He gave me a brief, faint smile. "You taught me that."

"But wake up as what?" The words slipped out before I could stop them.

He tilted his head slightly. "What do you mean?"

Before I could answer, Alex appeared in the doorway. "I'm sorry to interrupt, but the person at the front desk told me I could come straight here."

Daniel stood, smoothing the front of his coat. "I'll talk to you later, Olivia. Remember, I'm here if you need anything."

"Thank you, Daniel," I said, turning to Alex. "Where's Matt?"

"His dad called. Something happened to his mom. He said he'd be back as soon as he's done there."

I frowned. "That's odd. Do you think it could have anything to do with her?"

Alex's fingers twisted around the strap of her bag. "I told him I didn't think it was a coincidence, but he still went. How's Charlie?"

I gestured toward the bed. "See for yourself."

Alex took a step closer, her eyes darting to Charlie's still form. Before she could say anything, Daniel rushed back into the room. "Olivia, you need to come to the ER. There's an emergency."

# MATT

I'd never pushed the gas pedal so hard in my life. Dad's call about Mom had thrown me off. She'd mentioned not feeling well the last time I saw her, but I didn't think it was serious. Now, every time I called him back, it just rang.

The highway was a mess, so I veered onto the side streets. I was reckless—blowing through yellow lights, swerving into oncoming lanes—fully aware I might catch the attention of a cop. But right now? I didn't care.

Why now? I smacked the steering wheel in frustration. It felt like the universe was hell-bent on throwing everything at me at once. Damn it. And her—I knew she had to be behind it somehow. That woman. She was pulling the strings. But what could I do about it? Not a damn thing.

My focus snapped back to the road, and there they were—those damn birds. The same flock, just sitting in the middle of the street like they owned it. Panic surged as I slammed the horn, but they didn't move. Not an inch.

After a split-second of deliberation, I stomped on the brakes, the tires screeching in protest. The car behind me wasn't prepared for my abrupt halt— bam, it rear-ended me, sending my car into a skid.

I yanked the wheel, trying to get control back, but it was too late. The inevitable impact with a tree was like a surreal dream, a surreal nightmare. Out of the corner of my eye, I saw her behind the birds, and then they all took off at once.

A deafening crash followed, metal against wood, my head hitting the window, and then . . . blackness.

# ALEXANDRA

When Olivia dashed out of the room, I stepped closer to the bed. Seeing Charlie again after all this time felt... wrong. She still looked like the girl from the coffee shop—only now, all that spark and energy had been stripped away. She was frozen, stuck in some cruel limbo, like life had hit pause and forgotten to press play. She didn't look a day older. It wasn't fair. She'd been so full of plans, ready to take on the future, and now? She was just... here.

Olivia's explanation sounded like something straight out of a bad sci-fi movie. Charlie turning evil? The old me would've laughed it off, rolled my eyes so hard I'd need Advil. But after being trapped in an elevator with psycho lady and her supervillain vibes, I couldn't brush this off as fantasy. This was real. This was my life now.

I reached out and took Charlie's hand, careful, like I might break it if I wasn't. It felt so small, so fragile—cool to the touch—but there it was: the faintest pulse under my fingers. Proof she was still here, still fighting. I looked at her face—too calm, like she was just sleeping. Too perfect. Too still.

And I clung to one impossible hope: somewhere in there, the real Charlie was still hanging on, waiting for her way back to us.

"Hey," I whispered, "it's been a while, hasn't it?"

Two years had passed—two years she should've spent at Northwestern, having fun, joining clubs, making friends, maybe even falling in love. I could almost picture it: the parties, the late-night laughs, all the moments she should've been living. Instead, her life had spiraled into this nightmare. I remembered that day at the coffee shop—the way she talked about the future, her eyes shining with excitement, with dreams.

I brushed a strand of hair away from her face, a tear slipping down my cheek. What else could I do but wait? Maybe if I saw this so-called "transformation" for myself, I'd figure out how to help. But, honestly? What could I really do? Call for backup? Find a magic "How to Save Someone from a Supernatural Crisis" manual? The thought was as ridiculous as it was useless.

I felt the weight of it all, like I was sinking under it. I slumped into the chair next to her bed, still holding her hand, and closed my eyes for a moment. I just needed to believe I could fix this—before it was too late.

***

"I don't mean to intrude. It's just—the line is long, and I overheard. I just got into Northwestern."

It took me a second to realize where I was. Back at the coffee shop, two years ago. Charlie stood behind me in line, smiling, trying to strike up a conversation.

"That's amazing! Congrats. What's your major going to be?" I found myself saying—just like I had back then.

She grinned. "Thanks! Journalism. I hope it's okay I just started talking to you. I'm Charlie, by the way."

"Alex."

But then, without warning, her tone dropped. "Come with me," she whispered.

"What?" A chill ran through me.

This wasn't right. This wasn't how it went before.

"Come on, I want to show you something. Trust me." Her voice stretched out, warped, like it was bouncing off the walls, but somehow not quite reaching me. Her face flickered—blurring, twisting, warping into something I couldn't recognize.

"Leave me alone!" I shouted, jerking my arm back. But her grip tightened, impossibly strong, her fingers clamping onto me like iron. Then her other hand shot up, wrapping around my throat. I couldn't breathe.

I cried out and shot upright, gasping.

The coffee shop was gone, replaced by the sterile brightness of Charlie's hospital room. My breaths came shallow and fast. A dream. Just another damn nightmare. I dragged my hand down my face, trying to force myself back into the moment. My head throbbed, dizzy, like the world was spinning too fast. I glanced at Charlie. Still there. Still unconscious. Still not moving.

I checked my watch. Three hours. I'd been out for three hours. Where was Olivia? Still off on her so-called emergency? And Matt? No calls, no texts—nothing. I dialed his number. Voicemail. My stomach twisted, and that feeling—that gnawing feeling—wouldn't let go. Something was off.

I turned back to Charlie, and that's when I saw it: a faint smudge of makeup along her cheekbone. My entire body locked up. That wasn't there before. Someone had been here. While I was sleeping. Watching. Waiting. I scanned the room, my heart thudding so hard I could hear it in my ears. There was nothing. Nothing but the sterile quiet.

Before I could process what was happening, the door slammed open, and Olivia rushed in, grabbing my arm. "Alex, you've got to come with me. It's Matt."

I didn't ask. I followed her, my feet pounding against the floor like I was already running out of time. My heart was beating too fast, so loud I thought it would stop before we even made it to the ICU.

And then I saw him. Matt.

Lying there, wrapped in bandages, he looked like someone who'd been beaten until he didn't look human anymore. His chest barely moved, shallow, desperate breaths. His face—swollen, bruised—was barely recognizable. How was this real?

My throat tightened, like I couldn't swallow air anymore. "What happened?" I forced the words out, barely a whisper.

Olivia looked at me, her eyes glistening. "Police said he was speeding. Lost control and crashed into a tree."

We both knew this wasn't some freak accident. There was no way.

"She did this," I said, my voice cracking as it rose.

Olivia didn't flinch. "I know."

I couldn't stop staring at him. His chest moved, but it wasn't enough. My lungs felt like they were closing in on themselves. "He's not going to make it, is he?" My voice cracked, and when Olivia didn't answer, I begged her. "Just tell me the truth."

She hesitated, then gave the smallest nod. "It doesn't look good. But let's wait and see how the night goes."

My hands curled into fists, the urge to hit something—or someone—raging under my skin. "I knew it was a setup. Matt knew it too, but he went anyway," I snapped. "It's like she planned every second of this. First him, and now us. She's coming for us next."

A voice cut through the air, sharp and cold. "Well, well, well. What do we have here?"

I jerked my head toward the sound. There she was, standing by the window, like she'd always been there. The blinds slanted just enough for the moonlight to streak across her face. Her black dress was wrinkled, stained, and her makeup was smudged like she hadn't bothered to look in a mirror for days. The scar on her cheek—jagged, raw—twisted as she smirked. She leaned casually against the windowsill, like she was deciding how much damage she'd do next. For a moment, neither of us moved.

With a flick of her hair, she strolled to the other side of Matt's bed, her movements slow, almost lazy. "He's right where I want him—deep in a coma," she said, her voice slick with satisfaction. She glanced at me and smiled. "Shh," she whispered, putting a finger to her lips. "We must be careful about what we say around him. I suspect he might be listening."

I stepped forward instinctively, fists tight, my voice sharp. "What the hell do you want?"

She tilted her head, a smirk tugging at her lips. "Oh, don't be so dramatic, Alex. You were right—it was a trap. I called Matt's father, pretended to be an old colleague, and spun a little story about Matt losing all his money, spiraling into depression. His father's anger? His concern? Absolutely delicious." She let the words hang for a moment, her eyes glinting with amusement. "You thought only the three of you could see and hear me—and Officer Davis? Wrong. I decide who sees me, who hears me, and when." She paused, studying me, her smile widening. "And of course, I knew his dad would call Matt, dangling his mother's health as bait. Predictable, isn't it? But, oh, fate had other plans." Her tone turned mockingly sweet. "Life can be so cruel, don't you think?"

My fist shot through the air, aiming for her smug face, but all I hit was the edge of the pillow as she sidestepped effortlessly, laughing like this was some kind of joke. "Feeling better?" she asked, her laughter cutting off abruptly. "You can throw all the tantrums you want, but it won't change anything."

"Fuck you," I spat, my anger boiling over. "You're a horrible monster! Why did you do this to him? What do you want from us?"

Her expression hardened, the humor draining from her face like a switch had flipped. "I didn't do anything to him. I'm delivering justice. He was meant to suffer, just like the rest."

Olivia's voice trembled. "What do you mean, 'just like the rest'?" she asked.

The woman turned her cold, unfeeling gaze on Olivia. "Just like all those who suffered on June ninth, two years ago, in that coffee shop. Remember that day? Oh, I do. I remember every scream, every drop of blood, every life taken—young and old." For a moment, something almost like sorrow flickered in her eyes, but it vanished as quickly as it appeared. "Do you remember the youngest victim? Six years old. One bullet, and she was gone. And the shooters? They didn't even flinch." Her lips curled into a cruel smile, her voice turned icy. "But you weren't there to see it, were you? You were lucky. You, Olivia, and you, Alex, and Matt. The three of you walked away. But why? Why did you get to live when so many didn't? It wasn't fair." She leaned closer, her voice dropping to a whisper. "But don't worry. I'm fixing that now."

"Those men were monsters," Olivia shot back. "They worshipped some demonic force. We didn't have a choice—they manipulated us into choosing the number six."

She had this calm, almost bored expression on now. "I'm well aware. But even choosing a number is a kind of luck. You picked the fortunate one. You walked away."

"Who are you? What are you?" I asked. "Some kind of demon? Those shooters were normal before the accident—until someone changed them. And we know it was you. Their mom has a sketchbook full of your face."

Her smile faltered for the briefest moment, like she was deciding how much to give away. "Honestly, those men were wicked long before I came along. But," she said, drawing out the word as her smile returned, "I suppose the charade is getting old. My name is Charlie Moretti."

"Charlie Moretti?" Olivia's voice was barely more than a whisper. "That's impossible. Charlie's lying in the other room, in a coma."

The woman yawned dramatically, like she'd heard this all before. "Honestly, Olivia, you're exhausting. I'm telling you, I'm Charlie. Why would I make that up?"

I finally found my voice. "How is that even possible? You're here, and that poor girl is unconscious in the other room. You don't even look like her."

She smirked, clearly enjoying herself. "Ever heard of an out-of-body experience?"

"No," I said. "What's that?"

She smirked, savoring the moment. "Allow me to enlighten you. 'An out-of-body experience is a sensation of being outside one's own body, typically floating, able to observe oneself from a distance.' Quite impressive, right? My ability to quote the dictionary must be blowing your mind. But the real kicker? The truth is its own kind of horror. I can see the fear in your eyes—it's delightful. But don't worry, the game's almost over."

She stretched, like she had all the time in the world, then reached into her bag and pulled out a gun.

"And I must admit," she said, pointing the barrel directly at me, "I really don't like you. Looks like you'll be the first to go."

# OLIVIA

Alex slowly rose from the bed, her hands raised in a defensive gesture.

We exchanged a quick look, both of us silently questioning the same thing: Was the gun real? If this woman truly was some kind of out-of-body apparition, logic said that the gun couldn't be real either.

But in that tense moment, doubt crept in. The gun appeared solid, defying every law of reality.

Charlie sidestepped around the bed, the gun still aimed at Alex. "Not another word," she hissed, her voice low and threatening.

Alex hesitated, uncertainty flickering in her gaze. My eyes darted toward the closed door, only a few feet away.

She tilted her head, considering. "Actually, go ahead. Make a run for it. By the time you call the police, I'll be gone, leaving Alex dead. And don't mistake it—the gun is very real. You can see it glinting in the light, hear it cock. Even feel the chill in the air."

Could she be telling the truth? Was the gun real? I stared at the weapon, torn between belief and disbelief.

Charlie's voice cut through my thoughts. "Touch it if you dare. Feel the cold steel. It's not a trick. Not an illusion. This gun is as real as the fear in your eyes. Matt will meet the same fate. But mark my words, I'll return for you. You won't know when, but I'll be back. You'll live in the shadow of fear."

I glanced at the door again. How could I defeat her? The out-of-body experience meant the "real" Charlie still existed. If I could get to her body, pull the plug—end it all.

Her laughter filled the room. "Olivia, are you hearing yourself? If you want to kill me, that's the way. Go ahead. Try it. But I won't stop you. I'm not scared of dying. At least then, I'd be free. You won't do it, though. Even if I handed you the gun and we went to that room right now, you wouldn't pull the trigger."

Her words hit home. The girl in that hospital room, the one trapped in her broken body, still looked like the Charlie I had met two years ago.

Still, I had to ask, "How can you be so sure?"

"Because the guilt of taking a life would haunt you forever." She shifted her gaze to Alex. "Enough talking. Let's get back to business, shall we? Time to end you."

"Please, let me send one last text to my mother," Alex pleaded. "At least let me say goodbye."

Charlie shook her head, a smirk curling her lips. "No. Nobody in that café got a final goodbye."

I stepped forward, placing myself between the gun and Alex. "If you want to hurt Alex, you'll have to hurt me first."

Her eyes gleamed with malice. "I have no problem with that. Just tell me where to shoot."

Alex moved in front of me. "What do you want? Tell us, and we'll do it," she said.

"I want nothing from you. I want you dead!" she screamed, her anger crackling. "All three of you! Luck favored you at the cost of others. It's unfair that you get to live and enjoy life while others have died."

"But you didn't die!" Alex screamed back. "You're lucky compared to those who did!"

A bitter laugh escaped Charlie's lips. "No, I didn't die. I just wished I had."

"How does our death make your life better?" I asked.

"I don't want a better life," she said coldly. "I want justice. You three should suffer like the others did. And you . . ." She turned the gun on me, her eyes narrowing with pure hatred. "I hate you the most, Olivia. You betrayed me. You promised to save me, but you left me to die."

"I didn't abandon you," I whispered. "I offered to take your place, but the gunman pushed me out. Please, Charlie, just kill me. Don't hurt Alex or Matt. Kill me. I caused your pain. They didn't. Why Officer Davis? Why hurt him?"

"He failed to protect the hostages," she replied. "Failed to protect me. Simple as that."

Her gaze hardened, a disturbingly calm smile spreading across her face. "No, I'm not going to kill you. It's too easy. I want you to suffer. I'll kill Alex. And Matt. But not you. Your life will unravel. You'll decay from the inside out, and when you're at your weakest... you'll take your own life."

"You're beyond twisted," Alex said, her voice laced with disgust. "Why not just kill us from the beginning? Why these sick games?"

"It was more satisfying this way," Charlie said. "I wanted you to feel it—the hope, the love, the success, all torn away in an instant. I had it all—my future, my career, someone I cared about. And then it was gone." She looked at Alex with a twisted mix of sadness and malice. "Goodbye, Alex."

She pulled the trigger. A gunshot echoed through the room, and Alex collapsed, a bullet piercing her chest. Blood spread across her shirt.

"No!" I screamed, tears spilling uncontrollably. "Alex, no!" I knelt beside her, desperately searching for a pulse that was no longer there.

I turned my gaze on Charlie, hatred igniting in my chest.

"You're no different from those shooters in the coffee shop," I spat. "You're a murderer, just like them." Any shred of empathy I might have felt for her was gone. All I wanted was her life to end.

She shrugged. "They turned me into this."

A knock sounded at the door, followed by a shout. "Police! Open up!"

In an instant, Charlie fired again, hitting Matt in the chest. The machine beside him let out a long, monotonous beep. Matt was gone. I stared at her, paralyzed by horror and helplessness.

She shoved the gun into my hand, her voice cutting through the shock. "You know what to do now." She turned to leave, then paused. "Oh, and by the way, your husband has another woman in his life."

Sobs wracked my body. "What?"

Charlie smirked. "Yes. The supposed love of your life is a liar." She pulled several photos from her purse and tossed them on the bed. "He's planning to see her tonight. No client meeting."

She tossed the photos on the bed. The photos hit the bed with a soft thud. Stacey and Owen, locked in an intimate embrace. Owen's betrayal laid bare.

"It stings, doesn't it?" she sneered. "He never intended to stay with you, Olivia. I just nudged him back into your life for a while, to keep things interesting." She winked at me. "He abandoned you when you were at your lowest, and you took him back without hesitation. Where's your self-respect?"

"Die, you bitch!" I screamed. I fired twice, hitting her chest. Her laughter echoed before she evaporated into thin air.

By the time the police burst through the door, any trace of her presence was gone. I met the eyes of two officers and Daniel, both shocked and terrified.

"What have you done, Olivia?" Daniel asked.

What had I done? I glanced at my trembling hand, still clutching the gun. They thought I did this. "I didn't do this. You have to believe me. I wouldn't—couldn't—do this. It was all her."

But, of course, they didn't believe me. Why would they?

"Drop the weapon! Drop it now!" one of the police officers yelled.

She had set me up. That's why she gave me the gun, to frame me.

I started to lower it, but then something inside snapped. This had to end. I needed to finish it. To ensure Charlie was gone.

"Lady, drop the gun before we're forced to fire!" the officers shouted.

But Daniel stepped forward, blocking them. "Don't shoot, please don't shoot her," he pleaded. "Look at how her hand is shaking. She's not going to hurt anyone. Let me talk to her."

With his back to me, I acted. I pressed the gun against his back. "Don't move, Daniel."

"What are you doing, Olivia?"

"Daniel," I whispered, "I need your help. Please, trust me. I didn't do this."

He raised his hands higher, playing along. "Olivia, you've got so much ahead of you. Please, don't throw it all away," he said in a loud voice before lowering it to a whisper. "What do you need me to do?"

"I need you to walk with me to Charlie's room," I whispered, then shouted at the officers, "Put down your weapons! Drop them, or I'll blow his brains out. I swear I will."

The officers exchanged glances before lowering their weapons.

"Don't move. Stay where you are!" I instructed as we moved toward the door.

Once outside, I pulled Daniel along, my arm locked around his neck and the gun pressed to his temple.

"What's going on, Olivia?" he asked as soon as we reached Charlie's room.

I let go of him, shut the door, and locked it.

Charlie lay there, fragile, youthful. For a moment, doubt clouded my judgment. The steady beep of the monitor—she was still alive. I raised the gun, pointing it at her. "Charlie isn't who you think she is, Daniel. Not anymore."

"What are you saying? Don't do this, Olivia," he pleaded. "You don't want to kill her. She's just a girl."

She looked so innocent, almost angelic—how could she possibly be responsible for so much devastation? Tears blurred my vision. "I have to, Daniel. She's a monster. She killed Matt and Alex. And . . ." My voice cracked under the weight of my grief. "She'll kill more if I don't stop her."

"She's in a coma," Daniel insisted. "What are you talking about?"

Time was running out. My finger tightened on the trigger. "It's complicated, Daniel."

*Shoot her*, I had to. But as I stared down the barrel of the gun, doubt gnawed at me. Could someone so peaceful in appearance truly be capable of such harm? Her face, so serene in sleep, so innocent.

No. I couldn't let sympathy cloud my judgment. I had to do this.

"Say your goodbye," I said, my voice heavy with the burden of the choice I was about to make.

The gunshot rang out. Daniel screamed.

A searing pain tore through me. I stared down, stunned, as blood seeped from my chest, pooling on the floor. I crumpled, the strength draining from my body. As I fell, I saw her—black hair framing a face twisted into a malicious smile.

Her grip on the gun loosened, and her form flickered, insubstantial. The young Charlie, now draped in black, stood up from the bed. Our eyes locked, and in a voice as cold as death, she whispered, "Nothing is for nothing."

Then, as darkness swallowed me, I knew the end had begun.

# CHARLIE

"Ms. Moretti, there is something I want to discuss with you."

The voice was unfamiliar—flat, professional.

"What is it, Doctor Williams?" Mammina's response was quiet, hesitant.

"This will be a very difficult decision to make, but it's time to think about taking Charlie off life support. I don't think she'll ever wake up. It might be best to let her go. I'm very sorry about this."

*Taking me off life support? Why would this doctor even suggest such a thing?*

"What? What do you mean? No, it's not time yet. I want to wait and see if she wakes up," Mammina objected. "Dr. Olivia said—"

"Ms. Moretti—"

"I said no!" Mammina's voice rose, cutting him off. "I'm sorry, doctor, but—no. You're not even her main doctor. I know Dr. Olivia isn't here today. I haven't seen Dr. Daniel either. But that doesn't change my answer." She exhaled sharply. "I'm sorry for snapping. I just—please understand. I know what you think. I know you believe keeping her on life support is wrong." Her voice shook, but she pushed on. "But I'm her mother. I'm *Charlie's* mother. She's everything to me. And I still have hope. A glimmer, maybe. But it's enough."

Dr. Williams let out a soft sigh. "I completely understand, Ms. Moretti. I'm a father myself. I want you to know that my heart goes out to you. It's your decision, and I respect that. I won't bring it up again until you're ready."

"Thanks, Doctor." Mammina's voice was heavy, drained. A beat of silence. Then she spoke again, softer now, directed at me. "Charlie, can you hear me? Please wake up. You've been sleeping a long time. I want you back. Please wake up. . . But maybe you won't. Maybe the doctor's right. But I can't let go." A shaky inhale. "Wake up, Charlie. Please. Time to wake up."

*Wake up, Charlie. Time to wake up* . . . The world slowly crept back into focus—blurry, strange. My eyelids fluttered open, light spilling in too bright. I squinted against it. Everything felt distant, like I wasn't fully there. Then I heard it—a quiet sound, almost drowned out by the buzzing in my head. Someone was crying. Mammina sat beside me, her face hidden in her hands.

"Mammina?" My voice came out thin, more like a croak than a whisper.

She looked up, her red, swollen eyes going wide the second she saw me. "Charlie?" She sucked in a sharp breath, as if afraid to believe what she was seeing. "You're . . . Oh, my god, you woke up!" Her voice cracked, thick with something between disbelief and relief. "Doctor, she woke up!"

Her words drifted through the fog in my head, distant, hollow. My body felt wrong—too heavy, too foreign. I tried to speak, to move, but the tubes, the machines, the weight of it all pinned me down. My voice lodged in my throat, trapped.

A figure moved in the background. The doctor stepped closer, his gaze sweeping over me like I was some strange experiment. "She woke up," he murmured, like he didn't quite believe it. His face came into view—wrinkled, mustached, unfamiliar. Not Dr. Olivia.

With a quick press of a button on the intercom, the doctor summoned the medical team. Minutes later, nurses and staff rushed in. They moved carefully, like they were afraid I might break—or disappear. Their faces were wary, scanning monitors, double-checking numbers, waiting for the inevitable mistake. Then something shifted. A murmur passed between them. Disbelief. Relief. A flicker of something almost like wonder.

After a series of tests, the doctor nodded to the team, then turned to Mammina. "Step outside for a moment."

She stiffened. "Why? What's going on? Is it bad news?"

He shook his head. "No. It's good news. We're considering taking her off life support. But we need you to step out."

A pause. Then, silently, Mammina nodded and left. Her eyes flicked to mine just before the door shut behind her.

What felt like hours passed as the medical team worked around me, carefully removing the tubes and wires keeping me tethered to the machines. They moved fast, efficient. Careful, but not hesitant. Checking, double-checking. Making sure I was okay. The soft beeping of the monitors and the hushed voices of the medical team filled the room, making the moment feel quieter than it should have been.

As the last tube was removed, it felt like I'd been set free from invisible chains. I was still weak and dizzy, but just being able to breathe on my own felt like a win. The nurse smiled as she fluffed the pillow behind my head, making me a little more comfortable. "Welcome back," she said.

I let the breath out carefully. Managed the smallest nod.

The doctor asked Mammina to come back in. "She needs to rest now. We'll be back soon to check on her. Hopefully, it's a path to recovery from here on out." And with that, he and the others left the room.

"Honey, you woke up." Mammina's face was a wreck—swollen eyes, tear-streaked cheeks, her mouth twisted between a sob and a smile. "You woke up—thank God, you woke up." She pulled me in, her arms locking around me tight, like she was afraid I'd disappear if she let go. "You're here. You came back." A shudder ran through her, something between a breath and a prayer. "I thought I lost you."

"What happened to me, Mammina?" The words scraped their way up my dry throat.

Mammina cupped my face, her hands impossibly gentle—like touching me too hard might break me all over again. "It's hard for me to talk about this, and I don't know how much you remember. But two years ago, you went to get a cup of coffee, and you were shot." She swiped at her tears with her sleeve, but they kept coming.

It hit me like a hammer to the skull. The memories. My legs. The shooting. The moment my life caved in.

"It was such an awful situation," Mammina said. "You were shot, and the bullet left you—"

I looked down. Tried to move. Nothing. Dead weight. Useless. Like they belonged to someone else. Like someone had swapped them out while I wasn't looking.

"Paralyzed from the waist down," I barely recognized my own voice. The words felt stale, like I'd heard them before, like they were someone else's bad news. Mammina's eyes stayed locked on mine. She didn't speak, but she didn't have to. I already knew. Every awful detail. "I also slipped into a deep coma," I murmured. "Then I had to undergo multiple surgeries. After the second surgery, Dr. Olivia told you that I had just a four percent chance of ever walking again. I know, Mammina. I know everything."

Her breath hitched. "How?"

"I could hear everything." The words tasted bitter coming out. "But there's something I need to ask you, Mammina."

"Of course. You can ask me anything."

I swallowed. My throat felt tight. I needed to know—had any of it been real, or was my mind feeding me lies? "Can you tell me how many people made it through the shooting? And their names?"

She frowned, trying to recall the details. "It was you and three others. Dr. Olivia Jones, and then Matt, and Allison . . . or maybe it was Alex?" She rubbed her forehead, as if trying to clear away the haze of time. "I can't quite remember the girl's name. But I'm sure it was four people, including you. Dr. Olivia Jones said something about choosing number six, and that's how she survived."

"When was the last time you saw Dr. Olivia?" I asked, my voice tight, barely controlled.

Mammina furrowed her brows, thinking. "Not since yesterday. Now that I think about it, it was a little odd to see another doctor stop by this morning. I also found it strange that she didn't come into the room during the life support removal. But then I also heard that there was some sort of altercation last night. Why does it matter? Why are you asking all these questions?"

An altercation last night? Oh my god. It all really happened. And I . . . I was the one who caused it.

"Mammina, it all happened," I said. "Every bit of it. Even the out-of-body experience. I could hear and see everything around me. There was me, and then there was her, who was also me . . . I know about everything, Mammina."

"What out-of-body experience? What in the world are you talking about?" Mammina touched my damp cheek. "Baby, why are you crying?" She wiped aways my tears, her eyes searching mine for answers. "What's wrong?"

The confession tumbled out. "You don't know what I've done, Mammina."

"What did you do?" she asked me.

"I hated them, Mammina. I hated them so much." The words burned coming out, like acid on my tongue. I shook my head, staring at my hands, afraid to meet her eyes. Afraid of what I'd see. Disgust. Horror.

"They took everything from me. My luck. My life." My voice cracked, but I didn't stop. "Olivia, Alex, and Matt . . . they walked out of that coffee shop without a scratch. Not a single bruise. And me? I didn't." My hands curled into fists, nails biting into my palms. "The anger didn't just live in me. It fed on me. A storm, a sickness, something festering under my skin, sinking into my bones." My breath shuddered. "And then, she appeared." I picked at the blanket, my fingers restless. "This other version of me. She was... scarier. Darker. Meaner. She felt like a nightmare." A pause. Then, softer, almost to myself: "But sometimes, she felt like the truth."

Mammina just sat there, listening. My fingers trembled. A tear slipped onto the back of my hand. I wiped it away.

"And at the end, I . . . I . . . killed—"

The door swung open.

"Ms. Moretti, Doctor Williams told me to come see you. He said it's a surprise but wouldn't say more. I just arrived at the hospital, and he sent me straight here."

I froze. Dr. Olivia Jones stepped into the room. Then her eyes lit up, and she gasped, "Oh, my god, Charlie, you woke up!"

Relief flooded through me. She was alive. Everything I thought had happened—everything I was so sure of—was just a dream. The lady with black hair. The out-of-body experience. None of it was real. It was all just a dream.

Dr. Olivia's voice turned rusty, her words unraveling into a thin rasp. "You woke up." This time, it was barely a whisper. Then she turned to Mammina. "How does she seem to you, Ms. Moretti?" A pause. Then, softer, more careful: "The same Charlie?"

Something inside me coiled. Tight. A weird pressure clamped down on my skull. Like something wasn't right all over again. Why did she sound so tense? *The same Charlie? Why wouldn't I be?* She should be happy. Smiling, celebrating. But she wasn't. She looked worried. The uneasy feeling I'd had since waking up came back to me, stronger than ever.

"Yes, she does," Mammina said. "I'm so relieved, Dr. Jones. Charlie woke up, and it's a blessing to see you here as well. I was worried. Someone at the front desk mentioned there was an altercation last night, but I wasn't sure if it involved you or not."

Dr. Olivia shook her head. Too fast. But her eyes never left me.

"No, I wasn't involved in that," she said quickly. "It was a family member arguing with one of the doctors. Just a minor incident, nothing out of the ordinary."

"Dr. Olivia, I'm so happy to see you!" I said, and I meant it. Relief flooded through me. I was so excited, so grateful. I just wished she looked as happy as I felt.

Her face softened. A smile broke through—small, hesitant, like she wasn't sure she was allowed to have it. She stepped closer, wrapped her arms around me. "I'm really glad you woke up. Very, very glad." Her hug was warm. I held on a little longer than I meant to. Like I needed it. Like she did. "Things will be okay now," she murmured against my hair.

"Doctor," Mammina said. "I feel, or at least I hope, that the worst is behind us now. Thank you, thank you so much. You saved her life."

"Don't thank me," Dr. Olivia said. "I wish I could've done more for Charlie."

Mammina shook her head, tears pooling in her eyes. "Charlie is here now because of you. When she came in, everyone thought she wouldn't make it. Everyone except you. They said she'd lost too much blood, she was too weak, and the surgery was too risky. They said she would die. They said it would take a miracle for her to stay alive. But you did the surgery anyway. You made a miracle happen."

"Let's not talk about this now," Dr. Olivia said. "I'm just glad she woke up."

Mammina sniffled. "Thank you for giving my daughter another chance." She wiped at her eyes, let out a small laugh. "We can go to Italy now. We can do anything."

Not everything though. I still couldn't walk. My life would never be the same again.

"You two have lots of things to talk about, so I'll go now," Dr. Olivia said. "The nurse will come for tests. Now that you're awake, we can hopefully get you out of here soon. We'll also need to talk about physical therapy. I'm not sure how much Charlie knows about—"

"I know everything," I cut in. "I know I might never walk again."

"Hey, let's not give up so easily." Her tone was firm. "There's always a chance, even if it's a small one. You'll walk again. I'm going to step out now to give you some time to catch up with everything. I'm so relieved that this is all over. Everyone will be so happy."

After Dr. Olivia left, Mammina rose from her chair, heading toward the door as well. "I'll be back, honey. I need to call your dad and tell him the good news."

"My dad?" I asked, surprised.

She smiled. "Yes, honey, he called this morning. He said he's a changed man and he misses you. He wants to come for a visit. I told him he had to wait until you woke up so I could ask you. What do you say?"

I smiled back. "I'm okay with that if you are."

"You should also call Jason to tell him that you woke up. He's been waiting for you every day."

"Of course, of course. Yes, Jason," I said, reaching for the phone. "I'll call him right now. I hope he still has his old number."

"He does. Okay, I'm leaving now," she said, closing the door.

As I started dialing, a little spark of hope hit me. Maybe things would be okay after all. I took a deep breath, trying to hold onto that feeling. For the first time in forever, I actually let myself believe. Maybe tomorrow wouldn't be perfect, but it could be good.

# OLIVIA

I maneuvered through traffic, jaywalking toward the Daily Grind coffee shop, barely resisting the urge to run. When I heard that Charlie had woken up and seemed like her old self again, I called Matt immediately. He and Alex were at the coffee shop, and he suggested I join them. I didn't have much time, but this news felt like it needed to be shared in person. I had to see their relief, feel it, before I could convince myself that it was real. Maybe then I'd believe it too.

Even as I hurried toward the coffee shop, part of me still couldn't grasp it. Was this really happening? Could Charlie's "miracle" recovery be real, or was I just chasing another lie? The city pulsed with life, awake in a way I hadn't felt in years. But something about it felt wrong, a strangeness I couldn't shake. Like I hadn't fully woken up myself.

The coffee shop hummed with the usual morning rush. I spotted Matt and Alex in the corner. Alex looked effortlessly elegant in a blue summer dress, while Matt was casual in a blue T-shirt. Two coffee cups sat between them, along with a plate of half-eaten pastries—evidence of a long conversation. A third cup sat waiting, and Matt slid it toward me as I approached.

"Medium latte, skim milk," he said with a smile.

"Thank you." I took the latte, letting the warmth seep into my fingers, then raised an eyebrow. "I have to admit, I'm surprised you both chose this coffee shop," I said, glancing around. "Matt, weren't you the one who once said you couldn't imagine ever coming back here?"

"It's difficult," Matt admitted, setting down his coffee cup. "This place will always be Gio's to me. I want to keep his memory alive, to hold onto that."

I nodded, knowing exactly what he meant. This place would always be Gio's for me too, no matter how much time passed. His absence hung in the air, in every corner, in every detail he'd left behind. The shop didn't look the same—didn't feel the same—but it didn't matter. It would always be Gio's in my mind. Nothing could change that, no matter how hard they tried.

"And what about you, Alex?" I asked. "You didn't really know Gio."

"It's tough, no doubt," she said. "When Matt suggested coming here, I wasn't sure at first. I was afraid of the memories it might stir up. But he gave me the choice to pick another place, and I realized I couldn't keep running from the past. It's not easy, but I'm here."

I watched as Matt reached over and gently squeezed her hand. She squeezed back, a smile spreading across her face. The connection between them was undeniable—no pretense, no hesitation—just a quiet understanding that spoke louder than words. Their growing closeness was hard to miss, the chemistry between them so real it was almost tangible.

"So tell us more about Charlie," Matt prompted. "Is she really going to be okay?"

"I believe so," I said, taking a seat. "She seems like her old self again. I'm still not sure about her ability to walk, but if she's come this far, there's hope. With the right therapy and her determination, I think she can overcome this hurdle."

He checked his watch. "I have to leave soon," he said. "Lucas, my real estate agent called this morning. He says he's managed to recover some of my money. We're meeting to discuss it further. I might still be able to rent a space for my bar—not as big as I'd planned, but I'll make it work."

"That's great news," I said, genuinely happy for him. "Looks like your luck's turning around."

He gave a relieved sigh. "I hope so."

"I got some good news this morning too," Alex said, practically glowing. "Bruce called. He's decided to leave his job as well. He said he couldn't stand being there without me. It just didn't feel the same anymore. And when one of his clients heard he was leaving, she offered him a position at her company. Bruce told her he'd only join if there was a role for me too. I've got an interview next week," she added, her excitement shining through. "Bruce wants to meet up to discuss the details."

"That's fantastic, Alex," I said. "I'm so glad to hear that things are turning around for both of you."

And I was glad. But something about it didn't sit right. It all felt too easy. Too perfect, like the pieces were sliding into place just a little too neatly.

I brushed the thought aside. I was just being paranoid. After everything that had happened, my mind was looking for threats where there were none. This was a good thing. A new beginning.

My thoughts then slipped back to last night. When I finally made it home, well past midnight, I found Owen sound asleep, his phone on the nightstand. I tried to slip into the bathroom quietly so I wouldn't disturb him, but just as I was about to close the door, his phone lit up with a message. It was face up, and I couldn't miss the name: Stacey.

Glancing at Owen, still sound asleep, I carefully reached for his phone and tiptoed into the bathroom. My breath hitched as I clicked on the message, terrified he might wake at any moment. Thankfully, he hadn't changed his password.

"Today was amazing. I want you by my side all the time. When will you finally tell her?" it said.

I scrolled through the messages, each one worse than the last—explicit pictures, intimate confessions—proof of their affair laid out in cold, ugly detail. The kind of proof that didn't need any more words to explain it.

Owen had been lying to me all along. No surprise there. No grand gesture waiting for me. The vow renewal? Just another lie, one more thing to keep me on the hook while everything else fell apart.

Returning to the bedroom, I flicked on all the lights. Owen rubbed his eyes, blinking in confusion. "What's going on, honey? Why did you do that?"

"How long were you cheating on me?" I demanded, holding his phone out for him to see.

"What?" he stammered, but his eyes dropped to the phone in my hand. He didn't even try to deny it. Avoiding my gaze like a coward, he admitted quietly, "Three years."

"Three years?" The words burned my throat.

"So you didn't leave because of Charlie or because I wasn't around enough. You left because you needed an excuse—so you could blame me. Is that it?"

Owen said nothing. I pushed further. "Why did you come back?"

He sighed, still refusing to meet my eyes. "I thought maybe we could fix things, but I needed to be sure. I didn't want to throw away our marriage if—"

I cut him off. "If? Don't even finish that sentence." The words tasted bitter on my tongue. "I'll be leaving now, but when I come back, I want you gone. I don't ever want to see you again. I'll give you the divorce you want."

I slammed the door behind me. As I stepped outside, the pain was still there, but so was a strange lightness, like a door had finally closed behind me.

I finally understood what Daniel had been trying to tell me: never settle for less. Owen had left once—I should have never let him back in. But what's done is done. We live, we learn. This wasn't just about love or betrayal. It was about me—knowing I was worth more than the bare minimum, that I didn't have to shrink myself to be enough. I had spent so much of my life giving, fixing, making space for everyone but myself. But I wasn't just here to put others back together—I deserved to be whole, too. Helping others heal had always given my life meaning, but for the first time, I realized healing wasn't just something I gave—it was something I owed to myself.

I stayed with Matt and Alex for another twenty minutes, mostly listening as they shared their plans. After saying my goodbyes, I headed back to the hospital.

As I walked, a quiet sense of peace settled over me. Life wasn't perfect, but it was mine to rebuild. I still had so much—a future to step into, people to care for, a purpose that mattered. Charlie's awakening wasn't just a miracle for her; it was a reminder that second chances were real. That healing—true healing—was possible.

And as for Daniel . . .

It was late when I left Owen, but somehow, I found myself at Daniel's door. He opened it, his surprise evident as he took in the sight of me standing there at such an hour.

"You were right," I said, tears welling up. "About everything."

He opened his arms, and for a second, I froze. Was I really about to let someone in again? The thought almost made me step back—almost. But then his arms were around me, solid, warm, asking nothing, and something in me broke open. No more running. Not from this. And for the first time in a long time, I let myself lean into it.

I didn't know what came next. The future was still uncertain, still unwritten. But for now, this was enough. A quiet moment. A warm hug. A safe place to land.

And that was all I needed. The rest would come, one day at a time.

# CHARLIE

Mammina finally left for work, promising over and over she'd be back soon, but it didn't stop her from popping back in a few more times, kissing me again and again. Each kiss felt like a soft plea, her lips lingering on my forehead before she'd pull away, only to come back and do it all over again. I could hear the worry in her voice as she said, "Baby, I still can't believe you woke up. I love you so much, I love you so much," as if saying it a hundred times could make it real. She left, then popped back in one more time, kissed me again, and finally, the door clicked shut behind her.

Jason was on his way over. When I called, he was in the middle of class but stepped out to answer. "Oh my god, babe, you're awake!" His voice cracked, full of disbelief. "I love you so much. I'm getting in the car right now—I need to see you. I can't wait to hold you again. I'll be there soon."

I hung up, a grin spreading across my face. I could practically picture him—grabbing his keys in a hurry, probably dropping them, racing out the door like he couldn't get to me fast enough. The thought of seeing him again, being wrapped up in his arms, was exactly what I needed. I glanced at the clock, counting down the minutes. I couldn't wait.

My eyes started to grow heavy. It'd take him about an hour to get here, so I figured I could sneak in a quick nap. I still felt so weak, so drained. Just as I was about to close my eyes, a sound broke through the quiet behind me. At first, I tried to ignore it—too tired to care. But then it got louder, sharper, and a voice pierced through the stillness.

"We still have unfinished business."

I turned toward the voice and saw her for the first time. Long black hair, heavy makeup—purple eyeshadow, red lipstick—she looked like she stepped right out of my worst nightmare. Her dark eyes locked onto mine, and a chill crawled up my spine.

"What unfinished business?" I asked, my voice trembling.

Her smile stretched slow and cold. "First, we need to finish what we started with Alex, Olivia, and Matt. After that, we can move on to darker things."

My breath caught. "So, everything that happened—it was real?" I stammered. "But they're all alive, right?"

She tilted her head, eyes gleaming. "Everything up to Matt's car accident was real," she said. "But after that, I was just offering ideas. Showing you how to make their pain worse. I was also showing you what you could have, if you keep doing what I say. Like having your father come back. Don't look so shocked. Do you really think he would just show up, out of nowhere? I was just teasing you with the things you could get. The rest? That's up to you."

"Up to me? What are you talking about?" I asked, confused.

Her smile widened. "Think of me as your inner darkness. I'm here to do whatever you tell me. And you—you absorbed the gunmen's powers. Do you remember what one of them said to you?"

"I... I don't remember," I said, my voice faltering, but the memories rushed back.

The gunmen. The line-up. Dr. Olivia taken away. The shots. People collapsing. The bullet tearing through my back. The pain was blinding, like nothing I'd ever felt.

"She's special, don't shoot her again," one of the gunmen said. "She's the last one, innocent and sweet. Just how we want it. You know what to do now, Billy."

"Listen, girl," Billy leaned closer. "Don't be afraid. You're lucky, you know that? We serve the Devil now, and you're about to join our ranks. Part of the ritual, we'll transfer our powers to you, just like it was transferred to us. We'll end our own lives, our purpose fulfilled. Then it's your turn. Your mission? Inflict suffering, sow evil. Start with three sixes. Make their lives hell. After that, go bigger. Only then will you fulfill your mission. Fail to comply, the Devil will come for you. You are the chosen one, embrace it, get creative."

I clenched my fists. "I won't do it," I told her firmly. "I'm not angry anymore. I survived the shooting, thanks to Dr. Olivia. I won't hurt anyone. I'm grateful to her."

She scoffed. "Grateful? Grateful to her? Why? Look at you—crippled. She took your place. You're nothing now. You'll be like this forever. And Jason? He might stick around for a while, but not forever. He'll leave. You know he will. You're *not* the same anymore. You're a burden. It's all their fault. They took what was yours."

I flinched. *No. I'm not like this. I'm not crippled. I am not... I'm not.*

But the more I pushed against it, the more it felt like a truth I couldn't deny. A sinking feeling spread through my chest. What if she was right? What if I was just a burden now, someone people would only feel sorry for? Would Jason really stay? Or would he leave me?

She stepped closer, her voice softening. "I know it's hard to face. But you don't have to be powerless. You don't have to be their victim anymore."

I swallowed hard. "But... I don't want to be like those shooters."

Her smile was patient, understanding. "You won't be. You'll be stronger. And you don't have to go all in right away. Start small. Three sixes. Just enough to remind them what they did to you."

*I can't let this be my life. I won't.*

I tried to focus on Dr. Olivia's words—*there's a chance.*

I shook my head, forcing the tears to stay inside. "No, I won't let this define me. I'm strong. Dr. Olivia said there's a chance I might walk again—"

"Dr. Olivia is lying," she spat. "You'll never walk again."

Her words sliced through me. I wanted to fight back, to scream at her that she was wrong—but was she? *How could I trust anything anymore? How could I trust the future when everything felt so uncertain, when it was so easy to think that nothing was ever going to get better?*

"Can't I use these powers to heal myself?" I asked desperately.

She shook her head. "These powers only work on others. And remember, if you disobey, the Devil will come for you. You have no choice."

A knock interrupted us.

"May I come in?" Dr. Olivia's voice sounded outside.

"They stole from you," the woman hissed. "You're crippled because of them."

A cold clarity began to settle over me, drying the tears on my cheeks.

"They stole from me," I repeated, my heart growing icy. "Crippled, because of them."

She nodded. "They took everything from you."

A part of me screamed that this wasn't who I was. That I wasn't like them. That I could still walk away from this. But another part, the one that had been helpless for too long, whispered: *Maybe it's time to take control.*

I shivered. The thought terrified me as much as it thrilled me. *I should be scared.* But I wasn't. A dark acceptance starting to root itself deep inside.

"They took everything," I echoed, the rage simmering just beneath the surface.

"You understand now," she murmured, her smile widening again. A gun glinted in her hand. "Are you ready?"

I hesitated. One last breath. One last chance. Keep fighting, or let it consume me.

And then it came to me, clear as day. I've never been readier.

I smiled, slow and sure. "More than ever."

"Enter, Dr. Olivia," I called out. "I've been waiting for you."

# ACKNOWLEDGEMENTS

This book wouldn't have come to life without the love and support of so many wonderful people.

First, I'm deeply grateful to my parents. You restarted your lives in the United States, overcoming unimaginable challenges to give us a shot at a better future. I am forever thankful for your courage and sacrifice.

To my husband and kids—thank you for your endless patience and for putting up with my late nights and crazy ideas. Your love keeps me grounded and motivates me every day. You mean the world to me.

To my sister and brother, thank you for always being my biggest fans, believing in me, and lifting me up whenever I needed it.

I owe so much to my extraordinary editors. Your expertise, insight, and unwavering support have pushed my writing to new heights. You taught me the craft of storytelling, guiding me through character development and navigating the publishing industry. Thank you for giving me the courage to share my work with the world.

To all of my friends—I'm so fortunate to have you by my side. And to my mentors, your guidance and belief in my potential have meant more than words can express.

Finally, a heartfelt thank you to Reagan Rothe and Black Rose Writing for taking a chance on an unknown writer. Your faith in this book has made all the difference.

I'm forever grateful to each of you.

# ABOUT THE AUTHOR

Julia Shraybman is a bilingual, Chicago-based writer who was born in Belarus. She came to the United States at an early age, bringing with her a deep love for storytelling inspired by her rich cultural heritage. From childhood, books were her constant companions, and she would often lose herself in the world of words. Now, as a writer, she weaves those early influences into her work.

Julia lives in Deerfield, Illinois, with her husband, their two children—a daughter and a son—and their adorable toy poodle, Pepper. When she's not writing, she enjoys exploring the city's literary scene and connecting with fellow writers.

Visit her online at www.juliashraybman.com. This is her first novel.

# NOTE FROM JULIA SHRAYBMAN

Word-of-mouth is crucial for any author to succeed. If you enjoyed *Lucky Number 6*, please leave a review online—anywhere you are able. Even if it's just a sentence or two. It would make all the difference and would be very much appreciated.

Thanks!
Julia Shraybman

We hope you enjoyed reading this title from:

# BLACK ROSE
## writing™

www.blackrosewriting.com

Subscribe to our mailing list – *The Rosevine* – and receive **FREE** books, daily deals, and stay current with news about upcoming releases and our hottest authors.
Scan the QR code below to sign up.

Already a subscriber? Please accept a sincere thank you for being a fan of Black Rose Writing authors.

View other Black Rose Writing titles at
www.blackrosewriting.com/books and use promo code
**PRINT** to receive a **20% discount** when purchasing.